LANCELOT
AND THE KING
THE NEW EDITION

Previously Lancelot and the Wolf

First Published in Great Britain 2011 by Mirador Publishing as *Lancelot and the Wolf*

Copyright © 2011 by Sarah Luddington
Artwork Copyright © 2018 by Olivia Ryan

First edition: 2011
Second Edition: 2018

Any reference to real names and places are purely fictional and are constructs of the author. Any offence the references produce is unintentional and in no way reflects the reality of any locations or people involved.

A copy of this work is available through the British Library.

ISBN: 978-1-912601-26-4

Mirador Publishing
10 Greenbrook Terrace
Taunton
Somerset
UK
TA1 1UT

THE KNIGHTS OF CAMELOT
Book 1

LANCELOT
AND THE KING
THE NEW EDITION

SARAH LUDDINGTON

Also available through Mirador Publishing:

The Prophecy
Vampire
Seelie
Unforbidden: A Queer Collection

The Knights of Camelot Series:
Lancelot and the King
Lancelot and the Sword
Lancelot and the Grail

Lancelot's Challenge
Lancelot's Burden
Lancelot's Curse

Betrayal Of Lancelot
Passion Of Lancelot
Revenge Of Lancelot

Lancelot The Lost Years: The Spear

Sons of Camelot Series:
The Pendragon Legacy
The Du Lac Legacy
Albion's Legacy

The Rock and Roll Mysteries:
Chords for the Dead

To the story tellers, musicians and artists
who inspire me.

Also to my knight in shining armour.

CHAPTER ONE

LIFTING MY SHIRT OVER my head caused me to wince. The muscles still sore and the skin still ravaged. If I dressed as I should, the gambeson then the hauberk would rip the scabs off my back.

I sighed, pulling the flesh taut over my ribs. I had to leave today. The nuns protecting me had healed all they could and if I stayed, I may endanger them. At least they managed to remove the worst of the blood from my clothing. I rolled the padded undergarment and mail up, moving slowly. The dull steel sucked in the early morning light. Arthur's mail shone with the light of his soul, he seemed to glow from the inside out every time he went into battle or tourney.

I forced the memory away. I forced Arthur away. I swallowed my need to weep and tried to relax my clenched jaw. A gentle knock at the door focused me on the present.

"Come in." My voice sounded the same even if I felt different. Deep, rough, heavy with unspoken emotions.

The door opened and a nun stood in the entrance of the small cell. She looked at me and then at the small amount of things I owned and packed. "So, you are leaving us," she said.

"Yes, Sister Eliza." I straightened. "I think it's for the best."

"You are leaving too soon, those wounds will become infected," she told me. Her hands sat on her considerable hips. As the one to dress them, clean them and stitch them where necessary, I guess she felt a kind of perverse ownership.

"I promise I will keep them clean and I promise not to do anything too stupid until they are healed," I said, dredging up a smile for her.

She blushed, her round face in the nun's wimple all too obvious with no hair to hide behind. My smile can open doors for me in the most frigid of hearts.

"Humph, I don't believe that promise for one bloody moment," she cursed, then crossed herself. I had soon realised that the world of a nun didn't come naturally to Sister Eliza. "But if you are going to leave then at least let me help you pack."

She hustled me out of the way and began organising my few possessions. She did a better job than I could have done. My pack and saddlebags were tidy in moments.

When she finished she asked, "Do you have a plan?"

I laughed, a bitter, brittle sound making her flinch. "No, what is there to plan for? I am dishonoured. I am exiled. I have been thrown to the dogs by my King. I have no plan beyond the nearest tavern over the Channel."

She sighed. "This self pity Doesn't suit you, Lancelot."

I opened my mouth to snap back at her when I saw the deep well of compassion in her blue eyes. I dropped my gaze. "No, I know. I need God's Grace but I don't know how to ask."

She laid her hand on my bowed head. I stood almost as tall as she could reach, I felt her fingers nestle close to my scalp burrowing through my thick black hair. "You just have to ask, Sir Knight," she said as a way of benediction.

"I cannot ask for God's forgiveness when I cannot forgive myself," I said to the stone floor.

"And you won't forgive yourself until you have your King's forgiveness," she said, sadly. Over the last three days, she managed to prise my story from my reluctant lips. A farmer found me in his field, bleeding to death and carried me in his cart. I'd been lucky apparently. The wounds, though open, had been treated when I'd been cut down from the flogging post. No infection, no fever, beyond the one in my heart.

In those three days, I'd only really seen Sister Eliza and the Mother Superior of this small community near the monastery at Sherborne Abbey. I'd been deemed a dangerous influence on everyone else. They were probably right. Sister Eliza, after informing me confession would be good for my soul, proved a patient and sympathetic listener. I thought the only thing, which would be good for me, would be an arrow to the heart. I refrained from saying it aloud though; I didn't want to shatter her illusions.

"Arthur can never forgive me and I don't blame him," I said. "I earned every lash of that whip."

She opened her mouth to argue, realised how futile it would be and snapped it shut. "Well," she said, becoming brisk, "you need something more positive to do than wallowing in a tavern for the rest of your life. I suggest you find a cause or a war to keep you entertained."

I smiled again and caught her fingers to my lips. I kissed them fondly. "Sister, I will do as you command. I shall find a war and fight until I'm done, then perhaps I shall have some peace." I'd meant the words to be funny, but her eyes filled with sudden tears.

"I wish you well, Lancelot du Lac, but I fear the darkness in your soul will never see you happy." She turned away and left me alone, without as much as a backward glance. My last true friend in England.

I took the horse Arthur left me for my 'escape', saddled him and walked from the small community heading toward the coast. I wanted to avoid notice at the nearby castle, so I rode through the back lanes until I'd travelled several leagues. It took a day of hard riding to reach the port of Keyhaven. I sold the horse and carried my things to the nearest cargo ship heading for the mainland. Arthur had his wish. I was leaving English shores for good. I stood at the stern as the ship left the harbour on the evening tide. I watched my home for the last twenty nine of my thirty six years, fade under the light of the moon. A washed out shoreline in shades of grey and black with torchlight flashing like fireflies.

My throat tightened. "I will always love you, Arthur," I whispered under my breath. I closed my eyes and turned my back on England.

The crossing proved quick and easy, the wind kind in our sails and the swells gentle. I'd had some bad ones over the years when I'd been travelling to and from various courts and wars, but this voyage at least proved painless. We arrived late the following day. I stood on deck watching the sun descend behind the headland, the deckhands tying us to the shore.

I disembarked as soon as I could and breathed in the stink of Le Havre. For the first time in weeks, I felt alive and grateful for the privilege. The shock of my time in England slipped into the sea to be borne away on the tide. Having been in this town many times, I wove with purpose through the docks avoiding the fish guts, grubby children and the cheapest of whores, to find my favourite tavern.

The recent rain meant the mud stank of human waste, horses and rotting food. More than a little fastidious I tried to pick my way through the worst of the muck. The streets were busy, noisy and ignorant of my crimes. Although a man of my height is hard to miss, I felt anonymous. Le Rex, my favourite inn, stood in the centre of the merchant's quarter of the town, so it made good money. Most of it was built of stone, except for the upper level. Its tiled roof rose like a beacon of hope. The rooms had fresh sheets and the women were clean. The door stood open as I approached. A welcoming noise and light burbled into the street.

Night found me with a beautiful woman in one hand and a bad hand in the other. "Well, play or fold you fool," came the gruff voice of some sea captain. We'd been playing primo vista for a long time and I held most of the coins.

I squinted at the cards once more, they were fuzzy, I then peered up at the woman on my knee. Her fine blonde hair snagged me immediately, that and her beautiful smile. "What do you think?" I asked, "Play or fold?"

She smiled back. "If you play and win this hand, as I know you will, I will earn more of your money. So, I say play." She winked.

I laughed. "The lady says play, so I will play. All in," I said and she pushed everything I had left into the pot.

She knew her own game well this one. If I won with her help, she knew I'd pay her more of my winnings and the pot had grown large. I looked forward to the challenge of burying myself in her body and fucking until the sun came up.

The gruff sea captain studied us. He thought I was too drunk to make a wise choice and he might be right. He studied his cards, looked at the pile of money in the pot and the pile beside his elbow. Just as I'd grown bored and my fingers began to explore the whore's cleavage, he said, "Fold."

"Really?" I asked surprised. "Great." Before he could do a damn thing about it, I folded my cards and hid them in the deck. The whore scooped up the horde and we left the table. The sea captain's curses made us both giggle.

I followed the woman. Her hips swayed and I watched her tight waist in the unforgiving bodice. We walked upstairs and she led us to a room off the main corridor.

She dumped the winnings on the bed and lay back, the coin jingling as it and she landed, making a pleasing sound. I watched her, amused as she wriggled around in the money. I walked to a table. Wine sat warming by the fire and my belongings were in a pile alongside. I poured myself a large glass and one for the woman. I knew at this point in the game I should be feeling the lust stir inside me. There had been many women in my life, one I thought I loved, but right now, right here, I found it hard to focus on her. A ghost overlay the desire I needed to satisfy. A tall, blonde, strong and male ghost, with haunted blue eyes, full of so much pain.

I threw the wine down my neck and heard the woman rise from the bed to join me. Soft lips brushed my neck and soft hands pulled my shirt from my sword belt and hose.

"Hmm," she murmured, "I don't get to play with men as well built as you very often. The finest room, with the finest whore and you are fit enough to fuck into next week. I can't wait," she purred, kissing under my collar length tangled hair. "Those dark eyes of yours speak of promises you can do to women most men consider too terrifying to contemplate."

I turned in her arms and looked down into clear blue eyes. "You are a bad girl," I told her firmly.

"You need me to be very bad and very wicked so I wouldn't complain," she said, kissing my mouth.

The wine and the moment collided with my desperate need to escape the ghost. I wanted something normal, something I understood and could enjoy, a simple pleasure with a willing partner. I pushed her back against the bed and had her skirts up before she fell on the covers. The coins chimed cheerfully. Her deft fingers undid my hose with wonderful efficiency.

I closed my eyes. Within moments my companion began the task of ensuring I left a hefty tip, but I felt the tears burn the backs of my eyes as the unrequited love for someone I couldn't have and a desire I didn't understand, complicated a simple moment.

When the first flush of lust was dragged from me, it left an unsatisfied warmth behind. A peculiar longing despite the warm arms and soft kisses.

"Whoever let you go to make you that desperate in my bed, was a fool of a woman."

I laughed, trying to cover my confusion and strange dissatisfaction. "Is there no way of hiding a broken heart from a professional?"

She pulled my shirt over my head and kissed my chest. "No, no way, but with a body this fit I'll take a broken heart and work hard to mend it." She licked from my belly button over my tight stomach and up my chest. I climbed onto the bed and she turned to attend my back.

"Oh, my God, what happened to you?" she gasped. I froze. For one blissful moment, I'd forgotten the healing scabs on my back.

I found words but they were rough, "I paid for sex not a commentary on my body."

She dropped her gaze. "No, sorry, sir, I had no right. We all carry scars, one way or another."

In that moment I wanted to run. Every muscle tightened to flee this damned woman and her prying eyes. What the hell must she think of me for looking like this?

Ever the professional and knowing she'd ruined the moment, the doxy rose from the bed and poured more wine. She smiled as she approached. "You look as though you are going to kill me," she laughed. "Don't be angry. It makes no difference to me what you've done or who you are. Just help me out of this damned dress and I'll make you forget you ever had a life before this one."

CHAPTER TWO

THE SOUNDS OF A scuffle drifted through muddled dreams of deep green woods and white Stags with wolves running as a pack alongside.

A small voice choked back a cry and a rough one snarled an order. I found myself unencumbered by my companion who snored with soft snuffles on the edge of the bed. I rolled and came up on my feet. My head throbbed at the sudden change of direction and my stomach rolled. My mouth felt like a leper's armpit and I decided I didn't need to know what happened outside.

A whimper and squeal had me reaching for my clothes, even as I told myself this was not my job. I opened the shutters over the window and peered out. I groaned at what I saw. The dawn just brushed the sky. I couldn't have slept more than two hours. A boy, almost man sized stood with his face pressed into the wall of the tavern's stable while two men held him still. One of the men fumbled at his crotch.

"Shit," I cursed and pulled on my boots. I opened the window wide, not wishing to break any of the expensive small glass panes and peered down. A wagon full of old laundry sat below me.

I turned, grabbed my sword and a knife before diving out the window. I didn't even think, just twisted in the air and landed on my back in a woof of sheets. It protested madly. I grimaced and struggled out of the suffocating fabric. I fell to the floor and then scrambled upright.

I saw the glimpse of a blade at the boy's throat and the wide eyes of panic as the man managed to freed himself so he could make use of his tiny dick. I needed to distract them.

"Hey, is this a free ride or are you charging?" I asked in my friendliest tone.

Both men turned to me and the knife dropped from the boy's throat. All the invitation I needed. I wanted them done quickly and quietly before they woke the town, so I used the hilt of my sword to smash one in the face while I cut the throat of the other. Blood washed from the large gash but the man dropped without a sound. The boy twisted away, his legs tangled in his torn clothes and he dropped, huddling over himself. I took the potential rapist by the hair and ran the knife over his throat. Done in moments without a sound. My heart beat a little fast. I swallowed my need for more death, coming back from the edge of the battle frenzy, it took too long.

Arthur told me I killed too easily. He said I would go too far one day and lose myself to the death call. A small sound made me rush back to the real world.

The boy crouched in a heap, staring up at me in fear. He'd managed to dress. He had short scruffy warm brown hair and terrified brown eyes. He looked older than I first thought but didn't seem to be shaving. His face was all angles and he was skinny.

"You alright?" I asked.

He blinked. "Yes," he said. Although his right eye started to swell and I could see blood on his lips and down his chin. There were bruises colouring his neck and wrists.

I held my hand out to help him up but he ducked away and scrambled upright alone. His eyes were averted from me and the bodies. "Thank you, sir."

"You the stable boy?" I asked.

"I was." He did look at the bodies then, his expression grim. "I guess I won't be now, they are the sheriff's men. I've been avoiding them for weeks." His eyes filled with tears and he folded in on himself. My heart melted.

"Damn it," I murmured. I knew, whatever the rights and wrongs of the matter, when they found these bodies, which they would, they'd find the boy and he'd give them me. He was alone and scared. As a stranger in the town carrying scars on my back, evidenced my bed warmer and looking like a fighter, I'd draw all the wrong attention.

"You know this place inside?" I nodded at the tavern.

"Yes, sir," he said, keeping his eyes averted.

"My room is the one above the cart, go and find everything. The girl is not to be disturbed. The coin on the floor and in the bed..." I thought about it for a moment. "Find as much as you can but leave a fair share for her. Then meet me at the horse market. If you aren't there by the time the town gates are open I'm leaving alone and you can shift for yourself. Understand?" I had no idea what the hell I thought I was doing. The last thing I needed was another problem in my life.

I turned to move the bodies and I heard a sharp intake of breath. I'd forgotten about my shirt, again. "Get a fucking move on," I snapped.

The boy glanced at my face and ran to the tavern. He'd know how to enter the place without being noticed. I reached down, grabbed the ankles of one of the stinking rapist bastards and hauled him into an empty stable. His friend followed. I pulled a coat off one of the bodies, shook out the lice and hoped my wounds were still closed. I didn't feel blood whispering down my skin so I assumed I wouldn't pick up an infestation. My arms were too long for the coat, but it would do for the few minutes I needed to reach the horse market. With the streets still quiet in the pre dawn light, I ran to the edge of the town, just inside the walls.

A small wooden house sat surrounded by horse pens and everything associated with horses. I banged on the door. "Dillon, you old horse thief, wake up," I yelled as loudly as I dared. Muttered curses, several loud crashes later and the door opened.

"What the bloody hell?" He sounded as angry as he always looked.

"Dillon, I need Ash and I need a good safe gelding," I said. "Oh and it's great to see you."

"Lancelot?" He rubbed sleep from his one good eye and stared up at me. He smiled, the mouth full of gold. I wondered how many of those teeth I paid for over the years. "What do you want that beast for now? It's still dark."

"It's not dark, you just drank too much," I told him, encouraging him out of his small house and into the yard. I knew how he felt.

"Ha," he said, "And I thought for sure you'd died this time and I'd get to sell that monster of yours."

"I gave you gold for at least a year of keep and it's only been ten months, don't exaggerate," I said.

Dillon the horse trader grinned. "You certain it was a year's keep? You are in an awful hurry for a year's keep." He eyed my clothing.

I groaned, "Fine, but the gelding better be good."

Dillon, his beady eyes shining with a new deal, stomped off on his short fat legs to find a stable boy to help with Ash. I followed him, if I left Dillon's boy to attend the horse alone I'd be waiting another hour at least. No one should have to deal with Ash but me, so the least I could do was try to saddle the brute.

Just as we reached a stable yard, I heard a scrabbling behind me. I turned with my hand already on my sword hilt. The boy from the tavern appeared with my things.

"Here, sir," he said. He'd run the entire way, and stood panting but ready with my saddlebags and bedroll in perfect order. He held with my shirt, doublet, cloak and a bag I didn't recognise slung over the boy's shoulder.

I blinked in surprise. "That was quick."

"I am, sir."

"Can you manage a warhorse?" I asked.

"Yes, sir," he said with utter confidence, just as a yell issued from the stable and I heard Ash's trademark neigh, or snarl, if horses could snarl.

"Find that horse and saddle him," I said, taking my belongings from the boy. His right eye had almost swollen shut but he ran for the stables.

In no short order I'd bought a fine looking chestnut gelding with saddle and bridle all in. I'd also bought equipment for the road, such as cooking pots and something to put in them. The boy appeared with Ash, my horse, whom I left with Dillon every time I travelled to England for a short time. This trip had meant to be short but my arrest kept me occupied for quite a while. I hated forcing the crossing on my equestrian companion. It seemed however, that I now travelled with a boy dedicated to the dark arts of horse management. My foul tempered stallion followed the lad meek as a lamb. Dillon stared in shock, as did his stable hand.

I handed the reins of the gelding to my boy and said, "This is, Mercury."

My stallion gnashed his bit in protest at the company. Ash had belonged to me for five years. I'd won him in a card game and wondered why his owner didn't seem to mind. The colour of wood ash, with a black mane and tail, he hated everyone. I kept him because he'd given up hating me most of the time and he was the finest damn horse I'd ever ridden. He had my back in a fight and knew exactly how I would move into an enemy when we faced one together. We didn't love each other but respect goes a long way in my game.

I took my own reins and mounted before the damned stallion nipped my backside. He danced in circles and pulled on the bit. "He's grown fat," I said to Dillon.

"He's the devil's own horse, that one," said the trader, watching the boy mount. The town gates opened. I waved a farewell to Dillon and rode out of Le Havre.

CHAPTER THREE

WE HIT THE OPEN road and I allowed Ash his head. We raced into the morning, the smaller lighter Mercury keeping pace well. The boy did know his horses, he rode strongly. After a league, we reined back the horses, they were sweating hard and my hangover had faded. I turned towards my companion.

"So, having risked my neck to save your arse, what's your name boy?" I asked.

"Else, sir," he said, clipped and tight.

"Unusual, but all right, it's your name and call me, Lancelot. I am not a, sir, not anymore," I said. Ash shifted under me sensing my sudden tension tighten his reins. I relaxed.

"Thank you, Lancelot," Else said. My name sounded strange on the boy's tongue and I glanced at him. I realised someone had done a hatchet job on his hair and his hands were narrow, his wrists small. He looked almost delicate. Beautiful with those long lashes over soft brown eyes. He had full lips under the swelling and slim hips.

I raised an eyebrow. "I can see why you had trouble with those men."

He glanced at me and I saw the fear flash through his face. I spoke quickly, "No, don't worry, Else, it's not my style." A memory surfaced from my past and I squashed it flat. Thinking about Arthur never helped. "But with a face like that you will need to learn to fight."

"I can fight," his light voice trembled.

"Then you will learn to fight better," I said trying to sound softer and kinder.

We rode in silence for a long time before I grew bored with the sound of the horse's steps. "How long had you been at the tavern?" I asked.

"Three months, Sir," he paused, "Lancelot."

"You are good with Ash," I said.

"He just needs someone to love," Else said and reached out to pat the warhorse's neck.

Love and Ash were not two words I'd use in the same sentence, but still. "Can you clean armour?"

The boy glanced at me, eye contact did not happen often. "Yes, I know a squire's duty."

I nodded as an idea started to take shape in my head. A daft one, because even in the best of times I lived hand to mouth and this would not be the best of times, but I'd had enough of my own company. Maybe a squire would help me have a plan like the good Sister wished.

"Well, I'm not worth much and my reputation as a man is dirt, but I'm a fine fighter and we might just make some money if you want to join me on that basis then you may," I said.

"Can I ask what happened to you?"

"No," I said.

"Those men," his voice grew even softer.

"Don't think about it, Else. These things are best forgotten as quickly as you can manage," I said.

"So, we never talk about either thing?"

"Never," I said.

"Deal," Else replied and I had myself a squire.

I pushed us on during the day, going for distance but alternating between walking and cantering, both easier on the horses and us. We'd covered many leagues and I hoped we'd gone far enough not to be worth finding for murder. There were times when I wished I learnt to think before acting but looking at Else's face as he rode beside me made me glad for my intervention. I'd seen too many innocents hurt to bear it happening when I knew I could prevent it.

I found my favoured spot in which to camp, somewhere off the main road, near a river in a small wood. Hidden shelter. When we stopped for the night I realised I'd taken on far more than I'd anticipated. Else proved to be scarily efficient. I went to find some dry wood, when I returned I found the camp organised with ruthless efficiency and the horses tethered and eating. Else took the wood from me and before I'd settled he began cooking. He smiled as I stared around me at the bedrolls and my armour laid out with care.

"I'll clean it before the rust sets in," Else said pointing to my hauberk and plate armour.

"Good," I said. I'd never kept my own squire, never needed one and the times I could afford the luxury were rare. I couldn't afford this one and as I was no longer a knight of the English court I didn't think I should have one, but I was lonely. I'd been lonely for a long time.

We ate in silence, I went to the river to wash before bed and watched Else slip away to perform similar rituals. He seemed to be a very private lad. Quiet but self assured. The main bonus his ability to make food out of scraps and control my damned horse. This made him worth his weight in gold, I just hoped he'd decide to stay when he realised I would never be able to make him any more than a servant. I lay back and stared at the night sky, trying hard not to think. After the activities of the night before, I grew tired and sleep overwhelmed me far sooner than usual.

The dream felt more real than any waking moment I'd known, on or off the battlefield.

A White Hart and Doe raced through a mist covered forest. The sense of panic overwhelmed any sense of reality. We raced together and then I realised I raced with the wolves, or Wolf. Yes, just one Wolf, dark and silent, running with the Hart, side by side, racing for our lives. I didn't know what kind of predator ran behind us, but whatever it was we had to run. As fast as we were, I knew it grew closer. I urged the deer on but they were unable to increase their speed. So, I stopped and turned to face my enemy in the shrouded forest. I bared my fangs and growled, waiting. Fear washed through the wood, fear and horror. Whatever approached would kill me, no doubt remained, but I must try, I must try for the White Hart's sake.

"Lancelot, please, wake up." Small hands shook my shoulders.

My eyes opened, my hands lunged for my enemy and dragged them over my body. I reached for my knife under my bedroll.

"Oh, shit, no!" Else screamed and I woke.

"Else?" Dawn, the sky in the east a little lighter than the moonless rest. I dropped the boy in an instant.

"You were dreaming. You woke me." He scrambled upright and moved away. "Sorry, but it sounded bad."

I took a few deep breaths to calm my nerves. "We need to move, break the camp." I felt grim, worried about some unnameable threat I didn't understand. I'd been dreaming heavily ever since my punishment. When I'd been pressed hard against the flogging post I had seen in my mind's eye the image of a Wolf. A Wolf I'd known as a boy.

"Do we have time for breakfast?" he asked with caution.

"No, we move now," I rose, still in shirttails for warmth and pulled on my leather hose, then my boots. Else began moving around the camp and in no time had it packed. I made certain I covered our tracks as well as possible, breaking up the fire and spreading it to make it appear old. Else tacked the horses but found lifting my bedroll with my armour wrapped inside, impossible. He was too short and not strong enough.

"Here, let me help." I stood behind him and took the bundle out of his arms. "You need to grow squirt."

He turned under me and I looked down. Beautiful brown eyes stared upward and he smiled. "Maybe you should buy a smaller horse, or a donkey?" he suggested.

"Or maybe I should get a taller squire," I said with a smile. I felt my cock respond to the boy's scent. Warm with a hint of spice. The sensation confused me a great deal. "Get the rest of the things loaded on Mercury," I said. I pushed him well out of my personal space.

He moved away, unaware of his effect on me. I muttered to the horse as I tightened various straps, "What the bloody hell is going on with me? Am I mad? Is that it? I don't fuck young boys, this is madness."

A memory of my time as a squire surfaced. Lying next to a tangled blond mop, a firm strong body in my arms. And I in his.

I growled, forcing the reminiscence away. "I don't do this," I told myself firmly. "He needs help not more bloody problems." I promised myself another night in a tavern with a good whore as soon as possible.

The day started cool and dewy but soon turned into a blue sky, fresh breeze day. The kind of day that lightens the soul and makes the birds boisterous. I began to relax the effects of the dream leaving me.

"Were you planning on staying in that town?" I asked my silent companion.

He glanced up at me. "No, I was just passing through really but needed the money, so stayed a while."

"Where are you from?"

"Here and there," came the evasive reply.

"Okay, Else, what shall we talk about?" I asked.

He considered for a moment. "How about the duties of a squire and where we are going?"

"Where we are going is easy, anywhere we won't get hanged for killing the Sheriff's deputy."

Else grunted at that, but we continued to talk. He proved to have a quick mind. He already knew much of what I'd be expecting from him. He told me he'd picked it up from listening to people in the tavern. I doubted that somehow but didn't press the issue. As most men do, we soon began talking wars and tactics.

"Phoen, what?" I asked at one point.

"Phoenicians," Else said for the hard of learning. "They fought the Greeks."

"Well, your education is a great deal better than mine," I said surprised.

"I just listen a lot," he mumbled. I declined to comment. We were both allowed our secrets.

My stomach began to protest so much even Ash's ears twitched. "Time for lunch and your first lesson in looking after yourself with more efficiency."

We stopped, we ate, we sparred, we rode. That night we stayed in a small village with a simple inn. We shared the only room and I slept.

A week passed like this with no sign of us being chased. I allowed us to ramble about and chose not to push our pace. The weather remained kind and I enjoyed Else's company. He made me laugh and the safer he felt the more he talked. There were times I'd catch him wool gathering and his face would soften, his eyes almost amber in the light. I wondered what he thought about before he slept or who kept him warm in his dreams. My dreams were quiet for the most part. A few I wouldn't confess to myself never mind anyone else but my life felt calm and I began to heal for good.

The eighth morning things grew dark and my world once more changed on the throw of the dice, which belonged to the Fates.

CHAPTER FOUR

"THIS LOOKS LIKE A good place to spend the evening," I said feeling cheerful. The Sword and Shield appeared to be the kind of place in which I could be drunk and happy for days.

"I don't see why we have to stop in this place at all," Else said. He'd been grumpy since we rode into the large town.

"Oh, just cheer up. We can restock, I can win a few rounds of cards, we can drink ourselves silly and sleep with a few willing women. Really, Else, you need to relax." I clapped him on the shoulder and we walked into the tavern. I paused on the top step and inhaled noisily, "That is a good stink," I announced.

The smell in question consisted of male sweat, cheap perfume and ale. We walked to the bar and I ordered two tankards and two rooms. Our surroundings were comforting and familiar.

"We can't pay for it," Else hissed, eyeing the barman as he poured from the barrel.

"We can when I win," I told him. The large heavyset barman plonked two ales with dark foamy tops beside us. I drank quickly and finished my ale just as an over painted but pretty young woman appeared at my elbow.

"Buy me a drink?" she asked, her hand straying to my crotch. She smelt as if she'd already had her share. Else's eyes narrowed.

"Leave him be," he snapped. "My Lord Doesn't want the likes of you."

I blinked as the girl said, "Seems your pretty boy here don't like to share you, my Lord." She began to vanish from my side. I grabbed her arms.

"Just hold on there, girl and I'll get you that drink. My young friend is just out of his depth and it's making him rude," I said while making significant eye contact with Else. "Now if he drinks his ale we won't say another word and you and I can have some fun." I laughed as she whispered in my ear a suggestion even I'd struggle to find redeemable.

"I'm going to see to the horses," Else said, leaving his ale and walking out before I could stop him.

My new best friend and I continued to drink. I found myself winning at cards and my usual routine and habits carried the night forward. I saw nothing of Else. I found my things secured and stowed in my room. The woman proved as inventive as she promised and I had a good night, with no stray thoughts of wide shoulders, slim hips and laughing blue eyes.

The White Hind lay exhausted, the Hart stood over her, trembling on equally exhausted legs. The Wolf, me, stood before them. Blood dripped from many wounds and the mists turned the same dark colour. I heard a sound and my black muzzle picked up a scent. The scent of death and damnation. Unknowable evil. The Hart stirred behind me, walking forward on his long legs. His great antlers lowered as he prepared to defend the Hind alongside me. The evil came then, all pain and anguish to fill our hearts with fear and shrivel our souls in dread.

"Lancelot, please, wake up," urgent calls and pulling on my shoulder.

I woke with a jerk once more but knew Else instantly. He stood by my bed and had his hands on my bare skin. The first time he'd ever touched me in such a personal way. I shook my head, the random thought unhelpful.

"What?" I asked, hungover again.

"We have to leave," he said. His fear made his brown eyes huge in the dim light of the room.

"It's only just daylight, Else. Please, go away."

"No, we have to leave." Else reached into his doublet and pulled out a crumpled piece of paper. He spread it flat, two faces peered up and the word 'Reward' hung over the heads.

"Is that me?" I asked.

"Yes, you fool. Now as delightful as your companion doubtless is, we have to leave, we are being hunted."

"Why? The damned Sheriff can't have that much of a hard-on for us." I felt the woman stir beside me and I shifted so I wasn't in her way. I didn't need her waking up.

"He can if you killed his brother," Else said, not meeting my eyes and keeping his voice quiet.

That nugget of information took a good few seconds to be fully appreciated. "I did what?"

"I didn't think it would matter, so I didn't tell you," Else said.

"Fuck," I cursed as I ran my fingers through my hair. "You stupid prick."

"I'm sorry," he said as he backed away from me.

I frowned. "Where were you last night?" I asked, realising he hadn't been there.

"Watching you piss away your life isn't my idea of a good time," he answered. The prim attitude was beginning to piss me off.

"Where did you find this?" I asked. At least my hangover was manageable for the moment.

"Down by the town gates. I went for a walk when I couldn't sleep for all the noise you were making. Well, she was making." Else scowled at the woman in my bed.

"You ever spent the night with a woman who knows what she's doing?"

"Don't be ridiculous," Else said. He actually straightened his shirt cuffs.

"Well, until you do, don't nag me about whether it's a waste of my life or not," I snapped. "I feel like I'm fucking married," I muttered as I stood up. The bedclothes fell away from my long legs. Else jumped back, gasped and turned a new shade of red. He snapped his eyes shut and turned.

"For God's sake, boy, we aren't that fucking different. You need to learn to relax." I reached for my clothes, then I paused. A noise outside jarred, it was out of place. I approached the window on silent feet and peered through a gap in the shutters. A tall man with red hair stood in the yard below. He wore a very fine sword at his hip and his spurs were what alerted me to his presence. As he paced, he chimed.

"Shit," I said. He'd have a man in the stables looking for Ash. I glanced at Else. "Are we packed?"

He nodded, pale but calm. "Right, finish in here while I dress." I began to throw on clothes and for the first time in weeks, I climbed into my gambeson and hauberk. It felt strange and unfamiliar I'd been without it so long. The skin on my back flinched but it was more imagination than real pain.

"We have to get to the horses and they'll know about Ash. If he's tracked us this far he's good," I said. My thoughts were quick, quiet and I had control, but also an insane piece of inspiration. "Here is the plan," I said picking up the doxy's dress. "You wear this and go into the stable with me. We deal with whatever we meet in there, quickly and quietly. We mount and we ride as hard as we can for the town gates. We stop for nothing."

"I'm not wearing that dress," he said. His chin jutted out with stubborn determination.

"If you don't, I'll leave you here," I threatened.

His eyes flashed. "Fine." He snatched the dress out of my hand and shrugged into it. His small deft fingers did things with it that had it tied up and fitted in moments over his usual clothes, it looked strange hung on him. The blue, though faded, made his eyes more hazel than brown. I didn't know what to say, for a moment he looked so vulnerable.

I coughed to hide the sudden confused emotion. "We need to leave and I need you to help me fake our way out." I grabbed my cloak and covered myself.

"Why are you doing this for me?" Else asked.

I paused. "Because you need me to, because I need me to." I'd thought about the answer to that question a great deal over the last week.

He nodded as though he understood and we left the room maintaining careful silence. The woman in my bed had no idea. I left her enough money to cover the night and a new dress. We all needed to make a living.

On quiet feet, we carried my pack and sword downstairs. I didn't want to fight if I didn't have to and I didn't intend on killing anyone. This sheriff might forgive the death of his brother with enough time but if I slaughtered more of his men, I'd have a bigger problem on my hands. I unlocked the front door of the tavern. The well oiled hinges opened without a sound. I couldn't see the redheaded man and decided a daring approach would be best.

"Give me your arm," I ordered Else.

He frowned, opened his mouth to argue and snapped it shut. His arm slipped through mine and his small body blended with mine. I hid the sword under the cloak and made certain the hood covered my face.

We walked straight out of the tavern; I intended it to be a bold move. Else's arm trembled on mine but his grip remained strong. There were no men in the yard. We walked toward the stables, remaining calm. My nerves pinged and the skin on my back crawled, screaming at me to turn around and check for arrows targeting my back. I held my breath, a stupid move. I forced the air out and focused on even breaths. If we were caught, we'd be hung. No argument and I doubted there'd be much of a trial. We were steps away from the stable when the tall redheaded man walked out. Else whimpered and clutched my arm. We'd covered his head so his short hair couldn't be seen but would the sheriff believe the ruse?

"My lady," the sheriff had a quiet precise voice. His eyes were a green hazel and reminded me of an eagle, as did his nose. "You are awake early."

Else curtsied beautifully and withdrew his arm from mine. "I have to reach my father as soon as possible, sir. My escort and I are here for only a few hours." He smiled and I stared, a horrible idea beginning to surface.

"You are returning to your father?" the sheriff asked.

Else smiled again. "Yes, he is very sick and my brother sent for me. My husband gave me his best man to escort me." He waved a negligent hand in my direction as though I were no more important than a dog. .

"Did you happen to see a man with a boy in there?" asked the sheriff.

Else frowned. "As we walked through the tavern's drinking hall late last night, I think I might have seen something. A tall man, with a whore on his lap, making a fool of himself at cards. A young man stood near him but seemed to be unimpressed by his master's behaviour. I noticed them because of the amount of noise he made with the strumpet." His tone made me aware of how he felt about my behaviour. If we managed to escape this threat unharmed, we were having a long chat.

"And where are you headed to reach your father, if you don't mind me asking?" The sheriff's eyes twinkled as he tried to catch the scent of a lie.

Else didn't miss a beat, he named the town we'd come from. The sheriff's own town, Le Havre. Then he named a man, a stonemason. The sheriff nodded.

"I know the man. He has a daughter married down here somewhere." The sheriff stepped back from the door of the stable, with reluctance he bowed. He knew something was wrong but he couldn't quite work it out. We walked past him and into the dim light of the stable.

Now, I had to hope he wouldn't offer to help with the horses because Ash stood in the largest stall and I wasn't leaving him. Else glanced up at me. "Well, man, what are you waiting for? Saddle the horses." His ringing imperious tone caused me a moment of reflection. I glanced at him. The fear in his eyes came from more than the sheriff's presence. He silently begged me not to challenge him.

I nodded and saw relief flood through his small body. We moved with our usual seamless cooperation, Else to Mercury and I saddled Ash. The sheriff didn't come to check on us and no men were in the stables. We brought the horses out of the stalls but mounted in the stable. I bent low over Ash's neck to stay in the saddle.

"Be ready to run," I whispered. Else nodded. We walked out of the stable. I kept my sword in my right hand and I knew Else carried a long knife in his left. No one stood in the yard. Were we really going to be this lucky? We walked from the yard, into the pre-dawn street. Nothing. We headed toward the south gate of the town. A hush over the town ate at my paranoia. There should be movement by now. The bread sellers, the flower markets, something should be moving.

We walked on, Else by my left elbow. I saw the town's well built wall and its open gate. It came into full view as we rounded a corner and so did half a dozen armed men across the street.

"And I thought you wanted the North road," said the sheriff. "The stonemason's daughter died three weeks ago. He is a friend of mine. A bad choice boy."

I'm not into heavy rhetoric when it comes to a standoff. There would be no point in trying to convince this man to release us. There would be no point in apologies. The only objective would be escape.

"Ride," I snapped. I dug my heels into Ash. Crossbow bolts flashed past my head as I moved, I heard Else cry out in shock but Mercury remained at my side. Your enemies rarely expect a suicide run and this would be one of the best. I crashed Ash into three men. Three others were reloading their crossbows.

"Just go," I yelled at Else as he turned to fight. Someone waved a sword in Ash's face and he screamed in rage. His hooves lashed up in the air and I rode his rear. He pirouetted on the spot to strike out. This was why I put up with his bad moods. He is the finest horse a man could have in a tight spot. I lashed down with the flat of my blade and knocked a soldier's helmet off his head. He collapsed to the floor. The sheriff ordered the gates closed. His voice loud but calm. They stood open to lure us into the trap, but hadn't considered how damned desperate we would be to escape. I watched Else cut down at a man trying hard to shut the gate. He jumped back and Else held the position waiting for me. I slashed down, bellowing a war cry at the top of my voice. Ash wanted to continue the fight but I forced him toward the gate and ordered him forward. Now was not the time to face the guards of two towns.

We galloped over the cobbles, sparks flying. Else turned Mercury and we rode, shoulder to shoulder out of the town. More arrows whizzed over our heads but aiming a crossbow at a moving target isn't easy. If they'd had a long bow, we'd have been in trouble.

CHAPTER FIVE

WE RACED DOWN THE main road scattering people and livestock everywhere. Chaos erupted in our wake. I glanced at my companion in the dress and realised blood stained the faded blue cloth.

"You're hurt," I cried out.

We galloped past a hay cart causing its old horse a fright. Ash tugged at the reins asking for his head so he could really race Mercury. I held him back.

"I'm fine," Else gasped. "Just find a way off the bloody road before they catch us." We both glanced over our shoulders. Men on horses with hounds at their heels were already leaving the town.

"This way," I yelled and I headed for the fields. We began to jump low stone walls and our passage became marked by the shouts of outraged crop farmers.

"The forest, we have a chance in the forest," Else said.

I remembered the horror of something chasing me through the trees and the mist hiding me and my enemy. I remembered the fear, but we had nowhere else to run.

We galloped for the tree line, flat out, low over the necks of the horses. Mercury began to drop back as we hit an incline. Even Ash started to slow. I risked a glance over my shoulder. Soldiers were now on our trail. We did not have the luxury of easing off on the horses. I slowed Ash and waited for Mercury to reach me.

"Hold on." I smacked the smaller gelding with the flat of my blade. He lurched, Else tilted but they picked up speed. Ash surged forward determined to beat the gelding. We hit the tree line and kept moving. A wide track ran through this part of the forest and wanting to put as much distance as possible between us and the hunters, I just kept riding.

The forest consisted of beech, their bright spring leaves helping the sun to mottle the ground. Blue bells were dancing cheerfully as we crashed past. I'm certain it would have been quite beautiful under different circumstances. The track branched off and we took the branch. It proved much narrower and far more rutted than the main road through the forest. I pulled Ash up not wanting to risk his legs. We slowed and I watched Mercury's head drop instantly. His flanks heaved. He sweated all over. I hoped to God I hadn't blown him.

Next, I checked Else. The dress soaked up the blood and the cloth flapped, wet and heavy. The boy under the dress sat very still and held the front of the saddle as though it were his only lifeline. He looked as pale as a church candle. We continued in silence. I heard the distant sound of hounds, but so far, they hadn't found our tracks in the wood. I realised we were riding through a very old part of the forest, great oaks, beech and tall thin birch marked our way. Thick tangles of hazel and bramble forced us to weave. I heard the one thing we needed more than luck right then, a river. Grabbing Mercury's reins, I pulled us forward. There, rushing and gurgling like a cheerful friend, lay a wide stream or small river. A good five feet separated the rocky banks. I forced Ash into the water, turned downstream, so the mud we stirred up would be harder to track and forced him on.

We splashed through the river for a quarter of a mile when I spied a bank, which would be good for our exit. I steered Ash toward the sloping bank.

"No," Else said from behind me. "So far it's the only sensible place to leave the river. We need to continue on." He sounded dangerously week. The foliage over the trees cut down the light, hiding his face but a dark stain spread over the side of his horse.

"You need help," I said, trying to make Ash reverse enabling me to come along side. The horse didn't like the idea when he couldn't see his feet.

"I'm going to be fine, you can help when we stop." Else's voice sounded lighter and he wheezed.

I frowned. Indecision isn't something I suffer from because I often travel alone or have clear orders. He sat hunched over the wound, crooked in his saddle. If we were caught we couldn't run. We needed to be clever to avoid capture.

"Alright," I agreed and pushed past the exit. We were lucky; a long stretch of river on a bend had a shale beach and rocks, not mud, leading out of the river. We splashed from the water and I jumped off Ash. "Ride up there and find the path. Keep the horses still so we have a chance of hiding our direction. Then rip that bloody dress off. I've an idea."

Else nodded, expression and body tight. I watched him settle near the trees and try to undress without dismounting. I smacked Ash on the backside and he walked after Else. I used my hands to begin breaking up our tracks. I took my time over this, I couldn't hear the hounds right now and delaying them further would help. I swept the beach free of hoof marks and returned to the others. Else continued to struggle out of the dress. The dress was winning.

"Get down," I said.

"I can't." There were tears in his voice.

I stood still and looked up into my companion's face. Pale and drawn, Else's hands were weak as they fluttered with the ties. A knot of anger began in my guts. "Let me help."

I held up my hands and tried not to growl. He looked down, his eyes too wide. Else stopped moving, nodded once and with great care, I managed to help him down without touching any of the blood. He whimpered though.

I stood him on his feet. "Let me look at the wound."

"No, it's fine." Else backed up out of arms reach.

"Well, I need the damned dress to help hide the hoof marks, so hold still." I didn't want to frighten the little bugger. I'd seen how fast he could be with a knife when necessary but I had to have hold of him first.

"I'll do it," he sounded stressed.

I made a grab for him, running out of patience. He yelped and tried to pull back, but we'd done a great deal of sparring together and I knew how to take advantage of my height and weight. I also knew all the tricks he pulled to force people to let go of him. How that fat fool pinned him to a wall I'd never understand. Even when we first started, Else proved a good open hand fighter.

I pulled him into my body, he twisted and we ended up his back to my front. He began to thrash. I lifted him off his feet. "Damn it, hold still before you damage more of yourself." I grunted as an elbow hit my ribs.

"You have no right!" Else screamed, startling the horses.

I tore at the dress. I pulled at his doublet and beat his hands away from my face long enough to look at what I found. Wraps, linen wraps, tied around his ribs, thickening around his waist.

"I fucking knew it," I yelled as I dropped him and backed off.

Else collapsed on the ground, panting, blood once more pouring from the wound, staining the white linen dark red.

"You," I lost my words. "You..." I felt so betrayed.

"Girl," Else said with breathless bitterness.

"Liar," I qualified.

Else dropped her head.

"Who?" I thought about it. The questions, the lies I'd doubtless be spun, the tears and petty manipulations. "Actually, forget it. I don't care. You're on your own."

Else's head jerked up. "You'd leave me here?"

I threw my hands in the air and felt the anger surge out, "Well, what am I supposed to do? You lied to me. Do you know how often women have lied to me? Do you know what I've been forced to suffer because of women? Do you know some of the things I've been thinking about, having you lie in my camp night after night?" that last part I hadn't meant to say aloud.

I expected tears. I'm not good with tears. Instead, Else tried to stand, she almost managed it by holding onto Mercury's stirrup leather to help. The colour of her eyes darkened and her own anger crackled against mine.

"And do you think for a moment this has been fun for me? Do you think running and hiding as a boy is a good way for me to live my life? Constantly in fear of discovery, constantly in fear of attack, of being found. Do you think it's fun lying to someone who you care about? Who you owe your life too?"

A long howl screamed through the wood. Seconds later the baying of hounds coursed fear through my blood. They had found our entrance into the stream. I moved, I swept Else up into my arms and I pushed her onto the horse. I tore great stretches off the dress and wrapped Mercury's hooves, then did Ash's. We were both silent during the process. I swung into Ash's saddle. The cacophony behind us increased.

"I'm sorry," Else said. I looked into her eyes, she meant it but did I want to hear it?

I pushed Ash forward and we began to ride along another narrow path. We'd lost any advantage we had and I felt the pressure as I rode behind the small gelding. I thought about Else while I assessed our predicament. Something serious must have forced her to live the way she had been, hand to mouth, no protector, family or friends. She'd chosen to travel with me because she must have thought I'd be safer than anyone else, or going her own way. She could have run from me at any time. I'd have just lost the price of a good horse. Now I knew she wasn't a boy I couldn't believe I hadn't seen it before. She moved with a softness and grace no lad ever thought of mimicking.

How desperate had her life been to risk herself in such a way?

I just wished she'd told me, trusted me. Why would she think I'd be a threat if I knew her secrets? At least I now understood her prudish attitude toward my whoring. Women lied. She lied. All the women in my life lied and tortured. The terrible pain I'd suffered in England dimmed in Else's company. Now it all came back in a rush of misery. How did this happen to me? I was saving yet another woman by laying my life down for her.

The path became rougher, the incline harsh. Else pulled up and turned in her saddle. "Can we get the horses up there?" She pointed at a scree hillside covered in scrubby trees. The occasional large rock protruded from the loose shale covering the steep slope.

I looked at her and said, "I can but can you?" She was so pale. "We can't ride up it, we'll have to scramble and let the horses find their own way."

She nodded. "I can do it if you think it will help."

We rode to the bottom of the slope and pushed the horses into the small oak trees. They soon began slipping on the rocks but we found a path carved by the likes of deer and foxes. I slid off Ash and helped Else down. She felt strange in my hands, my body reacting to her presence in a predictable manner. I ached for her and was shocked by the surge of lust. I gasped and almost dropped her down the slope I tried to escape her so fast. I made it to Ash's head, grabbed his reins and pulled him forward, moving with brutal intent, I wanted to escape myself and the hounds. I tried hard not to think. The sound of the hunt echoed off the side of the hill we climbed. Dogs would have no trouble with the loose rocks but would their masters want the risk badly enough to come after us?

Else began to pant hard. Her breathing out of control. I looked down into the forest spreading out below us. Light flashed off steel helms. They would reach the slopes of our cliff face in no time. I glanced upward. Large rocks that appeared to be balanced on thin air hung over the scree slope. I struggled past Ash to avoid falling.

I pulled Else upright. "You take Ash, I'm going up there." I pointed. "If you hear them still following you just ride. I will slow them down as much as I can." I grabbed my sword and the short bow I used for hunting.

"Lancelot." She grabbed my arm when she realised what I planned. "Thank you."

"Just keep the horses safe," I said and I scrambled away from Ash. If I'd been alone I would have managed to outrun them but Else needed help. I needed to check that damned wound and she needed to recover.

On hands and knees, I made swift progress up the cliff face. Pulling myself from tree to tree where possible. I still had to dig my fingers into the sharp shale. They were cut and bleeding in no time. The damned mail shirt weighed me down and I sweated under the hot morning sun. Grunting, I hauled myself over the edge of the rocks. I lay for a moment wheezing, my lungs and muscles screamed at me.

"This better fucking work," I muttered. I rolled over and crouched low. I'd raced up the slope to avoid observation. I did not want to be seen from below. I watched Else half leading, half leaning on Ash. She'd tied Mercury to his saddle and the three of them moved quickly. The hounds circled below trying to find our tracks. The huntsmen closed in on their trail. I didn't want to kill any of them, they were following orders but I also didn't want to be hung for killing a worm.

If I worked hard enough I'd have time to get this right and save lives. I found what I'd spied from below, a small tree trunk, uprooted that winter because leaves still graced its small crown. I pulled and it moved. Every muscle in my arms and shoulders begged me to stop but I learnt to swing a sword at four years old and I'd been pushing myself ever since. I ignored everything but my end goal, survival. I forced the narrow roots under the rocks and worked the trunk like a lever. Up and down, the seesaw action pushed the trunk deeper and deeper every time the earth around the rocks gave. I heard the horses gathering at the slope and men's voices discussing the merits of following us. I heaved. The rock shifted. I pushed, it wobbled but the trunk couldn't give me any more. The earth too soft to take the pressure. I climbed over the tree and dug my fingers under the huge rock. I realised the impossibility but I'm a stubborn bastard. I heaved and lifted with my legs. The pain, the need to stop became anger and grief over Arthur and his cursed wife. I saw her. Long blonde hair blowing in the summer breeze, she laughed at me and caressed my face. Her betrayal snapped something in my mind and caused my heart to cry out in an anguish I hadn't released even as I'd been flogged. I thought about Else and how alone she'd been, how brave and how she'd never asked anything of me but her own space. The rock shifted. The rock fell. The rock tumbled away from me and I almost fell after it.

CHAPTER SIX

I DIDN'T BOTHER TO wait to see the chaos. I did hear it. Dogs barking, men yelling, horses screaming in fear. I prayed in silence that they all escaped the crashing hellish maelstrom of rock. The top of the cliff rolled downward gently. I ran on trembling legs. The forest once more became a gentle warm place.

Else stood holding Mercury but leaning on Ash. He didn't flinch even as her blood dripped down his leg. He just kept turning his head to check on her. He whinnied as I appeared, seeming to ask for my help. I rubbed his head when I reached him.

"Else?" I peered at her.

She raised her head and managed a weak smile. "We won?"

"For the moment. Now, let me check this wound," I said dropping to my knees.

She pushed off Ash. "Just where I like my men, on their knees." A laugh wobbled out of her and I heard a sob at the end.

"Well, if you behave yourself I'll be happy to kneel before you, my lady," I said peeling back the hole in her clothes. The arrow had cut down to her ribs, a clean slice. It would need stitches to close it, but if we kept it washed, it should heal. I gave her the news.

"Oh, good, stitches," she said as she tried to see.

I slapped her hands. "Don't touch it. Let me unravel some of these bindings and move them over the wound. We need time to stitch it well and I want to put a few miles between us and that accident."

"I can do it." She began to pull away.

"Worrying about your modesty isn't going to help us escape," I snapped. "For God's sake, woman just accept my help and be done with this game."

Else froze. "Sorry," she murmured.

Being very careful I pulled her doublet over her head. Its soft wool and leather smelt of horse and Else. The bandages around her chest and stomach, one to flatten nature, one to fill it out, were clean and neat.

I undid the one for her waist.

"Why did you lie?" I asked, concentrating only on the soft fabric in my hands and trying to avoid the bloodstains.

"I didn't mean to, I meant to tell you as soon as I could but when you offered me a job, I realised I wanted it. I wanted to stay with you and feel safe for a change. I've never travelled closely with one person before and I thought I could manage well enough. Even the Sheriff's brother didn't think he was raping a girl." She sounded detached. I didn't look up into her face. I didn't want this to be personal.

"I hate being deceived," I said.

"I know. I don't blame you. I would just beg you to dump me somewhere large enough for me to be lost."

"Like a forest," I snapped.

"I was rather hoping for a town," she said, a soft reprimand present. Her small hand captured my right one, my fist full of linen. "I am sorry. I never meant to hurt you or confuse you. I just wanted to be safe."

I stared hard at her hand and realised her stomach lay inches from my nose. Flat, tight, narrow waisted. "How long have you been living like this?" I asked, my voice rough.

"Five years, travelling from place to place. I knew it couldn't last, I'm not getting any younger and the crows' feet don't match the beardless face." I heard her frustration.

"Why did you do it?" I had to concentrate on something else other than the feel of her hand on mine. Her calluses were as rough as my own. My fingers still sore from the climb.

"I had to run and hide. I didn't want to marry the wrong man and my father isn't very forgiving."

"Who is your father?"

"It Doesn't matter," she whispered.

I looked up then, straight into her soft round eyes. How could I have thought her a boy? The brown, so warm, so precious. A gift. Was it one I wanted?

The moment stretched. I stayed on my knees looking up into that urchin's face with its short spiky halo of hair and she stared down into my rough, square jawed, features.

She smiled and her left hand moved of its own accord to trace the line of a scar over my right eye. The howling of hounds startled us.

"Fuck," I snapped. "Hold still." I became all ruthless speed and bandaged the wound up. Else whimpered at the feel of the linen but didn't cry out. As I stood, she swayed. I lifted her into my arms and pushed her onto Ash. I jumped up behind her and wrapped one arm around her waist and another on Ash's reins. Mercury remained tied to the saddle.

We moved off, deeper into the greenwood.

The canopy began to thicken and the light grew greener. Else remained conscious but she seemed barely aware of our surroundings. The sounds of the dogs dwindled behind us. Unable to climb the scree, they would have to find a way round and pick up our scent at random. Finally, we were able to put room between us and the sheriff.

We rode at a walk but I maintained a good pace. I wouldn't let Ash wander. I noticed other trees and flowers surrounding us, at one point we walked through a patch of wild garlic. The smell made all of us hungry.

"There is bread in my saddle bags," Else said quietly. I pulled Mercury toward me and raided his bags. We ate bread and some cheese, drinking water, as we rode.

Few words passed between us. I didn't know what to say to Else the runaway girl. I'd known what to say to my squire, but I spent my time with women doing one of two things. Either doxies in taverns or women so far above my station in life it didn't feel real. Else though, felt warm in my arms and far too small.

We approached a fork in the path once more. "We need to go right," Else said pointing. Her arm trembled. The path looked a great deal darker than the one to the left.

"I think we need to go into the light. If I need to stitch you up I need light to do it and this day isn't getting any younger." I turned Ash to the left fork.

Else put her hand on mine, "Please, Lancelot, go right."

"Why?" I asked.

"Just trust me," she said.

"Why?" I repeated my tone more loaded.

She sighed. "You are still angry with me."

"I just want to find you somewhere safe to stay. We will be safer if we are separated." The words were rough. Else had made me a criminal and she lied to me. Another woman in my life played games like that and I did not wish to repeat the experience. My freedom from trouble is all I wanted. Women came and went. This one made my heart ache and my loins tighten, but I knew how to control those sensations.

"You are going to leave me?" she asked.

"You have a better idea?" I didn't want an answer. "This has made a mess out of both our lives. If I leave you somewhere safe, we have a chance. I'll lead the sheriff away but that's all I can do for you."

"She really did a number on you didn't she?" Else growled quietly. Then more strongly, "Go right, it will lead us somewhere safe."

"How do you know?" I bit each word off. She had no right to judge me. I wanted Else gone from my arms.

"Because I have lived near here." She struggled, no longer relaxed against me, trying to assert her separation because of my rising antagonism. I allowed it to happen. The loss of her warmth felt like the loss of the sun in a desert, issuing in an ice cold night.

I decided I didn't want any more detail. We rode down the right fork into the darkness of the forest. The ground and the trees grew mossy. The air became damp and heavy. Large rocks rose around us, further cutting off the light and filtering us through deep crevasses. At one point Else tilted in the saddle and I realised she'd exhausted herself with her small act of defiance. I pulled her back against my chest and held her safe as we walked onward. The forest became still and quiet. It reminded me of my dreams. I wished I'd left Else at the fork in the road and gone my own way.

My thigh started to feel damp. I looked down, blood stained my leg. "Else, we need to make camp. You need to be stitched up. You're bleeding again."

She didn't reply. I twisted her in my arms, she'd sunk into unconsciousness. We had to stop. A small stream crossed our path. I rode Ash and Mercury off the track and draped Else over Ash's neck as I slipped off his back. I reached up and pulled her down, she lay in my arms. So empty, so still. Her pulse fluttered in her neck. I lay her down on the mossy floor of the bank near the stream and made camp. It took a long time. I felt stiff and tired. It had been a long couple of days. I gave up with the mail shirt and shrugged it off. I realised I'd been bleeding, my back having split once more due to the pressure I'd placed it under. It just made me feel more weary.

I started a small fire, but it spat fitfully, the wood damp. I collected fresh water and untacked the horses. They wouldn't wander far and I had to let them find some food. I wished them luck I'd not seen anything to eat for hours.

I sighed, I realised I could delay no longer. I had to help Else. I hated stitching people up. It's far easier to put holes in them than repair them. I retrieved a small kit from my bag and approached Else. She looked so small, lying still in the dark light of the forest. I took my knife, washed it and my hands in the stream. I had a small flask of brandy in my bag, so after one quick swig, I poured some of that over the blade of the knife. Keeping wounds clean is always hard, but the good Sister in England left me a large pot of her healing cream so I'd use that for afterward.

I retrieved the knife and simply cut through Else's clothing, then the makeshift bandage. Blood no longer seeped it flowed as I worked. I poured the rest of the alcohol into her wound. She roused for a moment but settled back into unconsciousness. A long strip of bone winked at me through her muscle and flesh. Rolling her onto her side, I started work. I tried to keep the stitches close together and small to help the scarring. She woke once or twice, but seemed unaware of my efforts on her behalf.

It took forever to finish and dress her wound. How she'd managed the day we'd had with a hole in her that size I didn't know, her strength seemed endless. Once I finished I woke her to make her drink. We managed a little water but she didn't manage full consciousness. The afternoon drew to a close. I tried to keep the fire going and find food. Neither worked well but the horses remained nearby and calm. I gave up and decided sleep would be a good idea. I knew I should sit on guard, but equally, if I didn't sleep I'd make mistakes. I left Ash in charge of our small camp. Else shivered in her delirium, so I took both our bedrolls, curled up around her and dived into sleep.

The dream came up in increments, unlike every other time I'd taken the shape of the Wolf. I lay before the Hind, who slept. I stood and paced around her. The Hart, his antlers low walked toward me, we touched noses as though we had loved each other for a long time. A woman, a tall woman with long brown hair, the same shade as Else's came forward. She was beautiful, regal, slim and elegant. Both I and the Hart bowed before her, she smiled and the world became lighter. She crouched before us and stroked our heads. It felt as though I'd been kissed by a goddess. She walked to the Doe and I rose to go with her, she looked so sad as she tried to wake the animal. Grief broke inside my heart and soul.

I woke, weeping, curled around Else's still form. Dawn had come.

CHAPTER SEVEN

"LANCELOT." ALMOST A WHISPER of sound.

I already knew who would be standing before me. I uncurled from around Else. She stood there, the woman from my dream, for the first time I noticed her eyes. Deep blue, startling and shiny.

With care I moved away from Else and placed my hand on my sword. The leather hilt a comfort. "Who are you?"

She smiled. "I am Else's sister."

"That Doesn't mean a great deal because I don't know who she is," I said. Ash looked as though he were asleep, some guard he turned out to be.

The woman laughed, a light sound, it made my belly feel warm, which made me nervous. "Else is strong, Lancelot, but she is dying in your arms."

That shook me. I glanced down to my companion. Her lips were blue.

I rolled her onto her back and she felt cold and still. The woman was right, Else was dying. "This shouldn't be happening," I whispered. "She can't have lost that much blood." The world began to fall a long distance from this moment.

"She hasn't," the woman said as she knelt on Else's other side. I glanced up at her, my sword forgotten. She looked sad. I found myself overwhelmed by sorrow. If Else died, I would be heartbroken. I knew it like I knew my name. Like I knew my crimes. Like I knew the number of lashes on my back.

"What can I do?" I asked those perfect blue eyes.

"Love her, Lancelot. She has given you her heart and you don't know what it is worth. You wish to reject her to protect yourself." The gentle chiding in her words were blades being buried in my gut.

"I cannot love her," I said. "I love no one." Those words made sense. Yesterday I reminded myself, I wanted to leave this creature in the woods and ride on alone. I did not want romantic entanglements. A squire is what I needed and would act as a balance to my morose loneliness, but a woman? No, I did not need a woman, I wanted something else. I shook my head trying to clear a leaking, sneaking fog.

"Yes, you do," the woman said and it seemed as though I'd been shoved into the centre of a hurricane.

My need to escape this madness left me dizzy but locked in place. The world took on the soft hue of dawn, the colours of pink and orange staining the forest floor through the green leaves. Mist rose as the sun warmed to the day. The deep green wood held me in its spell.

I stared at Else, her small elfin face at peace. Whispered voices overrode my struggling instincts. My thoughts turned and dived, shifting away from my control like river eels on a hook. Did I love her? Even when I'd thought her a boy I had wanted to bed her. She made me ache with desire and have some fevered dreams I didn't want to consider now. I enjoyed her company and admired her spirit. The determination she'd displayed when under pressure of capture had given me great pride, but she'd lied to me from the moment we had met. And now this mysterious woman claimed to be her sister.

"She lied to me," I said.

"She wanted to protect you. She knows you have a deep wound in your soul. She did not want to add to your burdens, but now she needs you. If you do not love her, she will fade and die. It is the way of our kind."

"I need time," I said.

"There is no time, Lancelot. A few more moments and her heart will stop. Just one kiss. The kiss of life. That is all she needs."

I glanced up. "Just a kiss? I don't understand."

"You don't need to. Just one kiss will be enough to begin her healing. Just one kiss, Lancelot du Lac, greatest Knight of Camelot."

"I am no longer a knight," I said bitterly.

"You will always be a knight of Arthur's Court."

I didn't even question how she knew. As the dawn light hit us through the deep green of the leaves over our heads, I took Else in my arms.

"Just one kiss?" I asked again.

She nodded.

"What harm can a kiss do?" I asked myself. I had thought about it often enough after all, but that was my Else, not this one. Still, I lifted her and lowered myself. Her breath whispered over my lips, her eyelids fluttered.

"Lance..." a whisper of sound but I heard my name. She suddenly felt so warm and safe against my chest. I wanted to hold her forever. I *had* to hold her forever.

I kissed her. I had never been so tender, so gentle. A small shock zapped my lips and I found my mouth pressed hard against Else's, my tongue seeking entrance to her body. Her mouth opened. Her hands moved around my back and neck. She responded. The kiss deepened. Something profound slid out of me and into the small body in my arms. The exploration grew more desperate. I felt as though I had dived into my companion and I'd begun to drown.

Else drew back. "Stop, love. I need more time." She smiled, lay her head on my chest and seemed to sleep.

I looked at the woman. "What's happened to her?"

"She is healing. You need to come with me. I have a safe place for you and the horses where you will not be hunted." The woman stood and walked to Ash. He stirred and bowed his head to her hand, just as the White Hart and the Wolf had done.

I rose. I didn't even consider packing my things or tacking the horses. They fell into step behind me while I meekly followed the woman.

"Where are we going?" I asked as we wove between vast oak and ash trees along a path I'd never have found alone.

"Somewhere safe," said the woman.

"What's your name." I realised my world had grown softer, less well defined. It didn't seem to matter.

"My name is irrelevant," came the reply. "Else is all that is important."

I frowned, knowing this was not a good reply but unable to argue my opinion. I tried another question, "What is this place?"

She glanced back at me and smiled. I realised her teeth were shaped to a slight point at the ends. "A safe place for you to rest, Sir Knight."

Before Else grew heavy in my arms we arrived at the edge of a stream. I thought it must be the one I'd camped near. All our things lay in a pile beside the entrance to a cave. The stream came from the cave and formed a pool before babbling off.

"How did that get here?" I asked.

"My friends brought your things. We want to keep you comfortable."

"What friends?" I asked.

"These." She waved her hands and the air stirred over the pool of water and hundreds of small bright lights appeared in the dimness of the woodland light. The world sparkled and shone. They danced and wove, a small chittering, like tiny church bells filled the air with harmonies. I smiled in honest joy, tears rose in my eyes for their beautiful dance and joy filled my broken heart.

"Come, Lancelot, bring my sister." The woman beckoned. She stepped with confidence onto moss covered stones, which made the stream race in tight formation to escape the coolness of the cave.

I followed her, careful of my footing but I didn't slip once. Else remained safe in my embrace. The cave soon widened inside the entrance and I found myself in a home. An area to my right contained a hearth, a low table and pelts to sit on, with rough rock walls on one side and the stream on the other. Natural light filtered into this part of the cave from the entrance. I looked back and all I could see where the trees, almost as though they conspired to hide the cave from the whole world.

Further inside sat a large bed. It had a low wooden base, I smelt the fresh hay and camphor in the mattress, with clean linens and thick fur covers. The air felt cool this far inside.

The woman stood by the bed and pointed. "Place her down there. We will see to her comforts soon."

I didn't want to lose Else from my arms, but compelled to follow the order, I knelt by the bed and placed her onto the mattress. She didn't stir.

"Come, rise, Lancelot, let us now help you to heal," the woman said. Her blue eyes shone in the dimness of the cave.

"There is nothing you can do for me," I said. "I will sleep at the entrance to the cave to ensure our safety." This was my duty. Somewhere in the dimness of my mind, a small voice screamed a warning. I didn't understand so I stayed waiting for orders or approval of my suggestion.

"No, Lancelot, now it is time for you." The woman approached and took my hand. Her skin soft and cool to the touch. She stood only a little shorter than myself. As she led me further into the cave, I began to see light once more and what appeared to be a mist.

The cave narrowed, the rocks changed quality, becoming smoother and veined with deep seams of crystal. These reflected the light from some unknown source. The stream created the mist, I realised it came from the ground, hot. The deep pool of warm water appeared bottomless and reflected the cave's ceiling perfectly. Long stalactites of limestone reached for the water but never came close.

Gentle hands were untying the laces at my wrists and chest. I reached up to stop them. "What are you doing?"

"You need to bathe," said my companion with calm resolve. "You cannot lay with my sister in your current state, it would be unbecoming. Besides, the water wishes to see what perfect gifts our Else has given us. You must heal and we will help. Just relax, Lancelot."

There were so many strange words, I found myself lost inside them and her gentle hands, as she took my shirt from my back. Then she bade me sit on a rock and she took my boots. Her hands were gifts in themselves making my skin tingle wherever she touched my naked flesh. I stood and her hands touched my belly to undo my laces, my cock stiffened instantly.

She giggled. "It seems you are feeling happy."

I pulled her hands from my hose.

"I'll deal with this," I said, my brain asserting some kind of control.

"As you wish, but we will all enjoy your company, mortal man," she whispered, moving away a little.

I stripped, my mind once more becoming complacent in the warm fog covering the pool of water. The woman slipped off the white gown in one simple shrug and walked into the pool, naked as a babe. I grew thick and hard just watching her elegant form gradually descend into the water and now she wanted me to join her, the long slim arm out in welcome.

I glanced back at Else. I could just see her lain on the soft blankets.

"Come, my sister won't mind," the allure and promise inside that voice broke the last of my resistance to this strange dream. That's it, I decided, I'd been dreaming all this time. We still slept in the wood and I was not walking into this warm water to lie in the arms of a woman who seemed less and less human.

I waded into the steaming liquid and found the rocks sloped down sharply. Within a few paces, I found myself waist deep. The water caressed my tired aching body more gently than any woman. I sank into its stillness and drew in a deep breath. My companion approached, her long dark hair trailing behind her like ribbons in the wind from a horse's caparison.

Her arms found their way around my neck and her legs were around my hips without me moving. She smiled into my eyes and my arms and hands were suddenly holding her close.

"Become one with us, Lancelot," she said. "Let the water heal you, let my body ease your pain. Let us become your world so you can join with my sister."

"I don't understand," I told her. I frowned, the screaming in my head growing frantic. I had to run. My hands slipped from the woman's waist and I turned to obey a warrior's instinct.

Her arms tightened, she bowed her head and kissed my neck. A thrill of erotic energy raced through my body straight to my cock. My balls tightened evilly.

"Stay, beloved. Stay and be safe for a while in our arms," she whispered. "Forget the world and its ways for a time. Stay with us and be with Else."

I turned back, the scream died. Desire swept away all thought of shame, guilt, pain and anguish. In this place, there could be only love, passion and warmth.

"Yes," I said as the woman's mouth descended on mine. I tried to turn away. Tears fell as I lost myself to lust even as my soul cried for someone I could never have in my arms again.

"Arthur," I whispered aloud for the first time in weeks.

My seed filled the creature who rode my strangely willing body but unwilling heart. It filled her belly and spilled onto the warm water all at once. Her movements relaxed and she sat still as I softened with her. She stroked back my wet hair.

"Now, you will heal and you will sleep. The next body you fill will be my sister's," she told me.

I nodded, words escaping me, as she led me from the water, meek as a lamb, dried me off before laying me naked under the blankets on the bed. Else also lay naked in the bed. I pulled her into my arms. Sleep stole my muddled thoughts from my head.

CHAPTER EIGHT

AT SOME POINT, I roused from that strange unconsciousness. The small warm body next to me woke at the same moment. I stared into soft brown eyes, which smiled up at me, a soft dreamy expression making her very feminine. I kissed the perfect full mouth. Else opened herself to me and we shared the most intimate of kisses for long moments.

I drew back and asked the silent question with my eyes. She gave a brief nod. I rolled onto her body and found I engulfed her with my height and weight, but her legs were open and her knees were raised either side of my hips. The messy fog inside my head relaxed for a moment and I drew in a deep breath.

"Else, I don't want this," I said.

She stroked back my hair. "Why? I am willing," she whispered. Her eyes were heavy, pupils dilated.

I tried to think of a reason to stop this game. "I have no wish to take your maidenhead. It would be wrong. I am not a man to bed virgins and we are not married." I lifted myself off her body, but her arms and legs locked around me.

"I need you, Lancelot. I don't want to wait. I don't want to think," she said.

A warm memory, unguarded and no longer repressed, rushed from the back of my mind. I lay over an athletic body, strong arms holding me. A sense of terrible loneliness swept through my heart. I buried my head in Else's shoulder, the soft smell and finer bones were wrong but I needed something, anything to take away the loss and confusion.

"I love him," I murmured soundlessly, my lips brushing over her skin making her shift. I never confessed this aloud. I never allowed myself to remember, to feel this deeply. The fog washed forwards again, taking control of my body and the memory of Arthur faded, the halo of golden curls vanished.

Time slipped away. Flashes of awareness mixed with physical need battled until I lost and Else became mine whether I wanted it or not.

I didn't think of, or even remember my past. I merely existed in my cave, held in the arms of a beautiful woman. Sometimes we left the cave and walked through the trees. Their leaves whispered to us of our desire and it seemed as though they stroked our skin as we moved. I thought I saw women, young and beautiful with bark coloured skin and green hair dancing in the shadows. We found our horses, both of whom were quiet, peaceful, Ash even asking for cuddles. We spoke of gentle things, of stories, passions, hope.

Every time we made love, I fell more deeply into the world of our small glen. I began to forget everything, Arthur, England, Camelot, my terrible grief. The peace of Else's existence held me in deep thrall.

I woke one night to hear terrible words.

"I can't do this to him. He's like a drug addled child." There were tears in Else's words.

"You must do it, everything depends on his loyalty to you," said that woman's voice. I hadn't seen her for days.

"His loyalty has never been in question," Else cried out.

"He was going to leave you," she said.

"That's because I lied to him, I am still lying to him." Misery in my lover's voice made my heart hurt.

"Once this process is over he will not leave you and he won't mind. Please, sister, understand our way, this is all we can do to defeat our enemies."

"By using Lancelot and forcing him back to Arthur under my control? It's so unfair. He deserves to be able to make his own choices. Just as I do," Else said.

"You will do your duty." The reply sounded like a slap to the face. "He would not have loved you without our intervention, you were failing, he has to be ours to control. Arthur needs him and we need to control Arthur, we cannot lose control."

"My duty is killing him," Else said. I felt her hand on my head but I couldn't move. A strange paralysis held me still.

"Your duty is changing him, that's all. He will be happy with you and do you not love him?"

Else sighed, "Of course I love him. I just loved the life in him and the rage. He is no longer the man I knew."

"Good, then the transformation is almost complete. Return to the bed and continue your duty." The woman's voice faded away and I felt myself once more buried in Else's body.

"You are weeping." The only words I managed before, once more, sliding into captivity.

"I am going to free you, my love," she said stroking my face. "I just have to pray you will learn to forgive me."

I woke to Else shaking my shoulders and calling my name. I remembered feeling fear whenever this happened and I forced myself awake. A flash in my mind as I surfaced jolted me, the Wolf, dead and the Hart dying. My mind cleared for one moment and I focused on my lover's face.

"What's happened?" I asked.

"Thank goodness." Else bent her head. "Drink this." She thrust a flask into my hands.

"Tell me what's wrong? You look scared." I reached for her. I had to protect her.

"Not now, fool, just drink. Do as I ask, Lancelot and we might both live through this." She rose and went to a pile of belongings. My armour and sword. I blinked, surprised, I'd forgotten all about them. I drank from the flask. Alcohol, brandy, it burned down my throat. I coughed, I hadn't drunk strong liquor in, well, weeks I thought. I'd been on a simple diet for a long time. Fresh spring water my only liquid.

The brandy hit my system. It burned in my belly and I felt my mind come screaming out of the darkness. A terrible, rushing sensation which threatened to destroy my sanity. I gasped and clutched my head. Images and memories ricochet through my head. I saw the day I became a knight, the day of the trial, a hundred jousts I had won, the day of my punishment and banishment from Arthur's side. I witnessed the courage of my friends as they tried to save me from my miserable fate. Lastly, I remembered the reason I felt so alone. My betrayal of my friend and my King. I remembered Guinevere.

"Lancelot." Else's voice whipped through my head. "We have to leave, get up and get dressed. Please," she begged.

"I can't do this." I held my head in my hands, my world crashing back into me. My soul shattering all over again. I'd spent weeks in blissful ignorance of my life and now I seemed to feel each wound a thousand fold. As though they conspired to make me suffer for the time I'd been absent from their company.

"I know it's hard, love, but please, I need you to get up." She stroked my face and the pain receded.

I looked at her. "What's happening to me?"

She smiled but her expression remained grim. "I will tell you everything but we have to leave and we have to do it now. Just sip the brandy. If you drink too much, the real world will come back too fast. It seems we have a fine balancing act to perform."

Her sense of urgency motivated me. My fingers fumbled, everything made harder because of my haste.

"The horses are ready," she said taking my hand.

She pulled me forward and the world became peaceful. "Why are we leaving?" I asked. "I want to stay with you." I tried to pull her to a stop. I wanted to take her in my arms.

"Lancelot, stop, we don't have time." Else squirmed out of my grasp and walked off. I needed her skin on mine. It drove me to her side.

The horses were tethered outside the cave and Else managed to force me onto Ash. She tied my kit behind me, struggling with the height difference until I began to help. Her stress and fear started to mean something to my fuddled mind.

"This way," she ordered, forcing Mercury downstream.

"I don't want to leave," I repeated for the hundredth time.

"Fine," Else snapped. "Then you can stay here and be fodder for the denizens of that cave. I'll go and save Arthur alone."

I frowned, more confused than ever, the dream like state I craved fluctuated violently. One moment I rode and my body felt heavy and tired. The next I realised I'd become immortal, strong and capable. The further we rode from our small world, the harder it became, my body started to shiver as if with fever. I felt sick, headachy, and my bones hurt.

"Else, we have to stop." My stomach rebelled completely. I slid off Ash and vomited heavily. Gentle hands soon stroked my hair back and with her comforting words, the pain eased.

Eventually, I sat back on my heels, my breathing hard and heavy but I felt better, "I don't think the brandy was a good idea," I said.

"It's all I could use to bring you back," she said.

"I don't understand." My mind glazed over with her contact. I tried to pull her toward me, wanting to make use of my sudden strength. She wriggled out of my grasp again.

"You have to get back on the horse and we have to ride out of this damned wood before we are found," she said. "Once we are out I will tell you everything, but we cannot stop, Lancelot. We don't have time. Please, just ride."

The rest of the night passed like a nightmare. My body, desperate to be near her, continued to rebel if we were apart for even a few minutes. I begged her to ride with me on Ash, but Else ignored everything except escape. She also wouldn't tell me what we were escaping. Time moved in fits and starts. It began to rain and the wind grew stronger. The trees moaned and cried our betrayal. I felt their grief as we left. At one point, I'd had enough. I pulled Ash up and told her I was going to stay.

"Fine, if that's what you want." She turned Mercury toward me, rode close and punched me full in the face. I rocked back in shock, the pain unbelievable. Before I knew what happened, she'd tied me to my saddle and taken Ash's reins. She dragged the horse and me after Mercury.

Blood filled my mouth and everything hurt more than any pain I had ever known. We rode on. The night turned to day. The dawn lost in cloud and drizzle and we broke free of the wild wood. Else slackened our pace and we rode through the widely spaced beech trees and coppiced hazel of common land.

Just as I'd begun to think death would be fairer than this evil existence, we stopped. She untied my hands and helped me down.

"God, you look terrible," she said, brushing back my thick black hair.

"What's happening to me?" I asked my trembling, shivering body almost unable to stand.

"Just sit and I'll make camp," she said. She guided me with great care to the trunk of a large beech tree. "We should be safe. They don't come out of the deep green wood anymore."

I huddled against the tree and wondered if I was going to die. The worst of fevers raced through my body, causing it to convulse out of my control. Else wrapped a blanket round me and built a good fire. She made me drink water and it helped the stomach cramps. Then she took my hands.

The feeling of her fingers on mine made the world softer, gentler. I stopped convulsing and shivering so much. "I feel better with you, come be with me." I tried to pull her into my lap.

She looked at me for the first time in what felt like days. She wept. "I didn't know it would cost you so much."

CHAPTER NINE

THE PART OF MY mind, which seemed forever to be the warrior, asserted itself. I looked around us properly, the trees were almost bare, the wind cold. It was autumn. I knew we had hidden in the wood for a while, but two seasons?

"What is happening?" I pulled my hands away from Else. My instinct for survival overrode my craving for her body. "Where have we been? Who are you?"

I remembered the questions I'd had in my mind the day I stitched her up. The lies she'd forced on me when she had revealed herself as a woman and the lies she had yet to explain.

"You must understand, Lancelot, I didn't mean for this to happen but we had no choice. We had to survive. It was the only place we could hide and I thought I could get us through safely. But I fell under its spell as well. I lost track and it's taken me so long to be strong again." Else plucked at her gambeson with nervous fingers.

I rose on shaking legs and approached my pack. I drew my sword for the first time in months. I turned back to her as fast as I could manage, Else gasped. "Who are you?" I demanded.

The sword point rested at the nape of her neck. It trembled but I now felt something like myself, broken and weakened, but me nonetheless.

Else raised her hands slowly. "I am nothing you can easily understand. Please put down the sword and I'll explain. I swear. The time for lies and tricks is so far gone. Please, love," she began.

"Don't call me that." I remembered my anger for the first time in months. I welcomed it and hoarded it close to my heart. Unfortunately, my body had other ideas. My stomach cramped, I jerked violently and my hand lost control of the sword. It clattered to the floor of the wood and I doubled over.

Else flew to my side. "You can't hurt me, Lancelot. Your body won't allow you to threaten me. I know you are angry but please, be calm."

"Just tell me." I almost collapsed into her arms, forcing myself not to weep like a babe.

Else held me. "I'll have to begin with my conception or this isn't going to make any sense," she began. I stilled, my head in her lap as I shivered. "I am a sister of the woman in the cave. Our mother is the same woman but I am half mortal, sort of, my father is Merlin." She stopped.

I groaned, "You aren't human at all, he's not human."

"He likes people to think he's not human but only one grandparent is fey, they just happened to be a very strong kind of fey. That's what makes him powerful."

"Alright, so you are Merlin's daughter, what more lies are there, Else?" My bitterness hurt us both. She trembled against my exhausted body.

"There are many lies and tricks," she said. "I was raised in the wild wood until I was five. That's how I found it this time. Then Merlin appeared and took me into the world. Your world. His magic eased my transition but I remember even now how much it hurt to leave my family. He took me to England and implanted me into a new family, the de Clare family."

She paused for a long time as my brain began to join up some hideous dots. "Shit…" I groaned. "You are Eleanor de Clare. The missing daughter."

"I am."

She'd vanished before being presented to court. I remembered the chaos it caused. I had even joined the hunt for the girl. She'd been sent to court in order for Guinevere to finish her training before Arthur allowed her to marry the man her powerful father had chosen. That had been over five years before.

I laughed and forced myself to leave her lap, but I couldn't bring myself to release her hands. "I've been fucking Stephen de Clare's sister. He's going to love me for that. He's the one who made Arthur give me these damned stripes." I referenced the lash marks on my back.

Else looked down. "I didn't know."

"I didn't think you needed to know. I thought you were my squire."

"Do you want to hear the worst of it?" she asked.

"Of course it gets worse. This is my life. It has to be worse." I did pull away from her at last and moved to the other side of the fire. The ground felt cold and damp but it kept my mind focused.

"Merlin helped me run. He hadn't meant to leave me with the de Clare's long enough to be married. He didn't think they'd find me a husband when I was barely fifteen. When he did find out he brought me to Europe." Else rose and paced. Her unhappiness a living thing, the tension in her body obvious. "He told me I had to wait, I had to survive and wait for the man who would save my people and Arthur. A man would come and rescue me when I needed him most. That man would be the one to destroy our enemies."

"What do you mean?" I asked.

She threw her hands up. "I don't know. He left me and said he would return but he never did. When you showed up and saved me from the sheriff's men, I knew it must be you. I'd never needed help so badly. And when I realised you were Lancelot. The *Lancelot*, that we all dreamt about at home, I knew you were the one to help. I used to listen for hours about how much Stephen hated you winning all the tournaments and fighting by Arthur's side," she ran out of breath.

Pausing she fought to calm herself. I watched, dumbfounded.

"Merlin told me that when the man appeared, I had to bind him to me with ties of loyalty and love. When you thought I could be your squire you were happy to be in my company. But I'd noticed the night you arrived how you are around women and we all heard about your love for the Queen."

I looked away from her at that point. My relationship with Guinevere is not something I chose to talk or think about. My love for her husband even more complicated.

She hurried on, "So, I thought being a boy would help you come to terms with my company. I didn't want to trick you or force you to love me."

"That worked so well," I said, aching for her once more.

She ignored me and more words spilled out, "When we were almost caught and we ran into the wood my homing instinct kicked in. It is the place of my birth. I felt it call to me and I followed that call. When I woke, it was already too late. You had been enchanted and I didn't have the strength or talent to fight my sister's desire for you. She wanted to bind you to me, so I would force you to save our family and Arthur. In making love to me, she bound us together, driving your essence into me and mine into you. She knitted my magic through your soul and you cannot escape me without great harm. It takes a full quarter cycle for this spell to be complete. You would have been my happy companion forever if I'd left it any longer and you would never have known what I'd done."

"I would have been your slave," I said.

"Yes," she murmured. "When I realised what we were doing to you I tried to talk to her, to explain this wasn't a good idea. That as a man you would have helped if I were just honest. That she needed to remove the spell. She needed to free you from me and the land of the fey. But she wouldn't. She told me I had to attend to my duty and my duty was to save our family by using you."

Else sat as though all this exhausted her. "But I know we have to save Arthur without lies and trickery. I wanted the love of the man, Lancelot, not the halfwit her magic was creating. That's when I knew we had to leave. So, I've been working on that for the last few days and nights but it's hard because the human part of me is as vulnerable to the spells of the fey as you are. I just knew I must take you from that place before the autumn equinox."

"So, now what?"

"Now you have to survive the withdrawal of the magic from your blood and your soul. Now you have a choice. Travel with me to England and help Arthur, or leave and try to survive without me."

"What is the threat to Arthur?" I asked.

"A rival fey family want him dead. They are using the de Clare family to cause trouble in Camelot. You are the only one who can help. You are the only one Arthur loves enough to trust."

"That's it?"

"More or less," she said.

"But I am addicted to you aren't I?"

"Yes," she whispered, hiding her voice from me. "I am sorry. I didn't know it was happening until too late. I loved you so much, Lancelot, I didn't have the will to stop you."

"Love me?" I began to shiver. "Love me…" I said, broken and disbelieving. "You have lied to me, tricked me, manipulated me and hurt me. You are just like all other fucking women and I hate you." The shiver turned into a jerking aching reaction to my emotional withdrawal.

"Let me touch you and I can ease your pain." She rose and came to my side. Her hand outstretched to my face.

I reacted with predictable violence. I threw myself backward and pushed her hard in the chest, sending her sprawling. "Don't you fucking touch me. Don't ever touch me again, you scheming bitch," I growled at her. She went white with shock. "I would rather suffer a thousand whips on my back than ever have you touch me again. I will save Arthur." As though it had been in any doubt. "But you do not come to me again, ever." My rage and sense of betrayal; my self pity and misery were the only things which made any sense to my beleaguered mind.

We didn't speak other than to see to the camp. When she left me alone to see to her toilet, I wept silently. Eventually I felt able to sleep, but I had vivid evil dreams of slaughtered white Doe's and bloody Wolf pelts. Of the antlers of a great white Stag hung on the wall of a dark castle. I woke fitfully, my body racked with pain. Else watched, her misery clear, but she maintained her distance.

When dawn came, I forbid her from touching Ash. I moved slowly, painfully, every muscle ached but I vowed I would break myself of my cravings for her body. My only goal to smash the spell placed on me. I would not love this fairy witch. She stayed quiet and small. My anger made Ash nervous and tetchy, he nipped and stamped every time I came close. It took a long time to saddle him and even longer to climb into my gambeson and hauberk. I mounted and a small whimper escaped my control as I settled in the saddle.

"Please, Lancelot, I beg you, let me ease your pain."

"Leave me alone," I growled. "I will kill you if you touch me. Now, just get me out of this fucking wood and back to England. If Arthur Doesn't kill me on sight we might find a way through this shit."

"Yes, my Lord," she said.

We rode. I sweated, first burning with fire through my blood and guts, then so cold I thought I'd rather die than move another step. Everything hurt more than I had ever considered possible. I knew every sinew and bone which laced my body in an eternity of pain. We left the wood around midday and that night we paid for lodgings in a farmer's hay barn. I curled around my pain and nursed my rage.

It took almost a week but we made it to the coast. It rained, a near constant dripple, adding to my misery. We were too impoverished to pay for transport across the channel but Else vanished at one point and reappeared with a purse of small coins. I didn't ask. I didn't care. England beckoned regardless of my state of mind. I suppose I became accustomed to the pain and the terrible convulsions almost stopped. I just ached, a hidden wound in my chest, which refused to heal, bleeding constantly.

"I have enough to take the horses," Else said. She watched me drink strong liquor of indeterminate heritage. I'd taken to drinking even more than before as we travelled, it helped ground me and made the withdrawal less agonising.

"Well, I'm not leaving Ash here," I snapped. "He'll kill anyone other than Dillon." I hid my relief from her, I needed Ash, he steadied my nerves and acted as an anchor. He gave me something real to hold onto, something that needed my concentration and dedication.

We were in a town I didn't use to reach England, Mont St Michel. Else knew it, she'd used it to hide her identity for some months. She now wore a simple dress of deepest green, a warm woollen cloak around her shoulders. The curls from her brown hair kissed her high cheekbones. She looked beautiful. I spent a great deal of time not watching her.

I stared at a woman, who touted for business in the tavern, her dark blonde hair tied back neatly. An idle thought wandered through my head about how she might feel in bed. Then I realised I didn't care. I didn't ever want another woman in my bed. I never wanted another woman in any capacity in my life. Arthur might well be in danger and I would go to him, but once he knew of the threat, I planned on leaving Else. I also knew Stephen de Clare would cause chaos when he realised I brought his sister home, and I'd bedded her. Else and I needed a conversation about how she wanted to handle the situation but I wasn't ready.

She sat with me while I tried to drink myself into a stupor and didn't say a word. When the tide came in, we left the tavern, collected the horses and I spent a long time coaxing Ash onto the ship. He consented when Else took his bridle. We were a long way from England. It would take almost three days to reach the south coast and another two weeks, maybe more to reach Camelot. Once there, I'd either live or die at Arthur's behest. I'd given up caring to be honest. I had nothing left to live for; I'd given my heart and honour to one woman only to have her marry my best friend, then turn him into a cuckold. When I'd escaped her I'd run into Else. She had lain in wait for me, taken me and used me. She had dishonoured herself using my body and I would have to pay.

I spent the whole journey drinking alone. The Capitan watched me warily. The sailors gave me wide berth. Misery became my only companion.

CHAPTER TEN

AS A HIGH FUNCTIONING alcoholic, I managed to pack and organise Ash just as land came into view. The rough trip meant I'd spent the whole time on deck, battling sea sickness, constant drunkenness and Else's presence on board. She felt like a huge flea bite under my skin, which needed scratching. I hated her being near me. She'd lost all colour in her warm skin and seemed to be losing weight. Else spent as much time as possible below decks with the horses.

When we docked, I couldn't see her with Mercury, which surprised me because he stood with his usual patience waiting for her. She'd brushed and tacked him up, even tied her bedroll on the back of his saddle, but I didn't see her anywhere nearby. The itch she represented grew to be a pain. An ache under my heart. Where the hell was she? That ache began to spread into my chest. I hated it. That ache meant I'd need to at least see her to ease its pain. When she vanished from my sight for too long it hurt and the pain just grew worse until I couldn't breathe around it or think.

"Damn it, fucking woman," I cursed. I didn't want to admit I felt scared for her, Else had never been anywhere she shouldn't in all the months I'd known her.

I tied Ash and stomped up the ramp they used to help the horses in and out of the ship. We'd paid extra to have them housed under the deck, helping to keep them safe and warm.

I reached the deck and looked for her tousled head and green dress. Nothing. She must have decided to change. I walked into the galley and down into the cabin area of the ship. I heard a muffled cry.

"Else," I whispered, already moving as though I'd never drunk a drop in my life. I crept forward on light feet. I drew my knife from my belt and wished I had room to use my sword. The Captain's cabin came into view and seemed to be the site of interest. I reached it, four men were present. Four men and one woman. Three holding down my squire and one about to make use of her. Her dress lay torn over parts of her body and bruises already coloured her pale skin. The world became a very simple place.

"Just hold the whore still," said the Captain. "Only bloody good for one thing and he don't seem to want nuffing to do with her. Maybe his Lordship has a limp dick but she ain't his wife, I knows that." He grabbed his stiff cock and moved to push it into Else. She tried to fight. I stepped into the small room.

"Is this a game for all comers?" I asked, feeling that quiet, calm place take over, echoing the challenge I made to the last rapist I discovered.

The Captain shifted back from his prize, I cut his throat. Blood leaked down his grubby waistcoat and a small gurgle escaped. He died before he hit his chin on the table. Two more went down in one big movement. The third tried to stab me with his own knife, but by this time Else found herself free. She flipped onto her feet. She reached for her torn gown and wrapped the sleeve around his neck, pulling tight. She heaved him backward, onto the small table. He reached for the garrotte, with a knife in his right hand. She grabbed it and cut his throat. Not one word passed our lips until it ended. We just stood, our heavy breathing filling the small space and stared at each other.

"This is becoming a habit," I said.

"Men are only ever after one thing," she managed through swollen lips.

"Not all men," I said trying to be gentle as I watched her eyes fill with tears.

She whimpered, a small sound of anguish. With no room to think I found my arms around her small body even before I realised I'd moved. I held her closer than I'd ever done before and she trembled.

The ship came into harbour, the movements gentle under our feet. We'd be at the dock in moments. I had to get her moving. We'd become fugitives once more, only this time I was in England. My territory.

"We have to leave, do you have another dress?" I asked as I untangled her from my body. The room began to stink of dead men. Blood leaked everywhere. I sighed, I did kill too easily. I felt nothing for these men. They had threatened my... The thought died. My what? Lover? Wife? Burden? Torturer? Squire?

She looked up at me, her right eye puffy again. "You didn't notice?"

"Else, now is not the time to criticise me for not noticing a new dress." I brushed hair out of her eyes.

"I have a blue dress," she said, her fingers picking at the green one. "This was my best dress though."

"We'll buy you a new one," I said. "Just get dressed into something decent." I lifted her over the dead men.

"Everything is on the horses," she told me.

I growled something foul and considered my options. "Fine, put this on and wait." I shrugged out of my cloak and pulled the dead men into the cabin, pulling the door closed. Else looked frail in the vastness of my winter cloak.

The ship bumped against the dock. "Do you trust me?" I asked.

"With my life," she said without hesitation.

"Then make like a sack," I said as I bent, folded her over my shoulder and lifted. Else grunted but lay passive over my back. No one could see her head or her feet. I might just pull this off by making it appear I carried my cloak rather than wearing it. I walked onto the deck. The pain in my heart eased with each step and my strength returned. I walked through all the sailors who were busy with the docking and down toward the horses. I slung Else as gently as possible over Mercury's surprised back and tied her in place.

"Stay quiet, no matter what, stay still and quiet," I ordered.

She looked up, a flash of her eyes, as I pulled back the hood. "Thank you. You didn't have to save me," she said.

"Yes, I did." I covered her head, unable to say more.

I tied Mercury to Ash and led the stallion out of the bowels of the ship. We walked up the ramp and the horse's hooves beat a slow tattoo on the wooden deck before reaching the thick planks down to the shore.

"Where's your woman?" asked the first mate.

"I have no fucking idea and I care even less. She's meeting me in Jack's Tavern," I said knowing this town well enough to name a favoured drinking spot.

He grunted, not really caring and we walked back to dry land. I heard the deck hands as we past them, English voices, from an English town, we were in Key Haven. The town from which I'd fled England so many months before. I mounted Ash, after pulling him off the dock and walked him to the nearest small, dark alleyway. The day conspired to help us with dark brooding clouds of the kind that keep even the most curious indoors. I didn't want to dismount to help Else just in case, so I almost lay over her to untie her from Mercury. As she came free, she turned on his back and the flash of naked thigh under my cloak almost unmanned me for good. She straddled the horse effortlessly.

"You aren't hurt?" I asked.

"Only my damned pride," she muttered.

"Four men of that size in such a small place would be almost impossible for anyone, there's no shame in that." I tried to reassure her.

"Bastards hit me on the back of the head." She rubbed her scalp.

I leaned toward her without thinking and touched her head. Throughout the whole terrible scene we hadn't made skin on skin contact. I'd worn riding gloves, only now removing them to help her. Our skin touched, a spark flashed into me, arcing out of her body. She yelped. I felt as though I'd been stung.

"What the fuck?" I snapped as I yanked my hand back.

Her eyes filled with tears. "It's the spell. It's trying to draw you in again," she almost wailed.

I felt my anger stir but I also felt pity for her, she didn't want this, I understood that at last, she didn't want to hurt me. I tempered the anger. "It's all right. Just so long as you are safe and we don't have to worry about you having concussion."

She sniffed and shook her head. "I'm fine."

"That's not true but we don't have time to debate it. I suggest we leave town. The gates will be closing in an hour."

"Can I change?" she asked. She still wore her boots.

"Can you do it quickly?" I asked. She nodded.

Else sat on Mercury and began rummaging in her packs. She pulled out a leather doublet and hose. Every now and again, a flash of pale flesh would fill my mind as she exposed an arm, breast or leg. I forced myself to move away. In a few moments and without getting off the horse she told me she was ready to move.

I did not want my actions on the ship to help draw attention to us, so we walked calmly from the alley and wove our way through narrow back streets to reach the main road half way through the town. The port made the place busy at all times of the day and night and allowed all kinds of people to blend. When we reached the town gates, I heard Nones being called in a small monastery to our right. We had maybe four hours of daylight left with the glowering sky hiding the sun. The men on the gates were half asleep and paid no more attention to us than they would flies on a pile of horse shit. We left without a fuss and I drew a relaxing breath at last. I was home and pushing into the English countryside.

Night soon became an urgent problem. I wouldn't risk an open rutted road with no starlight or moonlight so, we stopped and made camp. Else had organised us good provisions and we arranged our makeshift home with familiar ease. She started to cook a simple potage while I tethered the horses.

I brushed Mercury down with short efficient strokes and I considered my options. My choices were limited and they would affect the rest of my life if I could just find it in myself to forgive some stupid bloody decisions. I finished the horse, wanting to talk more than think, I'd been thinking too much recently.

I walked back to the camp and watched Else for a moment. A vivid flash of how she felt in my arms bounced out of my memory, a small sound escaped my lips. She turned, her smile faded as she saw whatever was in my face. I fought for control and won, walking back into the firelight calmly.

"We need to talk," I began. Else watched me, wary again. I sat on a log by the fire and looked into it rather than at my companion. "We need a plan for tackling Arthur. He's not going to be willing to listen to us without being forced to do so. And it's hard to make him do anything."

"Alright, well, I was planning on just riding into Camelot and asking to see him," Else said.

"If we do that he will have me arrested on sight and you packed off to your brother without considering any other option." I realised my hands trembled. I needed a drink. Great one addiction to control another. I have all the brains of a water vole.

"So, what's the plan?" she asked, dishing up a bowl of potage. The smell was fantastic. Thick and warming, I really needed to eat.

"I challenge Arthur on the tourney field. He can't resist a fight. All I have to do is beat him and he'll be forced to listen to me. He always offers his knights a gift, *'You can have anything you like if you win, but my wife or my kingdom.'* So, I'll just ask him to listen to me."

Else reached across the space between us with my bowl. I didn't think about the consequences as I took the bowl. Our fingers brushed and that dreadful spark bit us both. We froze, our hands held out with the wooden bowl between us, a part of us. Her eyes were so big, her lips parted, she looked tired. The ache in my loins grew painful. I drew my hand back, the bowl held in a crushing embrace. Else settled on her heels and stared into the fire taking deep breaths.

I continued with my plan but my voice thickened, growing heavy and desperate. "Once we have Arthur's attention, we will find Merlin and we can sort this mess out." I finished, plan gone to shit. I tried to eat, forcing myself now my stomach had lost interest.

"Can you win?" she asked.

I laughed. "Of course I can win. I'm the best he has."

"You've not fought for months and you are suffering under some great burdens," she said being tactful.

"You mean, I look like shit, my body is a wreck of addictions and my focus is all over the place? I know, Else, but I'm still the best there is, as I think I proved earlier." The thick stew warmed my guts and took the edge off everything I suffered.

"Well, at least you know your limitations," she said chuckling. "Pride not being one of them."

I smiled. "We will go to a friend of mine. I'll need some new equipment and we have no coin. He will not betray us to anyone."

"You mean my brother?"

"Among others," I paused. The shadow of the mighty Stephen de Clare towered over our campfire. I needed to perform damage limitation, saving Else's reputation should be a priority. At least some of the people at Court would remember a de Clare sibling. The words stuck in my throat. A confusion of emotion caused a logjam of thoughts. Part of me wanted to remain angry because I didn't know which of my thoughts were real or caused by her magic. Part of me just wanted to acknowledge I desired her even before knowing she was a woman. Part of me wanted to simply run. "Else…" I tried again, but she held up her hand.

"Don't, look, Lancelot, I know how hard this is for you so just listen. My brother need never know about what happened. It shouldn't have done anyway and if he tests my virginity…" She shuddered at the thought. "Then I can lie. I've been out of their hands for a long time. We will just play it that you found me, recognised me and convinced me to come home. Then I'll ask Arthur to interfere and stop Stephen marrying me to some idiot. If he won't then I guess I'll run again, or marry some man and breed his children." The anger and bitterness in her words shocked me.

She also sounded horribly resigned.

The thought of her marrying someone else did not make me happy. I'd taken her maidenhead and now I would lie about it so I didn't have to be burdened with her. My quandary lay in the fact I hadn't done it under my own volition, but I knew full well if I'd been cognisant of the all the information, her virginity would still be mine to claim.

"Else," I said. "Come here." I couldn't move to her. I didn't trust myself.

She came to me, not making any sudden moves, as if I really was the Wolf.

I felt like one. I would have my prey between my jaws. Her large brown eyes betrayed her fear and desperation. She looked down. I reached up and took her hands. The energy between us rushed and I fought for control of my mind at the contact. I began to lose. The fog rushed through my consciousness. She must have felt or seen it happen because she cried out and pulled her hands back.

"Damn it," I cursed, the fog receding. With every muscle in my body knotted and full of power, I reached for my riding gloves and pulled them on with sharp movements. I rose. Else backed off, I reached out and grabbed her hand.

"Please, don't run, it'll just make this harder." The need to hunt this woman made me sick. I pulled her into my embrace, thick layers of clothing between us, I possessed her and the predator in me backed down. He grew peaceful now he sensed my prey relax in my arms. I smiled. The gloves helped. I held her with the gloves and it eased the honest need I had to be with her without triggering the magic.

"It works," I said. "I can feel you but not the spell." I allowed my hands to move over her body, holding her waist and the back of her head. I pressed her close, tucking her head under my chin. We stood together like that for a long time.

"I wish I knew how I really felt," I whispered. "I want to know I feel something honest. But I don't know if it is honest. I do know I have no wish to hide behind your skirts when facing your brother and I have no intention of seeing you marry some fat fool."

Else sighed, "I cannot ask for your protection, my Lord, I have no right."

"You are my squire, you have every right."

"There is one thing I haven't told you," she murmured.

I felt the tension return to my body at her words. "What?" I couldn't hide the darkness. She withdrew from my arms and I let her.

"It's to do with the spell. I think we might be able to break it, so we could have an honest affection between us if that's what you want. I didn't mention it because you were so angry there didn't seem much point." She rushed with her words as though terrified I would turn into a monster again before she had a chance to speak. "Merlin will be able to break this spell. Then we can discover how much of this is right." Her eyes pleaded with me not to be angry with her.

The anger burned but I realised its pointlessness. There was nothing I could do except hurt us both. "Merlin can help?"

She nodded. I gently pulled her back into my arms, "Then we have a place to start, Else. I am not giving you back to your brother. I wouldn't have done it before this spell, I will not do it now."

I thought I understood how I felt. I did love this woman. What form that love took, I did not yet know, but admitting it existed seemed a good place to start. "We will tell them we are married. Then, when we find Merlin and when the spell is broken, either we can stay together or I will find you somewhere safe to live. But you are now my responsibility. You are my squire."

"I cannot give you anything in return," she said.

"You don't need to. We cannot afford for my mind to be lost in a cloud of fog, so sleeping together isn't a plan. We need time, Else." I gazed down into her brown eyes, without true physical contact and I knew, spell or not, I would give my life for this woman. She deserved it far more than some I'd known. I held her face and she turned into my hand, her warm breath against the leather covering my palm. I bit back a groan knowing she would bolt if I proved unmanageable.

"We should rest now," I said, needing very much to be alone. She stepped back and the void of her absence burned through me but this time, this time I could have her back if I needed her.

CHAPTER ELEVEN

THE JOURNEY TO FIND my friend proved uneventful, wet and long. Almost a week on bad roads in bad weather. We rode over a hill late one afternoon in the pouring rain. The trip did enable us to find our feet with each other under the new circumstances and we seemed to be managing our situation well. Every morning she broke camp and I trained with Ash if the weather and space permitted or I practiced sword techniques. When the pain of separation drove me to needing her or a drink too badly for me to continue, I'd stop. She would take my hand in both of hers and just hold me. I couldn't bring myself to look at her and we didn't speak, but the compromise helped my nerves and sanity. Thus, we managed my addiction. When she didn't have to give my body its fix we would wear gloves and causal contact became common. I still ached for her, but it felt different. It came from me, so I welcomed my desire and nurtured my feelings for the woman, not the fairy.

Geraint's holdings were large. His family had taken me in as a squire, so I knew his land well and we'd been inside his borders most of the day. We now sat overlooking his central home. I watched the bustle of the thriving township preparing for the night. The home of the Fitzwilliam's remained as large and imposing as always. A daunting prospect for any invading army.

The town lay in a tight sprawl under the watchful eye of a huge stone keep. Geraint's father built the keep and it proved its worth against marauding enemies. The walls were seven feet thick in most places, with small slit windows on the outside. What remained invisible to Else was the inside of the keep. Geraint's mother made certain it would also serve as a home. A large courtyard overlooked by full windows and open arches gave the place natural light and warmth. The back of the keep housed the great hall and kitchens, while the front, contained the living quarters. These overlooked the shoreline of the small cove and the sea. The cliff acted as a perfect defender. The land tumbled to the edge of this dangerous cliff, making the buildings around the keep sit on different levels. The effect was a haphazard smattering of stone and wood buildings, clinging onto the edge of Cornwall and threatening to tip into the sea at the prompting of a strong cough.

Surrounding the whole stood a wall, designed to act as a killing field between the enemies and the defenders. It danced up and down the land trying to marry together the different levels. If the wall were ever breached the enemies would be trapped in a no man's land. The whole town's populous fit inside the keep if necessary and helped defend their home. It worked; people loved having that level of safety provided by their Lord. In return, they helped to maintain their assets.

Else touched my arm to bring my attention to her. "We need to finish the conversation about what we are going to tell your friends."

I'd been thinking the same thing. "We tell them we are married," I said firmly.

"That's not fair to you and will cause chaos with Stephen. Please, Lancelot, I need to defend myself. I have no wish to use you to protect my reputation." She meant every stubborn word, the set of her jaw the only clue I needed.

I sighed. "Else, telling them we are not married makes you vulnerable in more ways than one. Accept my help and live on my honour for this."

"You are the Queen's champion," she continued.

I ignored that comment. "I am going to be your husband if Merlin manages to break this damn spell so I can care for you without losing my mind," I said, determined to keep my word.

We both sat on our respective wet horses and stared at each other. I'd just proposed. I hadn't meant to put my thoughts in those terms. Another complication I didn't need, but I also didn't want to take the words back. Else blended with me, she rode as well as I did, she'd proved herself on the road and against attackers. If I had this woman in my life, I would never be alone. I'd been alone for a very long time.

Silence for a long time, then, "Oh."

I nodded once, my gut clenching. "Good, now we know where we stand. We belong to each other and once this spell is broken we make it official, in the meantime Stephen can scream all he likes and he can't take you from me."

Else hesitated and then said, "Right." She rode forward, Mercury walking with his head down, plodding onwards.

I frowned. Somehow, that didn't feel like the correct response, especially under the circumstances. I didn't quite know how to or even if I'd have a definitive answer out of her. Did this mean she didn't trust me enough to marry me despite losing her virginity to me? I forced the problem to one side. It squirmed, protesting, wanting me to worry at it, but I knew how to control annoying thoughts. I forced the concerns into a dark corner and beat them into silence, informing them I had more pressing difficulties.

We rode down into the town, through yet another wet league. On the outskirts of the town, a man with dark red hair, slightly taller even than me, helped a blacksmith move a huge cart from the road. I forced Ash on and when I reached the site, I slid off his side and took hold of the same corner of the cart that Geraint lifted.

He didn't look at me, just said, "Lift."

I smiled. We lifted. It reminded me of the huge boulder I'd been forced to move alone in the wood. We both groaned with the effort. The cart lifted, we walked round the few paces necessary and dropped it off the road.

"At least something's gone right today," Geraint said forever cheerful, his default state. He turned to me to say thank you. When he realised who stood by his side, he cried out, inarticulate with joy and swept me into a huge bear hug.

We embraced for a long time. I hadn't realised how much I had missed him. Arthur refused him access to me when I'd been incarcerated, so we'd not been together for over a year.

"You're alive," he choked.

"You doubted?" I asked. He pulled back to look me over as though I was a prized horse.

"I tried to find you as soon as I could," he said. His voice tinged with emotion.

"I've been a long way from home," I said.

"You look..." he paused. "You look wet."

I laughed. "I am wet, my wife and I need shelter."

Geraint hesitated. I watched with amusement as he processed this information, "Wife? You've been busy."

"You have no idea," I said looking with love at my friend. His hazel eyes stared beyond me and I knew he looked at Else.

"Wife," he nodded. "A good idea for you, my friend, it'll keep you out of trouble."

I laughed. "I doubt it."

"And you still own that bloody minded horse." His face fell as he took in Ash.

"You're just not brave enough to ride him," I said, clapping him on the back. We moved toward the town. Ash fell in with Else as always.

"The only time I was stupid enough to try, I ended up on my head," he said as he walked with me under his arm. Geraint is the only man I know who makes me feel small. He suddenly released me and went to Else. "So, you've tamed my friend."

Else smiled. "I wouldn't go that far, my Lord. He's consented to be tamed."

Geraint laughed. "I have no doubt, but may I have your name, if you are to be a sister to our brotherhood?"

Else glanced at me. She didn't want to announce her presence under her real name without permission. I stopped Geraint and said very quietly, "Her name is Eleanor de Clare. But to me she is Else, and I think it would be wise to keep that name in public."

Geraint might look like a jolly giant but he had a razor sharp mind. "You married the missing de Clare girl? Bloody hell, Lancelot, you really don't like to make life easy." He stared up at Else and she smiled the apology in her eyes. "So, where have you been?" he asked her.

"Avoiding marriage," she said with a smile.

He laughed, then shook his head. "Lancelot, you are a fucking idiot but you do make my life infinitely more interesting. Now, why are you here? You risk hanging by returning home."

"It's a long story," I said. "I think we ought to tell it in the warm and dry."

It took the remainder of the soggy day to unpack the horses, for Else to dry Ash so Geraint's grooms didn't have to deal with him, and for me to dry my armour. We joined Geraint in a small room he used when he didn't have important guests to entertain. I headed straight for the fire and warmed myself while the servants scurried about with food. I realised one of the maid's had kept me warm in times past, she blushed and smiled as I noticed her. I smiled back, couldn't help myself, until I saw the expression on Else's face. Angry seemed to cover it. I coughed and turned my back on the girl. Geraint chuckled not missing a beat.

Once the room cleared, Else and I sat at the table and we ate our first decent meal for days.

"You need wine, my friend," Geraint said.

I stopped him pouring. "No, I don't. I'm in training and I have a few too many problems to be drinking right now."

"You're not drinking?" Geraint asked. I could hear the suspicion in his voice. "You've not taken to religion have you, Lancelot?"

I laughed. "No, not in the way you are thinking. Let me explain what's been happening to me since I left England." And I did. Everything. It took us the rest of the day and long into the night. Else took over when my memories began to muddle things up and she explained everything she knew about Merlin and Arthur.

"So," I rounded off long into the night, "we have to go to Arthur and I need Merlin to help him and undo the spell set on us by her sister. Merlin also needs to help Arthur defeat the fey that are using people like Stephen de Clare to seed chaos in England."

Geraint looked at us both. We'd moved to the fire and Else sat at my feet on a large rug. I stroked her hair with my gloves covering my skin.

"Let me get this straight," he said. "You are not human," he pointed to Else, "but you are the adoptive daughter of the de Clare's." She nodded. "You are destined to save Arthur from the rival fairy family which has control over the de Clare's," he said to me.

"Sounds about right," I said.

"You want to challenge Arthur in a tournament so he is forced to listen to you and pardon you for past crimes and to top it all you're under a spell so you can't touch the woman you married." Geraint sat back in his chair. "That's not complicated at all."

"The marriage part is a slight exaggeration," I said. "I just don't want Stephen to take her from me. If he thinks we are married he can't. But I can't marry her until the spell is broken because if we have physical contact it sends me to a bad place."

"Of course, why not make this even harder, what the hell?" Geraint said taking a large swallow of his wine. He thought for a while and I let him work through all the ramifications. "Fine," he said at last, "this is what we do." I smiled at the 'we', I knew he would not let me down. "We make you a black knight. You fight Arthur and you'd better bloody win without hurting him or I'll kill you, and we talk to him."

"You really think the fight is necessary?" Else asked.

"I think it is the only way Lancelot can deal with Arthur and the whole Court. He needs to re-establish his authority over the rest of us and become

Arthur's second once more. If there is one thing we dumb men understand it's war. But I fear beating Arthur is not going to be easy. He's changed since your punishment. Something in him feels broken and he is so angry with the world. At times I've worried about his sanity. He will welcome a fight but whether he will listen to you or not I don't know." Geraint frowned and studied me. "You too have changed, my friend. I cannot quite work out how, but you are different. Perhaps you can reach him, someone needs to bring him back, he's grown as hard as you used to be and the Court Doesn't need another relentless killer."

"I'm not a relentless killer, Geraint," I said as Else rose to put another log in the large fireplace.

"You are when Arthur needs you to be. Sometimes, I wish he'd used one of the rest of us instead of you to defend his lands. You grew hard, Lancelot, but I think this girl is changing that," he said. He stood and stretched. "Now we need sleep. We will plan this tomorrow and in the meantime you have separate rooms."

A servant appeared and we left Geraint to his thoughts. I followed the man who held up a small tallow lamp. The light flickered on the bare stone walls and the wooden floor. Else and I didn't speak but I sensed her apprehension. I had to admit my own emotions were unsteady. Walking to separate sleeping quarters did not seem like a good idea. We might have slept on different sides of the campfire every night but we were together. The man stopped, and showed us a simple wooden door.

"Your wife's room," he said. He eyed us suspiciously. His clothes were simple but warm, his small eyes and bald head shone in the lamplight.

"And mine?" I asked, willing myself not to punch him on the nose for his tone.

"Next door, my Lord."

"That will be all," I said. He left and took the lamp with him. Else and I were plunged into darkness, the only light came from the half moon through high arches.

As my eyes adjusted, I realised she stared hard at the ground. I took her hands in mine. "It will be all right."

"You will suffer alone," she said.

"I'll live," I told her. Though after some of the nights I'd recently suffered I might wish I didn't.

"If you need me, come to me." She looked up, her warm brown eyes earnest.

I ached to hold her close, to take her into that room and make love for hours. I wanted to hear her cry out my name. "Fuck," I muttered. I'd learnt that even thoughts of sex with this woman were enough to cause an ache so intense it almost broke my resolution.

Else released my hands and stepped back, well out of arm's reach. "I'll see you in the morning," she said and vanished into her room, closing the door and turning the lock.

I stayed where I was until I heard her begin to cry and I realised I couldn't do a damn thing to help her except leave her alone. I walked to my room. A fire crackled, warming the small space. A single bed stood against the wall and an arrow slit for a window the only items except rugs and tapestries trying to keep out the cold and damp. I sat on the bed and put my head in my hands, running my fingers through my hair.

"If I didn't love Arthur so damned much this would be a really bad idea," I muttered to myself. I began to undress slowly because the effort sapped my will to finish the job. Sleep came in drips and drabs, the small body next door called constantly.

CHAPTER TWELVE

THE BRUTAL COAST AIR bit into my naked chest but my effort made the sweat flow nonetheless. I'd been awake since before dawn. Training hard took my mind to a simple place. The dull light of another blustery early winter day left my blade, hard cold steel. No light glinted as I wove the weapon through the air. It felt good to be in Geraint's training ground. In my youth, I had spent almost every waking moment, other than the times I had formal duties, being here, becoming the best of us. Just taking this time, the quiet time of dawn, to work alone made my mind relax in a way sleep did not.

"Those scars are bad." Geraint appeared at the edge of the sand pit.

The training ground lay beside the main living quarters in the first circle of the defence near the stables. I heard the sea pounding the rocks below.

I stopped and grabbed my shirt from the rail. "I didn't hear you arrive," I said throwing it over my back trying to avoid the subject.

Geraint looked at me with his hazel eyes taking on a greenish cast in the dawn light. "We need to talk about that," he said pointing at me, meaning my back.

"No, we don't." I wiped sweat off my face with my sleeve. "I did what I had to do, so did Arthur."

"But you plan on fighting him and I'd like to keep both of my best friends alive," Geraint said.

"I hold no ill will toward Arthur for this, it wasn't his fault." I pushed my blade into its scabbard. I used a little more force than necessary, a fact not lost on my friend.

"Lancelot, I need to understand all of this. Your intentions." He paused and sighed. "Helping this girl, helping Arthur, it can't be the only thing you are doing."

"Why not?" I asked. "I love Arthur, I always will, what happened was my choice. I will not hurt our King, Geraint."

We stood assessing each other, he wanted to believe I held Arthur no ill will, I could do no more than let him see I meant what I said.

He sighed again. "I don't understand how you could forgive him. He should have protected you and stopped you sacrificing your honour for that bloody woman."

Anger flashed through me. "That is your Queen, Geraint, have respect."

I watched Geraint's jaw clench and he looked away. Else appeared, smiling. "I wondered where you'd managed to hide yourself," she chirped.

Her arrival broke the tension, Geraint's fine temper evened the keel of our friendship and before I knew what happened I found myself sparring with him. We fought for a long time and Geraint started throwing his own men into the fray against me. It felt good, testing myself even as I grew more and more exhausted. Geraint relented and decided we all needed feeding, so the training stopped. I walked to the rail, my shirt sopping wet with rain and sweat. Else smiled, a twinkle in her eyes I'd never seen before, I felt hunted.

She helped me through the rails of the ring and she handed me a rough blanket to wrap around my shoulders. I rubbed my hair. "You are so beautiful when you fight," she said, catching me by surprise.

I stopped, I realised there were gloves on her hands and no flesh peeped out to tempt me to some misdemeanour. I burned for her, the fight having set so many things straight in my head. The more I fought, the more clarity I found in my life and my thoughts. Her fingers brushed my chest and her hips were in my hands before either of us thought about the consequences.

"Bloody hell, woman, I want you," I growled low in my chest.

Her eyes dilated with her lust. A heavy hand on my shoulder pulled me back.

"No, Lancelot." Geraint yanked me out of Else's reach. I turned, furious at having been thwarted, my fist already halfway to Geraint's head. Geraint however, had other plans. He blended with my attack, I turned as he over balanced me having redirected the punch and I found his arm wrapped around my throat. Breathing became optional.

"If you don't hold still, I will choke you to death," he said close to my ear. "Get a grip or I'll have Else sent away to a nunnery until this is over. I've watched you suffer at the hands of one woman for years. I'll not watch it happen with her."

I struggled. Horror filled Else's face as she realised what she'd done in being so close to me.

"Let me go," I snarled desperate to fill that small tight body.

I fired my elbow backward, Geraint grunted but his grip on my neck tightened. "What the hell is wrong?" Geraint yelled over my struggles.

"It's a new assault of the spell, they must be trying to strengthen it," she cried out, sinking to her knees and bowing her head muttering, rocking back and forth.

I redoubled my efforts to escape Geraint. I must reach the object of my desire regardless of the consequences. I would die if I did not possess her body and soul. I would kill anyone who prevented me. Just a few moments before I had maintained perfect control, I had been at peace for the first time in months. Now, a monster raged through my soul screaming Else's name.

"Stop him!" Else screamed as her back bowed and every muscle in her body grew tight. Geraint's choke hold tightened and he yelled for his men to help hold me down. The world began to go spotty and black. I fought like a mad man to escape my enemies. The pressure on my throat increased until, my lights went out.

I woke with her name on my lips but Geraint stared down at me. I also realised I lay in my room.

"Where is she?" I asked, struggling to rise. I found my hands tied to the wooden base of the bed on either side of me. I pulled on the leather bindings. "What have you done?"

Geraint laid a hand on my chest and pushed me back down. "Lie still, you can't run or fight, so just listen and when I'm certain you are sane I'll release you."

I lay down. He nodded and continued, "Else is fine, she's next door trying to work out what the hell just happened. She thinks her people are growing desperate. They need you to help Arthur but on their timetable not yours."

"What's their timetable?"

"She Doesn't seem to know. If it's any consolation, this is hitting her as hard as it is you. She thinks they need you with Arthur as soon as possible. I've already begun the preparations. I suggest you leave Else here, where she is safe." He sat still, his great hands resting between his knees, his face mournful. "I have the feeling no good will come of this, but we must try to help Arthur. If this is the way the fey magic works and this is the good stuff, what is being thrown at him by his enemies?" As I said, Geraint was not stupid.

"You can let me up," I said. "I'll be good."

Geraint paused for only a moment before unpicking the ties. "So, will you leave the girl here?"

I rubbed my wrists, but in truth it was my pride which felt bruised. I still couldn't control the power that damned fey witch had over me and I didn't mean Else. I'd always known one day my dick would get me killed, never mind enchanted.

"I can't leave Else with you, Geraint. I wish I could, but she is as much responsible for my breathing as I am." I swung my legs off the bed and we sat side by side.

"You never make life easy for yourself." He shook his head. "What happens if they attack you when I'm not around? I saw the look on your face, even if the girl tried to stop you she couldn't have. You'd have hurt her and you would never forgive yourself."

I placed a shaking hand on his shoulder. "I have to get her to Arthur. I have to find Merlin. Neither thing can I do without her at my side. I just have to pray we move fast enough to satisfy the damn witch who is controlling us."

"If this is all true, Lancelot, it will mean war with the de Clare's. If they are being driven as you are, if Arthur is being attacked and used as you have been, they will come to blows." His green hazel eyes were anxious.

I hugged him. "If we find Merlin and help Arthur, we will prevent a war. The rival fey want the English throne. I have to stop them. Merlin has to stop them. If it means civil war then that's what we have to live with until we win. Which we will, because we are on the side of right."

"Civil war is a serious thing, Lancelot," Geraint said, his anxiety clear as he leaned into my hug.

"If I don't fight for Arthur we will lose him and still have war but with Stephen de Clare winning and I don't think any of us wants that," I said. "For a start the arrogant shit will force you to do homage to him and can you really kneel before de Clare and not puke on his boots?" I grinned at my friend.

He laughed. "War for Arthur's soul it is then. Anything to stop me having to puke on the bastard de Clare's boots."

Geraint rose and helped me stand. A long morning of sparring and the tussle with the fey magic made my legs wobbly. As tempted, as I was to hunt down Else, just to talk you understand, I followed Geraint like a shadow all day and helped him organise me, enabling me to face Arthur.

By the end of the day, I possessed black armour, which the smith fitted to my requirements. A black banner, with a Wolf's head in white on it, stitched by Geraint's servants. A black horse, thanks to a brave soul who dyed Ash's hair, and a mule to carry lances. A larger tent than I usually used and all manner of sundries Geraint pressed on me. We left his home together, travelling toward Camelot as a unit, half a dozen of his men for company. It felt good to be on the road with Geraint and I enjoyed his companionship. He and Else soon became firm friends and she earned the respect of his men by working just as hard as any of them with the horses. Once we grew close to Camelot, Geraint pushed on, riding straight to Arthur, hoping to smooth the way. Or prod him in the right direction if necessary. I planned to camp half a league outside the city and use Else as my squire. Once inside Camelot, my squire would call Arthur out to fight.

We would fight, I'd win, Geraint would come help Arthur, the three of us would talk and I could begin protecting him again as I have always done.

A simple plan.

However, it relied on several things. Me keeping my sanity around Else. Me winning against Arthur. Him not trying to lop my head off the moment he realised it was me he fought and also trying to convince my King that fairies existed.

Real simple.

CHAPTER THIRTEEN

ELSE AND I MOVED fast enough not to annoy any of her cheerful relatives, because neither of us felt a desire to touch beyond the usual. We were careful however to maintain as much distance as possible. I realised my clarity and strength as a warrior were hampered by her presence but that very presence brought me a sense of peace and I needed to maintain control and focus. When the morning arrived for us to declare ourselves at Camelot we were both nervous and I realised I'd begun to ache for her.

"Try to stay calm," she said, tightening the straps on my breastplate. The armour did not fit me as well as my own and I found it hard to adjust to the changes it forced in my fighting. I made a non-committal noise to her request.

She stepped back and surveyed her work. Then she looked up at me. "I know it's hard."

"Hard? I'm about to challenge my King to combat. Hard isn't the word."

"The more agitated you become the difficult it is for us to control our desire." She frowned and fussed with more straps.

I grasped her hands and brought her fingers to my lips. I watched her eyes widen, the spell raced into me from the soft contact we shared. I kissed her fingers. The rough leather of my gloves and the weight of the metal plates covering my hands, made me feel strong. The faith I had in this small creature standing before me, made me both invulnerable and terribly weak at the same time.

"Else, what you mean to me..." I whispered.

She gasped and struggled uselessly against my grip. "This," she swallowed trying to gain control over her own desire. "This really isn't helping."

I smiled and released her, just as the pain of her contact became too much for me to bear without taking things further.

"No, but it does remind me how much I have to lose if I don't make Arthur listen." A soft clank accompanied my movements as I picked up my sword, strapping it to my waist.

I watched Else put on her hat, she spent an age forcing her female curves into the narrow straight lines of a youth. She tucked her growing curls under the hat having lost the argument when she'd offered to cut it short once more. She moved around picking up my sallet and snapping the visor down. I felt a wave of peace wash through me, like a fresh breeze full of the scent of rose blossom. We were on the right path and I would be with my King once more, soon to have my wife at my side in more than just name. The sense of optimism felt almost alien to me, it had been so long since I'd sensed hope and joy over the horizon. It made me heady and confident. I smiled as Else, pulled on the soft padded coif, which protected my head under the great helmet, the final part of my disguise. She frowned at me, wondering why I smiled so broadly, I just smiled wider making her shake her head and laugh. Her laughter reminded me of the softest of raindrops after a drought.

Ash whinnied and stamped as I approached, he knew armour meant war or games involving war. I stroked his now black neck, "Sorry, old man, this one is for politics. Tomorrow we will joust, I promise." My words didn't stop him bouncing around like a fresh colt as soon as I lifted myself into the saddle.

Else swung into Mercury's saddle and we headed toward Camelot's imposing walls. From our position, the estuary remained obscured behind Camelot and the sea glittered to our left, the last of the fields rolled downward in gentle greeting on this particular day.

Camelot is a strange place, part palace, part castle and all city. With the Pendragon bloodline going back many generations as England's kings, it had grown and spread over decades. Arthur, a man who sought unity in all things, tried to blend the exaggerated fortified keep of his grandfather with the overblown palatial influences of his father's period. As such, there sat like a brooding hen the glowering tower of the central keep, high on the hill, overlooking the River Cleddau. The mighty keep evolved to be greater in height and width than any other in the country. The dark stone gave it a menacing air. Circling this was a wall, fifty feet high and heavily crenulated, with huge doors, gatehouses, a moat and drawbridges. There were squat round towers placed evenly around the walls, designed to make it hard for trebuchets and sappers if anyone laid siege to the keep. These walls would not fall. Beyond the traditional structure, there sprang throughout Uther's reign, large villas. Two and three storey buildings of dressed white stone with columns, courtyards, fountains and gardens. Their red tiled roofs made them look like a ploughed field when viewed from the surrounding hills. These homes belonged to the powerful and wealthy of Camelot and cascaded down from the keep's mighty wall.

The lower classes, right down to the villeins and serfs, lived in traditional homes. Heavy stone and wood, wattle and daub, thatch roofs and wooden lean-tos. With crazy streets, from narrow lanes almost too small to walk through, up to wide roads forced through various quarters by the government, the streets contained the blood pumping life to the heart. Many of these roads were paved, but most of the lanes were not, so the mud filtered throughout the city.

Arthur, as his token, tried to encourage the building of good drainage, sensible water supply to the city and proper housing for the vast network of poor who lived in his city. He built sensible low level buildings and tried to improve the roads. His finer buildings emphasised his desire to reach for the ideal of kingship. Over the last fifteen years, he'd ordered the building of community centres, churches and municipal markets. They were all of the same style, high arches allowing light to filter into all buildings, huge spires and flying buttresses to hold the walls and columns in place. They were vast buildings of beautiful proportions. This mismatched city housed thousands of people and Arthur lived with his court in the keep itself.

Else and I rode through the noisy throng in the streets toward the imposing walls. Ash stomped prettily as people, both rich and poor, stared at the black knight. Else rode ahead of me, holding the banner, which snapped in the breeze, the Wolf's head undulating. The day dawned bright but cold and I felt the steel cage surrounding me, leeching the warmth from my body as I rode. Word would race ahead that a black knight walked toward the keep. Arthur would be waiting. The idea of the black knight is simple, you hide your identity for several reasons; you are from a foreign court and want to join Camelot under your own steam, not because of reputation. Or, you need to ask a boon of your king without judgement on your family crest. Or you are a criminal asking forgiveness. Guess which category I fell into? The Wolf's head indicated I stood outside the law of at least one kingdom and yet I hoped it spoke more personally to Arthur.

We rode at a steady walk up the hill and I began to realise Camelot felt different. It wasn't the oncoming winter and all the trials it brings, it was something else. Something unnameable, a sense of dread? I hesitated to use the word but I saw fear lurking in the eyes of more than one person as I stared through the narrow slits of the visor. Why were these people afraid? This was Camelot, the centre of Arthur's crown and his jewel.

We reached the moat, the bridges and the wall. Guards stood in pairs at each end of the bridge and stopped Else from continuing by crossing their spears. They wore the gold and blue of Arthur's colours, their tabards stitched with the insignia of an oak tree, a crown encircling the trunk. When I joined Arthur as a knight, he gave me the emblem of the ash tree saying, 'Where there is oak, there is ash, my friend.' The memory hurt.

"Halt," the guard said. "State your business."

We had agreed I'd leave all the talking to Else. Too many people knew my voice, so I sat mute and she laid our case before the guard.

"We are here to speak to King Arthur. My Lord wishes to challenge his right to join the Court as is his prerogative," Else said just as I taught her.

The men should have broken ranks and allowed us through without further comment, instead they stayed still. The man spoke again, "If you are not a knight of our Court, you are not welcome here. Leave now and you can go in peace."

Else fidgeted but barely paused, "Since when are noble men unable to offer themselves for the King's judgement? We are here to offer trial by combat so my Lord can prove his worth to the best of kings. We are not here to offer harm."

I had not anticipated this, the thought of not seeing Arthur at all made my hands begin to sweat and stomach roll.

Else pushed Mercury forward, she leaned down from her saddle and the guard approached. The visor obscured my view so I couldn't see what she did as he approached but he said, "Let them through, they are of noble blood and mean no harm." I think she caressed his face.

I rode past and I stared down at the guard. His eyes were slightly glazed and he stood a little unsteadily, clutching his spear. He also sported an enormous erection. Someone would be having fun with his wife or whore later. I wanted to ask her what the hell she'd done to the man but couldn't while in the walls of the keep. This new development in my companion worried me. Her capacity for such magic came as a surprise.

The horses clomped noisily over the bridge and we met with no resistance on the other side. I didn't know whether the guard had been a job's worth or if we would have a real problem seeking an audience with Arthur. We rode through the wide killing field and I glanced at the training grounds for the squires and soldiers, forges and schooling rings for the horses filling the space. There were dozens of people moving around in this area, a hundred paces wide. We rode up to the main gate of the keep, offset from the front gate, so enemies could not run from one to the other unimpeded. A huge arched entrance protected by vast oak and iron doors with a portcullis towered over the horses. The keystone at the top of the arch taller than Else. The cobbles under the arch were higher than elsewhere, helping keep the enemies footing unsteady. Arthur's grandfather had been paranoid about attack. Once wet, these cobbles made difficult footing if you wanted to batter the doors down. I should know. I'd fallen on them often enough returning from the city too drunk to remember to be careful in the rain.

The guards at the final gate stopped us, just as I knew they would. "State your business," said a gruff voice. I knew the man, a good sergeant who had served Arthur for years. Why he stood on guard duty concerned me, this was a job for men below his rank.

"We come to declare a challenge to King Arthur, so my Lord can prove himself in open combat as worthy of Camelot," Else's voice rang out. As a woman, she had a deep voice, as a man, the sweet tones sounded almost wrong. Or maybe my knowledge of her status made that true.

I watched the scarred face crease in a deep frown. "If your Lord wishes to join Camelot then he should declare himself openly and not as a Black Knight."

Else stared down at the man. "His reputation is such the King will want him without testing his worthiness. My Lord has no wish to curry favour in such a way."

The sergeant sighed, his shoulders slumping as he looked at me. "Fine, but I'll take you to the King myself and God help you."

I almost asked why we would need God's help but the sergeant moved off before I spoke. Just as well I supposed but something felt off about Camelot and it made me nervous.

We walked into the great courtyard and two boys appeared to hold the horses. We dismounted. My feet hit the stone and I clinked. Ash bit the boy holding him the moment he realised we weren't fighting and proceeded to make life difficult for everyone within kicking distance.

"That's a fine horse," said the sergeant as he watched Ash's antics.

Else said, "My Lord has taken a vow of silence until King Arthur accepts him in his Court."

The sergeant shook his head. "Damned foolishness."

I took the banner from Else and she fell into step behind me. The sergeant walked ahead and we entered the main part of the keep. Granite steps led the way to a set of doors almost as large as the front gate. We went through the open doors and into a vast entrance way. Once more, this area had been prepared as a killing ground. A high stone balcony ran around the top, a place for defenders to fire down into the hallway. The whole space remained almost bare of furniture but for huge tapestries of hunts and stories from myth tumbling down the walls. There were many doors off this room, but no obvious access to the upper levels. All the stairways were through more doors, again creating killing grounds for defenders.

We walked to the back, the heavily decorated doors the only indication we were heading for the throne room and council chamber. I felt both calm and thrilled with anticipation at seeing Arthur again. I had missed him so much for so long. I only hoped Geraint would be there too, seeing my friend would steady my nerves. There were two more guards on the doors, who opened the portal ready for me to see my King.

CHAPTER FOURTEEN

THE DOORS SWUNG INWARD on silent hinges. I stood, waiting for the sergeant to announce us. I had seen this ceremony done a dozen or more times over the years as new men came to fight with Arthur. I looked into the chamber through the limited vision of my helmet and smiled because it hadn't changed in all the months I'd been denied entrance. Unlike many of the other rooms inside the keep, this room glowed with light. Arthur, wanting to stamp his reign firmly on the Court, changed its interior almost as soon as he ascended the throne. Vast columns ran through the long room, forming great fan vaulting over our heads. In the centre of each fan sat a stone boss, representing each of the knight's and their coat of arms. I wondered if mine were still close to Arthur's, then decided I didn't want to know. To see it defaced or gone or worse, replaced, would hurt too much. The floor remained clear of rugs and rushes, polished granite reflected more light from the huge arched windows Arthur punched through to the outside. A cloister type walkway ran around two of the walls, one at the back the other to my right, for private discussion and meetings. Stained glass in some of the windows gave the floor beautiful coloured puddles. Four rows of columns made the room appear wide and tall. There were tables along the walls and chairs but they were used for banquets. Arthur's stone throne sat in the centre, hidden by the throng for the moment. He only used it for high ceremony, preferring to mix with his people.

The room held many of my friends and enemies. A low level hum came from their conversation. All the men wore swords but none wore armour. Women graced the room in flowing gowns, sitting on couches doing the things women do, lute, stitching, talking. None would hold a sword and defend my back like my Else.

I didn't see Arthur until the sergeant spoke, "Your Majesty, I am here to announce the arrival of a Black Knight. He wishes to ask for the right to fight for his place in your Court as an anonymous petitioner." The man's voice boomed over the crowd, just as it would in the training yard. I'd never understood how a good sergeant manages to make his voice heard over the cacophony of a fight, but you never fail to understand them.

The crowd stilled and parted. They revealed the throne and Arthur. My breath hissed out of me in shock. The man before me was not the King I knew. A table stood on the raised dais, a large flagon of wine with a glass beside it, half empty. Sext had yet to be called, the sun still in the eastern half of the sky. Geraint stood to the right of the throne, his expression grave and worried. Arthur, his bright blonde curls in lank tangles, rather than their normal short tight ringlets, lounged on the mighty stone chair. We walked forward. I realised his face looked puffy, his eyes red rimmed and his hand shook when he reached for the wine. The clear blue eyes of the man I adored were dirty and faded. I had never seen Arthur like this; me yes, without his influence to steady me, but he had always been the strongest of us. He looked so weary.

Arthur rose and walked down the dais steps toward us, the sergeant and Else dropped to their knees. I remained still.

The blue velvet doublet Arthur wore, which must have matched the colour of his eyes once, appeared crumpled and stained. He approached, his expression grim and amused at the same time. I smelt the wine on his breath.

"So, you have come like so many before you to present yourself to me for combat. Believing you have the right to join Camelot," he said turning and sweeping his arm out in a gesture of grandeur.

"My Lord has taken a vow of silence, your Majesty. Until he has won the right to bear arms as your man he will not speak," Else spoke with her head facing the floor and eyes downcast.

"Arthur," Geraint said, walking forward. "Maybe you should ask the knight in private why he would want to present himself to Camelot. Perhaps he would talk to you then and there would be no reason to fight."

My friend told me that Arthur was in no condition to fight, as if I needed the warning. Else's eyes shot to Geraint and he stared at me with pleading eyes. He did not want me to challenge Arthur. My King however had other ideas.

"You," he stabbed a finger in Geraint's direction. "Are a fuss pot. I," he pointed a finger at his own chest. "Need a man able to fill that gap." He pointed upward.

I knew what sat over the spot in which we stood. My boss, my coat of arms.

I knew without looking it no longer existed. One of the original four, which radiated from his own coat of arms over the throne, it now sat in some stonemason's yard broken and destroyed.

Arthur turned back to me. "Do you think you are worthy of Camelot, Black Knight?" he hissed with real menace. "There are things in this Court which break men's hearts and minds. Things which tear at the soul in the dark of the night. Things which make even a king beg for mercy. Do you still want to be a part of my world?"

Seeing the pain in Arthur, so clear and so blatant almost broke my resolve. I wanted to raise my helmet and beg for his mercy. I wanted to take him in my arms and hold him until he stopped hurting. I had never seen my friend like this, darkness oozed from his eyes and the Court shifted with nerves.

"My Lord," Else said before I did anything stupid, "will prove his worth on the tourney field. All he begs in return is the right to speak with you, alone, when he wins. You may pick any one of your champions to face him, so long as he speaks with you once it is over." She modified what we had planned to say, trying to help Geraint force Arthur into making one of the others fight me.

Arthur laughed, a terrible sound dripping with anger. "The King of England is not a worthy opponent? Is that what you are saying, squire?"

Else looked up shocked. "No, your Majesty, that is not what I am saying at all. It would be an honour to face you on the field." She had no choice but to give Arthur what he wanted.

"Good, then we fight, this afternoon," Arthur announced.

A ripple of noise seeped around the room. Kay, another friend, stepped forward. "I believe the Black Knight would rather face you in the morning, Sire, when you are both fresh."

Arthur turned to Kay. "You mean when I'm sober." I watched my friend's face blanch as Arthur's bitterness ripped into his heart. "Stop trying to manage me, my Lord Spencer. There is only one man I would choose to face this Black Knight and he is not here, so I shall do it."

He meant me. I would have fought in his place. It was my right as his champion, until the Queen stole me from my Lord. Then Arthur had to ask Guinevere's permission to use me for these games. A joke that grew sour over the years.

"Sire, I am happy to fight in your place so the Pendragon line comes to no harm," Kay persisted. "We cannot risk you against an unknown opponent."

This was true. Arthur however did not see sense and Kay was always sensible. "Bollocks, if you faced him, Kay, he would win and Camelot's honour would be in tatters. At least I will present him with a real fight," Arthur snapped. "This afternoon, at Nones, we will meet in the tourney field."

"Your Majesty..." Geraint began.

"One more word and I'll start talking about treasonable charges because you think your King is weak," Arthur said. Talking to the crowd but looking at me, he said, "I need a challenge and I need the hole in my heart filling." His voice dropped until only Else and I would hear. "I need a man I can trust, Black Knight, are you that man?"

I opened my mouth, spellbound by his sudden intensity to say yes, when he turned away and vanished from my vision.

"You have the detail of our date, make certain to be there, knight," he bit the words off. "We will see if you are worthy to call me, King." Arthur swept to the back of the hall and vanished through a small door I knew led to his private chambers.

I bowed. Else and the sergeant rose and we left the room in silence. I had just hours to prepare before facing Arthur and winning, without hurting him. We walked to the courtyard and I retrieved Ash, who stood alone in the large square space except for Mercury, he munched on some hay. Ash had proved himself too dangerous to stable. As I approached, he laid his ears back and gnashed his teeth.

"I knew a grey like that once," said the sergeant. "Damn fine horse and his master was the best knight I knew. Most of these tosspots couldn't fight their way out of a wet cloth bag, but him, he knew how to fight. Just like his Majesty Does. They were fine men to watch and finer to know. I can only hope you are here to bring the King back to his senses. He needs stopping fast. His anger is such that even the best of men are in danger. He lost his friend to politics and he cannot forgive himself or his Court for making it happen."

I didn't think the good sergeant knew so many words. I also realised he'd twigged as to who lay under the black armour.

He grinned at my sharp intake of breath. The price on my head for returning to England would be more than a year's pay. I tensed ready for the yell bringing dozens of soldiers, instead he said, "There are many things a man can hide, but the way each man touches the hilt of his sword is unique. It is a good way of finding friends and foe on a battlefield when colours are gone and armour covered in blood. I wish you luck, my Lord." He gave me his knee to stand on to mount, an offer I could not refuse. I mounted and rode off after Else.

"That was bad," she said. The horses clomped on the paved road covering her voice.

I didn't know what to say. I had never seen Arthur in such a state and it seemed as though I carried the blame. Had losing me to the trial and banishment really changed Arthur that much? Or was it the publication of the original betrayal, of others knowing of the infidelity and it proved too humiliating? How often had I begged for that time back, so I could undo the damage?

I felt Else take my hand through the thick gauntlet on my left side where she rode beside me. "This is not your fault," she whispered as though reading my thoughts.

"Yes, it is," I said hearing the weight of my sadness. I had broken the heart of the noblest man I had ever known and I did it for a fuck. I think I hated myself more in that moment than at any other time in my miserable life. Once I fancied myself in love with a woman, so I took that woman. Now I knew what real love should feel like and I couldn't have it. I also didn't deserve it, if what I had done to Arthur should be repaid in full.

In three hours, I would face Arthur on the tourney field and all I wanted to do was lay my head on the block so he could have full reparation for my sins. We rode out of the city and back to our small camp on the edge of the woods surrounding Camelot. Else hustled me into the tent and took my helmet and gloves off, then removed the coif, gorget, breastplate and backplate, enabling me to move but redress quickly. I sank onto the small bed I'd used the night before.

I ran my fingers through my sweaty hair and over my face. "This is madness, I should just walk up to Arthur and beg his forgiveness."

Else knelt on the ground at my feet. "No," she said, putting her hands on my metal knees, the poleyn stopping me feeling her touch. "You need to prove yourself to him once more. You need to shock him into remembering you are worthy of his love. You need to make him listen to us. Do you really think you are the only reason he is suffering? Can't you see the dark magic which is influencing him already?" Her brown eyes beseeched me to understand. "You are all that can save him from himself."

"You don't know what I did to him," I said.

"Yes, I do," Else said, her eyes gentle. "I made you tell me when we were in the cave. You wept in my arms."

That should have made me angry; it just made me more depressed. "So you know why I was flogged. How can Arthur forgive that?"

"Because you accepted another's punishment and he knew it." I saw her hands clench with the need to touch me. "Sweetheart, you are a good man who made a terrible mistake."

"I am not a good man," I said. "I am a killer."

"You saved my life, twice, three times if you count the hunt in the wood," Else said, her kindness overwhelming me. "You didn't have to do any of those things, especially after I had lied to you so badly."

I felt tears prick my eyes. "I thought I loved her."

"I know and while others were ignorant Arthur lived with the infidelity because he stole her from you in the first place. But, Lancelot, she is not innocent in this." Else continued, "You took her punishment because she let the secret out to try and control you."

I looked up. "How the hell do you know that?"

Else rocked back on her heels and sighed. "Geraint and I had a long talk before we left. He wanted me to know how Guinevere is capable of manipulating you and Arthur, hoping I think to aid me in protecting you. Your friends blame the Queen for your disgrace, not you. Geraint told me you held out against her for a long time but finally fell to her seductions."

"We were out hunting, all of us, Arthur asked me to stay close to Guinevere in case anything happened and she fell off the damned horse. No one else was close and I found her in my arms. Like a fool, I fell for it, for her. I had lain with many other women but never loved them, only her and there she was, just as she had been the day I asked her to marry me. Which happened to be the day Arthur asked her the same damned question." My voice echoed the bitterness I still held in my heart. "Who would you choose a penniless knight or a king?"

"I choose you," Else said. She had pulled on her gloves without me noticing and held my face in her hands as she spoke. "I choose you because you tried to leave her over and over again, but love can be a harsh mistress and Guinevere would not let you go."

"Geraint talks too much," I said.

"He is trying to protect you," Else said. "He loves you a great deal and wants to see you back at Arthur's side."

"Geraint is a romantic," I mumbled. I considered her words though, for the first time I was able to think about Guinevere without falling into a rage. "You said she was the one to make our affair public?"

Else rose and began gathering what we needed for the tourney. "Geraint didn't think you knew. He tried to tell Arthur but almost received banishment himself for his pains. Guinevere knew she was losing you, knew you would throw her over for Arthur and she wanted you stopped. She is jealous of your relationship with her husband and with good cause I have no doubt." Else looked at me and I ignored her implications. "But that is irrelevant. What is important is that she wanted to hurt you and Arthur, but she didn't understand, or chose to ignore the consequences. So, she leaked the affair. Never realising how much havoc she wreak in the Court, the damage to Arthur's reputation as a king and man, and what you would have to suffer by taking her punishment and your own."

I remembered the tears in Arthur's eyes when he decreed the full flogging for our adultery. He had begged me with his eyes to offer to take Guinevere's lashes. I said as Queen's Champion I would, the charges were untrue and we were committing no crimes. I wanted to take as much of the burden and pain from Arthur as possible. I knew he would not survive his wife being flogged in public. The relief and gratitude on his face that day the only thing that held me to this world as I took first my lashes and then hers in succession.

"She betrayed me?" I asked. I shouldn't have been surprised. I long realised Guinevere the woman was not Guinevere the girl, I once loved as a squire.

"She betrayed you, no one else. I am sorry. But now Arthur needs you to hold his way clear. To give him a new life. He needs you to protect him from her, from the de Clare's and from the fey who wish to control England for their own reasons. You have to help him or our world will be lost." Else pulled me to my feet and began strapping my armour back on. "So, stop with the maudlin introspection, and go bag us a king." She pushed me into the dull afternoon light and bullied me back onto Ash. She gave me a lance to carry and we set off, back toward the keep and my afternoon joust with Arthur.

CHAPTER FIFTEEN

WE RODE UP THE hill to the castle and the weather closed in. The clouds lowered, the wind rose, snapping at my pennon, the Wolf's head shimmering in the flat light. It would rain before too long, making footing dangerous. I mentally prepared, once more going through simple combinations of sword movements in my mind. I brought forward all I knew of Arthur's fighting style and remembered every fight we'd shared. Calm filled me, I remained centred and back in my world. This I knew how to do, I knew how to fight. Women, politics, they were a mystery to me but fighting I understood.

We approached the castle and I realised a great crowd swelled and rolled, like a huge wave of humanity. King Arthur always drew an audience. I wished we didn't have a crowd but Camelot's all about spectacle.

Once we reached the main gate, the throng parted. We walked over the moat and through the wall into the killing fields. The soldiers lined the way to the tourney field, keeping the people back. We made short work of reaching the site. Without the time to set up a tourney field outside the city, we were squashed into the practice area. There wasn't a great deal of room for the castle's inhabitants never mind the city folk. The walls began to close in on me, the armour became heavy and my vision too restricted. The noise of the crowd and the stink of bodies made me wish for the open fields and my simple life with Else.

I saw Geraint, Kay and many others scattered through the crowd of wealthy merchants. My eyes slid to the centre of the heaving tableau. I saw two things at once, Arthur, sat astride Willow, his mighty warhorse and Guinevere stood beside him but not touching him or looking in his direction. She stared directly at me.

I knew she couldn't see who sat under the black armour but her ice blue eyes captured my attention so thoroughly I stopped breathing. Across the distance of the tourney field, I realised Guinevere's beauty still made me breathless. The wind moved her cloak and with it her hood, giving hints of her slim figure and hair spun from the light of the sun.

"Hey, lover, focus," Else snapped.

I turned to her and looked down into her elfin face. Her eyes had turned the colour of dark honey when she felt calm and at peace. Her skin always retained a warmth in its tones which reminded me of summer. Her body's slimness came from hard work and hours in the saddle, not contrived eating habits.

I took a deep breath and willed myself to snap the chains Guinevere placed on my heart so long ago. "You mean the world to me," I said.

"Bloody good job," Else said. "Or I might be forced to release that damned spell all over you again."

I chuckled, suddenly preferring all the complications of my relationship with Else, to Arthur and Guinevere any day. I studied my opponent. He sat on Willow, the great black stallion looking sleek and perfect as ever. Unlike Ash, Willow had the temper of a gelding but the brains of a true destrier. They were a fine pair, even if Ash's temper usually meant he'd rather fight with Willow than beside him. Jealousy in horses is not attractive. Because of Ash's colour change, they appeared to be brothers and Ash shifted as he recognised the scent of the other horse. Arthur himself sat straight in the saddle and the lance in his hand did not waver.

Else rode forward. "My Lord is here and prepared for the tourney," she said her voice carrying over the hum of the crowd.

Arthur, his visor raised, said in return, "As is traditional." His voice rang clear and strong. Arthur had sobered up. "The knight has the right to ask for anything from me if he wins, other than my crown."

"All he asks in return is the chance to plead his case to the greatest of kings, in audience alone," Else said.

I frowned. Arthur always included his wife in that speech. Guinevere stood beside him as if a statue made from chalk. Her eyes blazed with the fury of a smith's forge. It meant, if a knight were brave enough he could ask for the Queen. I tried hard to ignore the implications but I felt them like poisonous demons on my back pulling my hair for attention.

Else distracted me by handing me the black shield I needed for protection. "Good luck and don't get hurt," she whispered. I just grunted in return.

Kay stepped forward. "Are we ready for the joust? Rules as always, the first to yield or the first to blood is the winner." Just two rules existed in this contest, don't aim to kill, don't maim on purpose.

Arthur lowered his visor and gathered his reins. Willow stepped forward. I gathered Ash's reins and fought him for dominance until he realised he couldn't grab the bit and run for his enemy. We lowered our lances. The crowd grew quiet. I focused on Arthur's great shield. The crest of the oak emblazoned on its surface. My own felt heavy on my left arm, a comfort. Kay gave the order to charge. Ash had already begun moving before Kay finished the word. The thunder of his hooves at full gallop filled my head. We were on the outside run of the lists, nearest the wall rather than the keep. I couldn't see anything other than my opponent racing toward me, lowering his lance as I did mine. I knew we were matched at the quintain, so the chances were we would not unhorse each other on the first pass. I also knew the more often we did this the more likely one of us would be seriously hurt. I had to unhorse Arthur regardless of our skill.

Ash reached for greater speed, as was his habit just before we met our target. He lengthened his stride, I braced my lance against my besagew and angled it a little too far to the left so it would glance off Arthur's shield and not splinter into his body by accident. I needed to use his momentum to unseat him by taking his balance. The horses were a thunderous noise in my head. I tensed my right side while relaxing my left so I could turn in the saddle if necessary.

One moment I moved freely, with the endless power of my horse racing forward. The next, the world stopped moving with the brutality of a hammer hitting an anvil. The anvil being my shoulder. Arthur's lance shattered against me, my lance struck his shield and shattered to one side. He hit me square. Hunkered down behind my shield the splintered wood cascaded around me. I twisted to accommodate the force of his momentum. Arthur however, was not so lucky.

Galloping past each other, I realised I'd struck home. I'd hit him a strong glancing blow. His seat in the saddle had overextended toward me, enabling him to hit me with accuracy, but it meant I'd encouraged him too far past his centre of gravity. Arthur twisted to stay seated but as I pulled Ash up, having discarded the shaft of my lance, I saw him overbalance. Instead of fighting the fall, Arthur flipped his right leg over Willow's neck and almost stepped off the horse. The stallion slowed, the other half of a perfect team. Willow snorted and stamped, returning to Arthur, allowing him to pull his great two handed bastard broadsword from his saddle. Arthur carried the thing on his back in battle but

Willow's calm nature meant the horse returned with it even in the joust. I couldn't have done that with Ash. Whenever I fell off, he trotted away in disgust.

I'd earned the right to fight from horseback but I would never choose to do so, the unfair advantage was not my way. I threw my leg over Ash's neck and slid off the side, drawing my sword as my feet hit the ground. My own favoured weapon was a hand-and-half broadsword. Big, but I could wield it either one or two handed. I chose two for the moment and approached Arthur with great care. His weapon was longer but heavier than mine and I knew from experience he intended to finish this fight quickly. I had never known anyone move as fast as he could with that monster. However, he couldn't move as fast as me and I was fitter.

"You did well in the joust, Sir Knight," Arthur said. I approached watching, gauging, assessing.

I tilted my head in acknowledgement of the compliment. He often engaged people in conversation and then sprang into attack in the middle of a sentence.

"This vow of silence Does not need to continue, we are alone, tell me who you are and why you want private audience with me," he said, circling me.

The noise of the crowd cheering started to filter through the adrenaline. I did not want a conversation. I moved into an obvious overhead strike, Arthur raised his sword and blocked the strike. The swords crashed, sparks flew and my blade slid off Arthur's. We began the fight in earnest. The weapons wove patterns in the dull winter light and as predicted, the rain put in an appearance. We were both good. I realised even if Arthur had been drinking, his skill remained sharp and there seemed to be a driving force to his fight which never existed before. He attacked with unfamiliar recklessness. I managed to slip under his guard and smashed my blade into his breastplate, but at the same moment, I felt him smack my backplate with the pommel of his sword. It threw me forward me and I headed for the dirt. I tucked and rolled. The unfamiliar armour made it a hard, slow movement.

"Fuck," I cursed as I came up. I turned back to Arthur, just as he came in for a strike, which would have taken my head off. I threw myself backward. This was supposed to be to the point we yielded, not died. I gathered my senses together and realised this fight had become serious.

Did he know who was under the black armour? Did he care or did he want me dead?

He came at me again and it dawned on me I might lose this bout. If I did he would unmask me in front of the crowd and I couldn't give him due warning about my existence. He'd have to arrest me without listening to me. He lunged. I deflected and led him into a pattern of movements. The crowd screamed their approval. I caught a glimpse of Kay and Geraint, they stood side by side, grim faced and silent. Arthur relaxed; he thought he'd worn me down. I caught the rhythm of his strike toward my legs, swept his blade, rather than allowing it to smash into me, and forced it into a circle. Arthur's body had already began to turn into the next attack and I took control of his momentum. I stepped into the attack, closed the distance, hooked my leg around his ankle and pulled back, while smashing my armoured elbow into the top of his breastplate. He crashed to the ground and grunted, air rushed out of his lungs. Arthur, always the scrapper, rolled away from me fast. I knew he'd move, so as he rolled onto his chest I dropped over his body. The weight of me, my armour and his own, pinned him down. I hooked my arm under his chin and pulled back against his helmet. Arthur grunted in his discomfort.

I said, trying to hide my voice despite my breathlessness, "Yield, your Majesty, you know you cannot win from here."

I felt him strain against me. Our armour ran slick with rain. He would not yield. If I didn't hold him and we ended up fighting he would know it was me. He'd be able to smash me to death. I wouldn't be able to pin him again this easily. Despite my weight bearing down on him, Arthur heaved and managed to raise himself off the ground, twisting as he did so.

"Please, Arthur, just fucking yield," I cried out trying to force him down. The crowd didn't hear me but he did.

Arthur locked rigid. He now lay on his back, his left arm free. He raised his visor. He panted hard but he looked more alive than he had that morning.

"Lancelot?" he whispered, his expression confused.

"Please, Arthur." I eased my weight off him. "We need to talk. You are in danger."

For just a moment his dark blue eyes filled with joy, before ungovernable rage contorted his face.

"I will never yield to you traitor," he screamed, pushing against me. His heavy gauntlet smashed into my head. The fist bounced off my helmet but the whiplash and noise were enough to disorientate me for a moment. The shock of seeing the loathing in Arthur's face made my brain disengage from the fight. I found myself rolling back with Arthur on top trying to wrench my helmet off.

I heard feet pounding toward us. Arthur almost yanked my head off trying to open my visor. I saw Else running and Geraint's voice booming at Arthur to stop. His fist came up as he saw my face. I just lay there, unable to stop my King from trying to kill me. His fist came down. Pain radiated through my head and my mind finally knew peace from the hate in his eyes.

CHAPTER SIXTEEN

I WOKE WITH A dull ache where my face used to be and sharp stabbing pains in my shoulders. I frowned. It hurt. I remembered to open my eyes, my nose realised it lay against something it didn't like and my brain agreed as my vision cleared. I stared at mouldy straw. It stank of piss and old food. I lay on my side, twisted up and without my armour.

"Fuck," I muttered and tasted blood in my mouth. My lips were split top and bottom. I took a breath and realised my nose remained intact. My right eye had swollen almost closed and my cheek burned in pain. I shifted my head and the world revolved on a new and interesting axis. Used to concussion I held still and waited for everything to settle before continuing my journey upright.

My shoulders hurt because I'd been chained to the wall by my wrists and I'd been hanging just off the floor of the cell. My neck also suffered with the cold metal of a rough iron collar biting my soft skin, like wood ants. Torches in the corridor lit a small window in the door, but no natural light filtered into the dungeon. I could hardly see the bare stone walls. I did however, feel the cold. I sat in my shirtsleeves, thin wool doublet and hose.

"Fuck," I said again. I realised my eyes swam with tears and they leaked over my cheeks. "Arthur," I sighed his name and closed my eyes, my grief overwhelming me for long moments. I lost the one thing, the one man who held me to this life more than any other. I know I'd been banished, but with Else's news that I must return to save him, I'd allowed hope in my heart. Perhaps he would forgive me and we could repair the damage we had done to each other. Apparently not. I just sat in the cold and the dark unable to unravel my predicament, only able to think about how Arthur must hate me to have done this to me.

Time passed, I realised I'd begun to shiver and I felt sick. "God, Else," I moaned. A wave of fresh agony ripped through me because we'd been separated for so long. I pulled my feet under me and tried to roll up despite the bite of the manacles on my wrists and neck.

The pain withdrew for a short time, giving me a respite. I struggled upright and stood. The chain forced the collar tight against my neck. That tipped me over the edge. Anger, shame and pain coalesced inside me. I pulled against my bonds and screamed. The sound bounced back off the stone walls of the cell and hit me in their turn like small spiteful lashes.

The effort cost me dear. When the emotions subsided, exhaustion swept in. Utterly drained and defeated, leaning against the cold stone wall, I just stood, quiet, blank, alone. Waiting for the pain to return.

I have no idea how long I stood there in that dank hole. I did think Arthur really needed to take better care of his prisoners. They should not be chained to the walls and should have somewhere clean to sleep, but I guessed he might have had me thrown into the worst place possible for a reason. Much later I heard movement outside the cell and the light flickered. A key turned in the lock and I realised I hadn't eaten in a long time. A tall, broad figure stood in the entrance, silhouetted against the torches. I'd know that figure anywhere.

"Hello, Arthur," I said, my voice dry from lack of water.

The moment hung, suspended in the air like motes of ash. He tilted his head, looking down. I still couldn't see his face.

"You shouldn't have come home," he said. He sounded as hoarse as I did.

"I had no choice," I said.

"So I hear." He stepped over the threshold and approached. He looked so tired, his eyes were shadowed and his face drawn. For a moment I saw the old man he would become if he lived that long. "I've sent for Stephen de Clare."

He couldn't have hurt me more if he'd punched me and the bastard knew it. He watched the pain radiate from my guts and sweep through my limbs. I collapsed to my knees before him.

"So, you do love her," he said, manner cold and distant.

"If you want to punish me, fine, I understand." I choked on the words. "But I beg you, Arthur, leave the girl alone. Don't send her back to Stephen. He will sell her to the highest bidder, once he gets our marriage annulled."

Arthur snorted and approached. "He Doesn't need to annul it, you both needed my permission which I haven't given, so it Doesn't count. It just makes the girl your whore, not your wife," he snarled close to my face.

The heat of his anger washed over me. It met my rage and I found myself on my feet, reaching for his throat. Arthur stepped back and laughed as I fought the chains holding me to the wall. "This is what it is like to be impotent when someone takes the woman you love from your arms."

That pulled me up short. I stood, quivering with the residue of unspent emotion. "I never wanted to take her from you, Arthur," I said staring into his heartbroken blue eyes. For a moment, I glimpsed his soul, desperately alone and burdened. He felt he had no one and his one consolation in his isolation had been me and I'd ruined it. I'd stolen it. I'd stolen it because I wanted something I couldn't have but being close eased the terrible ache.

He half turned in the cell. "Let her go, Geraint."

I heard muffled curses and a small, strong body hurled itself toward me. I gathered Else up in my arms and kissed her head where it lay against my chest. The spell ignited, making us both groan and fight for control. We sank to our knees and I held her face in my hands as we shared chased kisses. She wept.

"Let her go, Lancelot," Geraint said. He stood in the doorway of the cell. "If you don't it will be harder on you both."

"You don't believe this rubbish," Arthur snapped, pointing at us. "This is just a pathetic manipulation."

Geraint sighed, he looked as tired as Arthur. "You're wrong, this is very real. You send her back to Stephen and they will both die long before you have the opportunity to hang your best friend."

There were some unpleasant things happening I didn't understand. Arthur knew about Else and the threat but didn't believe it. He also wanted me dead.

"Then it will save me the cost of the hangman," Arthur snapped. He grabbed Else by the scruff of the neck and pulled her out of my arms. "That is the goodbye I promised you so you would go to your damned brother quietly. Get her out of here, Geraint."

My big friend held Else and she sobbed with uncontrolled grief. His eyes begged my forgiveness as he led her away.

"Arthur, what the hell are you playing at?" I felt so shocked I didn't know how to react. I had never seen him manhandle a woman.

"What am I playing at?" He dropped to his knees before me, so we were face to face. "You left me." His anguish pieced my heart like a javelin.

I opened my mouth, now more confused than ever and then snapped it shut. I tried again, "You banished me."

"Because it was the only way I could save your life. I thought you were dead." Arthur rocked back on his heels and buried his face in his hands. His knuckles turned white, his fingers began to pull his hair. I had never seen anyone so wracked with grief.

His pain made mine a pale reflection. He said through gritted teeth, "I couldn't find you. Geraint couldn't find you. I thought you had died. I found a nunnery, a farmer said you'd been there but they denied knowing you."

I blessed Sister Eliza. Arthur looked at me, his eyes haunted, tragic. "I lost my sword, the one thing which gave me the strength to be king."

He hadn't called me that since we were squires.

He'd once said, as I had lain in a field with my head on his chest, *'Lancelot, you are the blade, the sword I shall use as my strength to carry the burden of kingship when the time comes. While you stand beside me, I know I will have the strength to go on and do whatever is necessary to protect Camelot.'*

That had been more than fifteen summers ago.

I vowed that day I would always be at his side to hold him safe and protect him, as a weapon should, strong and reliable, able to go wherever he pointed me.

Later that year, during Yuletide, I met Guinevere and life changed for us both because Arthur's father died and I knew my fate was sealed, I could not love a king.

I watched Arthur collapse before me. I wanted to reach out and wrap him in my arms. "Then let me go, Arthur and I will become your sword once more. I have always been loyal to you, my friend."

He laughed, his bitterness all the lash he needed to tame me. "If I do that, it will cause civil war, Lancelot. Stephen wanted your head even before he knew you'd been fucking his sister."

"In my defence I didn't know she was his sister until after we found each other and made love." Which was sort of true.

"Somehow I don't think that's going to matter," he said. I watched the king descend over the man and my broken friend vanished inside the bitter exterior of the leader. "I have no choice but to give the Court what it demands, Lancelot, and it demands your neck. My enemies will not allow us to become strong again." He rose in one smooth movement and stood over me. His eyes cold and hard. "I am sorry, I know you have sacrificed much for this Court but it will have all of you before it is finished."

Speaking of his world in the third person made me realise Arthur's home, his seat of power had fractured beyond his ability to control. There were factions, which ran too deep to stop, pulling his world asunder.

He turned to leave and I tried to stop him. The chains snapped tight, the noise made him flinch. "Arthur, please, don't do this. Don't give in, we can win, I know we can. The White Hart must survive." I hadn't meant to say the last part, with his hand on the door to my cell, he froze but didn't turn.

Arthur said, "The White Hart is dead."

He left and closed the cell door himself, turning the key. The room felt so empty without Arthur there, his blonde curls bright against the red of the torches and his emotions so strong. I leaned back against the wall, lowered myself to the mouldy straw and sat, trying to understand the last few minutes of my life.

I realised that either Arthur lay under a terrible spell or he'd lost his mind to grief. I thought about what I knew, Arthur would willingly sacrifice Else and I to the whims of his political enemies; he didn't believe in the attack of the fey; and he remained scarred and hurt by my actions.

Arthur did not want to forgive me and I would die in this mouldy straw. If I didn't manage to force him to listen to me this would be my end. The great Lancelot du Lac, slain in a dingy dungeon by his best friend because he couldn't control his damned cock.

Self loathing is an emotion I am all too familiar with and it burned in my guts like the foul brew used in a tanner's yard.

I even tried to ask myself if it had been worth it, the betrayal, the lies, the pain I had caused. Yes, Guinevere may well have led the seduction but I didn't have to give in. I should have left Court sooner and stopped her coming too close. I should not have betrayed my friend, and in the quiet corner of my mind – *my true love.*

The torch outside my cell guttered and began to die. I hadn't eaten or drunk in hours and everything in me ached for Arthur and for Else. It would take Stephen two full days to reach Camelot if he rode from Chester. Else had two days to escape. I prayed she would run, that she wouldn't stay and plead my case. I realised it was a faint hope, knowing Else as I did. Time wore on and I dozed in my upright position, my hands going numb because of lack of blood and my body growing colder.

A faint noise woke me.

"Great, rats," I said, my voice surprising me I'd been quiet so long.

No, I thought, *not rats, something outside the door.*

I heard the key turn and a single sheltered candle showed the figure of a man once more.

"Tell me about the White Hart," said Arthur's from the doorway. He sounded scared. I had never heard him sound scared before.

CHAPTER SEVENTEEN

I SPOKE THEN, WITH slow deliberation and great care, describing each of my dreams in detail. Talking about the Wolf and how I knew he was me. How I realised the Doe represented Else and the mighty Stag, my King.

"The enemy you face, who is it?" Arthur asked.

"I don't know," I said choosing honesty. "But I do know it's bad and it's going to become stronger. I believe it is the fey who wish you off the throne of Camelot and we have to find Merlin to help us defeat them."

"And to free you of the spell holding you and Eleanor under its control?" Arthur asked.

"Yes," I replied.

"Why is she a Doe and not another Wolf?" Arthur asked.

I had asked myself the same question and tried not to think about the answer. "I don't know that either."

"Does she?"

"No, I don't think so, but she's not always very forthcoming with information." See I can be tactful.

"Does it hurt to be away from her?" Arthur asked still in the doorway.

"Yes, but I have grown used to the worst of the pain. It is as though I have a broken limb and no chance of it healing without her contact."

Arthur walked in, his hand shook. "I had the dream. I had the dream where the Stag killed the Doe and turned on the Wolf in his madness. As the Wolf died on the antlers of the Stag the world became dark. The trees died. The fields shrivelled. Camelot fell and thousands perished." As he spoke, he came close and knelt before me once more. "Forgive me, my friend."

He knelt, within arm's reach. I moved my legs so I didn't startle him and rose onto my knees. I took the candle from his hand and reached for his neck with the other. My palm brushed his skin. Arthur groaned and threw himself into my arms. Despite the restrictions of the chains, I held my King to my body. He shuddered in relief, having released himself from his burdens and begun to follow his heart.

"I love you," Arthur mumbled into my shoulder.

"I know, I have always known. And you have always been the centre of my world, my King," I said. I could not consider what kind of love he meant. The love of a brother in arms or…

His hands were hot on my cold back and his musky scent filled my head. I felt his heart pounding against my chest. I kissed his tousled hair without thought, just seeking comfort for us both. We'd been apart for so long.

Arthur lifted his head from my shoulder and we were less than a feather's width apart. Memories raced from the deepest part of my mind, overwhelming common sense.

"I..." Arthur uttered the word on a breath, which tickled my swollen lips.

I stared into the most perfect dark blue eyes I had ever seen and forgot everything in the world but Arthur. "I..." I managed, more articulate with a sword than a word. "I love you," I breathed. The context differed from the many other times I'd spoken similar words as his vassal. The honesty surged through me, a simultaneous relief and a terror.

Arthur closed his eyes as if that was all that mattered to him. He withdrew from my arms and reached into his doublet, taking out a key. With shaking hands, he unlocked my shackles and helped me stand.

"I hurt you," he said touching the bruising on my face.

"I think it's the least of our worries," I said smiling, or trying to anyway.

"Come on, you need to eat and clean up before we leave."

"We are leaving Camelot?" I asked.

"We have a wizard to find," Arthur said with his usual firmness.

I grinned, then groaned because it split my mouth again. I followed him out of my cell and knew I cheated death once more.

We walked up the corridor. Arthur had slung me into the deepest part of the castle. After the first set of stone stairs, my legs weakened and my breathing came in short gasps. The cold and hunger now defeated my body. Dehydration is dangerous to all warriors, but to me it is a killer. I work hard and sweat hard. I needed water.

"Arthur, hang on," I said, leaning against a smooth stone wall. We'd reached the part of the keep with dressed stone. He returned to my side.

"Is it Else?" he asked as he placed his hand on my back.

"Partly," I said. I didn't tell him it was because I'd almost frozen to death, my face hurt from where he'd hit me and he'd starved me for the day. I pushed off the wall and Arthur slid his shoulder under my arm. I leaned into my King. His strength felt so good. We were almost the same height. Arthur is just an inch shorter than I am, broader and wiry, whereas I am more heavily muscled. His skin is light and freckles in the summer. We made slow progress, but he took me up narrow staircases and along corridors until we reached his suite of rooms. I wondered who slept in my room just down the hall.

There were guards at various points but they ignored us and Arthur's rooms were bare of soldiers. He opened the large oak door and a wall of heat washed over me like a comfort blanket. He helped me into his most casual suite. His bedroom lay next door and a washing room. Here, he was always at his most relaxed, where he discusses plans with friends and sits in quiet contemplation when he wants to be alone. He helped me to a large wooden chair covered in tapestry cushions right in front of the fire.

I shivered, unable to prevent the deep quake in my bones. He poured a glass of wine and thrust it into my hand. I stared at the dark liquid. "I'm not drinking," I said.

"You need it," he replied. "Is this because of Else, Lancelot? You look terrible."

"I don't know, I can't tell anymore, please, Arthur, if she is here let her come to me." My hand trembled as I raised the wine to my lips. The fire in the huge hearth warmed my skin but not my bones.

Arthur touched my head with fingertips. "I'll go and find her. She's nearby. I'll only be a few moments." He didn't wait for a reply he just swept from the room.

I sipped the wine with my elbows resting on my knees, my head down. I heard the door open, expecting to see Else or Arthur, I stared dumbfounded at Guinevere.

She ran toward me wearing her hair down over her shoulders. It flowed around my waist and a dressing coat of thick tapestry coloured red and gold. It lay tight to her waist, but her legs flashed bare as she approached.

She dropped to her knees in front of my chair. "Lancelot, my love." She reached up to my face. "We have but moments. Arthur has gone to find that funny little thing you arrived with."

I blinked several times, I thought she meant Ash, then realised she meant

Else. I gathered my wits, allowing Guinevere the upper hand would be dangerous.

"That is my wife, my Lady," I said, watching those large pale blue eyes carefully. I withdrew from her hands and sat upright in the chair.

Guinevere frowned and rested her hands on my filthy knees. "Don't be ridiculous, Lancelot. You can't be married to her, she dresses like a boy and she has a foul mouth," she said it with such confidence I almost believed her myself. As for the foul mouth, I'd had some cracking arguments with the Queen and she could let rip when she wanted.

I stuck to my principles. "Regardless of what you think, she is my wife, your Majesty." I tried to stand so she couldn't touch me. Using her title helped maintain distance between us in my head. She pushed me back with surprising strength.

"She isn't beautiful enough for you to love, Lancelot." Her repeated use of my name displayed her need to own me.

"Guinevere..." I wanted to manhandle her out of my way, but I also wanted to avoid contact. "Don't be rude."

"My love." She clutched my hand, avoiding the issue of Else. "Please, this is more important than some wife you've acquired." That's Guinevere, all heart. "Please, I must tell you, Arthur is mad, quite mad, look how he beat you today. And he..." I watched her eyes fill with tears. "He has beaten me," her voice became a whisper.

My heart froze in response to her words. "Leave," I said, a wave of loathing sweeping over me. I took her hands off mine and rose, moving around her. "Leave, Guinevere and I will forget your foolishness and lies."

She stared up at me stricken. "I am not lying. He has beaten me. I need you, my love."

"I am not your love and Arthur may well have pushed you in an argument but he would never beat you." I didn't know how much more of this I could take.

"You are the Queen's Champion," she snapped when she realised she would not provoke me into believing Arthur hurt her.

"I am the Queen's fool," I retorted just as Arthur walked in holding Else by the elbow.

Else wrenched herself from Arthur's grasp and ran to me. I helped to cross the distance and pulled her into my body. The magic flared and the pain eased. I held her in my arms, my hands buried in her hair. I sighed, unaware of Arthur or his wife.

Arthur however, once he'd checked on us was not unaware of his wife. "My Lady, it is late for you to be roaming the keep." His voice might have cut steel.

Guinevere went white. Even her lips drained of colour. "My Lord." She inclined her head, the formality of their game awful to watch.

I stared at husband and wife and realised their marriage lay shattered on the floor around us, sparking light into the air to burn and blind the unwary. The hate writhed between them, its tentacles reaching out to yank in the innocent. I pulled Else around me, hiding her behind my back, trying to protect her from the possible backlash.

"You have no business in my chambers, Madame," Arthur said.

"I wished to see to the comfort of my Champion," the Queen announced. Now, as subtle moves go that one resembled a war hammer.

Arthur's eyes narrowed. I opened my mouth to intervene. Else pressed her finger to my lips and shook her head. Arthur moved around Guinevere, behaving as if to avoid an adder in the grass.

"My friend," he said with his back to his Queen. "I have a question for you."

I glanced at Guinevere and then focused on Arthur.

"Sire," I said unable to hide my wariness.

"You have been thrown from Camelot. You are currently a knight without a master, am I right?" Arthur asked. His eyes were cold, a winter's day before the snow.

"My Lord, I have always been yours to obey," I said. Else melted from my arms and moved away from me. I stood straight before my King, my heart pounding. Would he return to me that which I most valued?

"Then," Arthur said turning to Guinevere. "I reinstate your title, Lancelot du Lac and as such, name you as a new knight. All previous ties have been broken so I decree you shall become the King's Champion. Do you accept this title, Knight of the Court of Camelot?"

Without hesitation I dropped to my left knee and offered out both my hands, pressed together palms upward as though holding a cup of water. "I will accept this gift, my Lord and I will protect your honour as though it were my own. I promise on my faith that I will be faithful, never cause you harm and will observe my homage to you completely. I will preserve you against all persons in good faith and without deceit." My head remained bowed. I felt Arthur lace his fingers into the tangled mass of my hair.

I did not waver. I did not think through the consequences. I obeyed my King. I heard Guinevere hiss in response to losing me for good.

"This isn't over, Sire," she said with more derision than I thought possible. "You may have your knight back but your love for him is a foul thing which turns you both into monsters. You are unhealthy and that has made me barren. You disgust me, Arthur."

Arthur's hand trembled. I did not move one muscle. Whatever had been said between them I didn't want to know or consider.

"I accept your fealty, Lancelot, Knight of Camelot."

His words were all the benediction I needed. A wash of peace flooded through me and I didn't give a damn what anyone thought of us or our friendship. No one knew the truth of our love for each other. Together, Arthur and I would defeat all his enemies and Guinevere could just seethe from the sidelines.

I heard the door slam and Arthur's hand moved from my head. "God, what have I done," he whispered.

CHAPTER EIGHTEEN

I RELAXED MY HANDS and raised my head from the traditional position of the vassal to his lord. "You've claimed me for your own, so Guinevere can't use me as a weapon against you any longer. It was the only thing you could do."

Arthur seemed to collapse in on himself. He sank into a chair and drank my wine in a gulp. His hands shook, causing the wine to spill, so he carried the glass to his lips with both hands, clutching it like a drowning man. I didn't know what to say or do.

I looked at Else, seeking guidance.

She sighed, rolled her eyes to indicate the idiocy of men and knelt before Arthur as Guinevere knelt before me. Raising her hand she stroked his face, I watched him turn into her palm and kiss it. How I wished it were my hand.

"What do I do now?" Arthur asked.

Else said, "We leave Camelot, Arthur. This place is draining you. You need to regain your strength. I cannot protect you here and neither can Lancelot. Leave others to gather an army because there will be war before this is over, but they don't need you. We need you to help us find my father."

"I miss Merlin," Arthur whispered. "I've missed him almost as much as I've missed you." He looked up at me. "I take it you didn't invite my wife into my chambers?" His blue eyes turned from calm cool lakes to stormy seas in moments.

"No, Arthur. I did not."

"What did she want?"

"Nothing important."

"Tell me, Lancelot." I heard the threat and the order.

I obeyed. "She wanted me to rescue her from your clutches. She claims you are beating her. I told her she was a liar."

Arthur nodded, his expression becoming sad. "I have never hurt her, no matter what she has done to me. I have never hurt her physical."

"Taking Lancelot has hurt her and she will have her revenge," Else said looking at me.

"She will never come between us," I said and meant it. I wouldn't give her the opportunity to reach my heart again, not now I had Arthur to care for.

I heard him choke back a sob. Else moved into his arms and held him close. A strange feeling raced through me as I watched her care for Arthur. I felt jealous of them both, but I also wanted them to be close. To need each other as I needed them. A dangerous game having already lost one woman to Arthur. Would I lose my Hind to the Hart?

Unable to handle any more grief I left them alone and went to Arthur's private washroom. The water had almost frozen in the large bowl but I took a clean linen cloth and washed myself, stripping off the foul smelling clothes I'd been in for hours. I dunked my hair into the remains of a bucket of clean water and ran my fingers through it, trying to take out the knots. It needed a good brush but Else didn't like me using the horses' brushes. Knowing Arthur as I did I found some old clothes and changed into them. They were finer than my best doublet and hose. I looked with longing at his soft bed and wondered if they would notice my absence. I ached to lie still for a few moments.

I heard voices and realised Arthur had summoned Kay and Geraint. I walked into the main room and a wall of muscle almost knocked me off my feet. Geraint hugged me to the point I began to feel my ribs bend. "I thought you were lost to us this time," he said with joy.

I laughed. "I will be if you don't let me go, you great bear." I smacked him on the back. He relaxed his arms. I relearned how to breathe.

"I'm sorry I had to take Else away from you," he said coming straight to the point.

I glanced at Arthur. He looked away, uncomfortable with his recent behaviour. "I think we all need to take a moment for forgiveness today. We have all done what we thought was necessary." I held Geraint's upper arm as I spoke but I gazed at Arthur. It was not lost on my friend. Geraint nodded and turned to Arthur.

I looked at Kay properly for the first time. Kay was about five years older than me, I'm a year older than Arthur and Geraint is three years younger. Kay and I should be close, but he found me impossible to understand. If he hadn't been born the son of a great noble, he would have made a wonderful bean counter. He stood shorter by a good hand than Arthur and his body already ran soft. A slight belly poked over his hose, separating them from his doublet and his hair had thinned dramatically, he appeared to have aged ten years in one. He looked the age that suited his personality. His hair had once been the colour of river sand and his eyes a washed out blue. He owned a strong straight nose, which sat in a face made too small for its fine structure. Kay married when he'd been a young man, a sensible girl who'd become a good wife. But Kay wasn't here because of what he looked like, Kay was here because he made a fine politician and his loyalty to Arthur had never been questioned. If I was Arthur's blade, Kay was Arthur's pen.

Kay smiled at me. "It is good to see you home, Lancelot."

I blinked, surprised. "I am glad to be home."

"Thank you for saving him," Kay said as he shook my hand. "You might have tried doing it in a less dramatic fashion, but thank you."

I grinned, or tried to; the bruises were making my face stiff. "If I'd done that you might have suspected I'd grown up. Then who would you disapprove of?"

He shook his head. "Lancelot, you will never grow up and use your head rather than your sword."

"And I thank, God, for it," I told him.

"All very nice," Geraint said lounging in a chair by the fire, "but why am I here at this ungodly hour?"

"I'm leaving Camelot," Arthur stated.

Geraint raised his eyebrows and Kay said protested, "Sire, you cannot leave Camelot. The Court is seething with unrest. If you leave it will cause a vacuum of power we cannot control."

"I have to find Merlin," Arthur told him. Kay's face closed down, he hated Merlin and the influence the strange man brought with him. Merlin offered no logic, just riddles and predictions.

"You can send Lancelot to find Merlin," Kay told him.

"No, I can't. Lancelot will be going with me, but I am the only one who might find my friend."

"So, you are leaving us in charge of the Court?" Geraint asked shrewdly.

"Yes, and you are to gather my army," Arthur said.

Kay blinked. "Army?"

"There will be war with Stephen de Clare before this is over," Arthur said.

"Civil war?" Kay said, "That is madness, Arthur, he wouldn't dare."

"Are you certain of that?" Geraint said sitting up. "You know as well as I that the man covets Arthur's throne. The whole Court thinks Arthur has lost his mind since Lancelot's banishment..." Geraint stopped and blushed, realising too late what he'd said.

"Don't hold back there," Arthur muttered coming to stand beside me.

Geraint grinned. "Well, that's the first time I've spoken the truth in the last year and you've not threatened to throw me in prison."

"Don't push it, I can still arrange for that to happen," Arthur said crossing his arms over his chest.

Geraint laughed. "I don't think you could do that now you have Lancelot back. Anyway, Stephen thinks he can use Arthur's instability to take his throne."

"Stephen's not the only one to watch," Arthur said. He sat, Else walked to him and I don't know how it happened but now he held her hand. Geraint frowned at me. I chose to stay blank. "My wife will move against me, doubtless using Stephen in the process."

"All you need to do is forgive Guinevere," Kay said, trying to be kind.

Arthur looked up at him and I saw the anger. Else brushed her free hand through his hair and Arthur calmed, Geraint opened his mouth, I shook my head.

Arthur said, "I cannot forgive her and do not presume to know what I need to forgive her for. Just watch her and control her movements. Do not give her easy access to Stephen when he arrives later today. We will be leaving before dawn, I do not want anyone to know where or why we have left. You will tell them I have gone on pilgrimage. Taking Eleanor and Lancelot with me."

"That makes no sense, Arthur," Kay said.

"It Doesn't have to make sense. I'm mad remember." He smiled at Kay.

"I don't think you should leave alone," Geraint said. "I know you and Lancelot can look after yourselves but do you actually know where Merlin is?"

I began to tune out the talk. I walked to the corner of the room and sank into a chair. It was a long time after midnight and the night sucked at my bones. We'd be leaving in a few hours and I had to switch off. My eyes closed and my brain slipped away.

"Lancelot, wake up." Arthur's voice dragged me from sleep.

"Time to leave?" I asked.

He smiled. "No, time for you to sleep." I realised Geraint and Kay still sat in the room. Arthur helped me stand. "I've been hard on you today, my friend. Go next door and sleep."

I looked for Else, but she'd vanished. "Where?"

"She's gone to pack your things and prepare your horses. She wants to make certain you are a long way from Camelot before her brother arrives." Arthur poked me next door. I watched, mesmerised by his hands as they rose and started to untie the doublet and shirt I'd borrowed. Those strong fingers brushed against my skin for the first time and we both paused. My heart raced so fast he must have heard it, or perhaps the fine tremble in his fingers occupied his thoughts. He pulled off the shirt. "Get into bed, Lancelot and sleep. I'll wake you when we leave."

His hand sat on my bare chest and pushed. I stepped back to the bed and sat. Arthur knelt and began unlacing my boots.

"My King, you don't need –" I began.

"Shut up, Lancelot, and hold still. I just want to help." Arthur sounded strange but my exhausted brain couldn't work it out. I think he'd been planning to say something else and changed his mind. His hand brushed up my leg and stopped on my thigh, the muscle twitched.

Arthur pushed himself upright and suddenly turned me around. I should have resisted but he caught me by surprise. His hand trailed down my back and I felt it move over the scars. "Oh, Lancelot," he sounded breathless. "What have I done to you?"

Enough, I couldn't deal with this any longer. "Arthur, it's over, please just leave it. It Doesn't matter." I tried to turn back against his hand but he just moved with me to keep the scars in his sights.

"I would give anything to take this back," he whispered. His fingers strayed all over the thick lash marks. He lowered his hand, once more catching me by surprise and kissed one of the long echoes of my pain.

I flinched against the hand on my chest, where he held me under control. This was a bad idea. For a start, Geraint and Kay sat next door.

Our desires had been forbidden and denied for so long, to give into them now, my reputation in tatters and Arthur a mess, would lead to mistakes and those could cost a king his crown.

My common sense asserted itself at last and I moved away from the bed. My damn cock thick and hard. How often had I dreamed of this over the years? Arthur remained with one knee on his bed, stood so close but his head turned away from me.

"Please, Arthur, we can't, not now, it's too much." I didn't know what else to say.

Arthur slid off the bed and just walked out. I sighed, the weight of Camelot squeezing my chest. This was not going well, Arthur hadn't made a move towards me in years. I finished stripping and lay on the bed, switching my brain off and falling asleep in moments.

The dream hit me like a series of huge waves crashing against endless cliffs. The images were frantic, the Doe and Hart tight together, the Wolf standing guard, something evil sweeping from the woods and covering them in darkness, until all I heard were screams but no images. Another, Camelot, fire dancing and laughing through familiar streets. I ran on four legs hunting and searching for something I'd lost. Again, standing on the top of a strangely shaped hill, looking down over long flatlands before me, mists creeping through them. A man standing beside me, he looked down at me, his black robes tattered and dusty, his staff blackened and burned. He seemed so tired.

His hand sat on my head, as he said, "We are losing. You must help." The sense of loss sweeping through the man, then into me made me whine.

I woke to darkness in a strange bed and felt sick. It took me a few minutes to realise I lay in Arthur's bed in Camelot. "I can't keep this up," I muttered to myself, exhaustion made the world tilt.

"I was about to wake you," Arthur said from the darkened corner of his room.

"Shit!" I sat up. "You startled me." I squinted as he struck a light and a candle flared.

"You were dreaming," he said. I looked at him once I had focused. His eyes were sunken dark pits. His flesh thin and drawn over his strong features. His colour grey.

"You look like you needed to sleep," I said trying to guess his mood.

He shook his head. "I needed to drink." He held up a skin of wine. Oh, joy. "Kay asked me how I could forgive you so fast," he said, the tone bitter once more. I remained silent, though the same thoughts occurred to me. "I told him about the dreams. He laughed."

"Kay has never understood your ties to other worlds, Arthur. He is a practical man. He has never understood signs and symbols. He has never understood our friendship," I said, treading with care.

"Our friendship..." Arthur echoed. He hung his head between his shoulders, his elbows on his knees. The shadows drew close to him and sucked at him. The thought disturbed me in a way I didn't understand. I felt drawn to him so strongly my legs moved before I'd realised I'd flung the blankets off. The cold air nipped at my bare skin. I walked to his side and knelt, taking the wine from his unresisting fingers.

I stroked the short blonde hair. "You need help, Arthur. Let me help you and we will bring Camelot back to you."

"You can't bring Guinevere back," he said.

I paused, "No, I can't. I am sorry."

"You weren't the only one," he said.

My breath hissed out of me. "I don't believe that."

He looked at me his eyes haunted once more. "You should. She never loved me, Lancelot, she thinks I am deeply perverted. She thinks I love you too well. I have been so jealous of your time with her but I knew it was the closest I could come to loving you so I let it happen."

I realised my mouth hung open. I had often wondered if I allowed Guinevere to seduce me for the same reason. "Arthur, I don't need to know this."

His hand reached back behind my neck and held me fast. His blue eyes were bright with powerful emotions I only half understood. "I need you to know it." The weight of his gaze and his hand became a crushing stone, trapping me.

I grabbed his forearm, more for security than any hope of disengaging us. "I will never leave you, Arthur."

"Promise me you will never betray me, Lancelot."

"I swear, my King, my brother, I will never betray you or give you cause to doubt me." I almost tasted the wine on his lips we'd come so close together.

"Am I wrong for loving you as I do?" Arthur asked.

"I don't know," I replied, just as confused as him. I knew what my body was saying but I had to think with more than my balls. "I do know you are deeply wounded, Arthur, and you need rest. You need to escape Camelot and you need time to heal. Ask me again when you are stronger and more certain of yourself. Until then," I paused, hating myself for saying it, "we will wait."

He closed his eyes, his face moved a feather's breath toward mine and our lips touched. The lightest of movements, his stubble rubbed against my face for a heartbeat or two. The world tilted, righted itself and I knew my world was changing for good. I had to wonder if I was brave enough to walk the path.

He pulled back more in control of his desires than I felt right then. He said, "As you wish, Lancelot. We will wait and I will heed your council." He rose and walked away from me, yelling for his squire. The energy in him flipped so fast I found myself reeling.

CHAPTER NINETEEN

WHEN IT CAME TO the final preparations, it didn't take us long before we were ready to leave the city. Arthur regained control of his somewhat erratic behaviour and I received a pleasant surprise when I walked into the stable yard. Geraint sat on his big ugly roan gelding.

I laughed. "I thought you'd be here, protecting Arthur's crown."

"What and let you have all the fun and all the glory, again?" Geraint asked.

Else appeared. "You alright?"

I touched her face for a moment and sighed. "I am now I've seen you." The confusion Arthur left inside me slipped away.

We travelled with three packhorses, our horses and the four of us. Gone were the days when Else and I travelled with simple packs and just each other for company. Arthur appeared and grinned happily. He was drunk. The haze in his eyes clear under the light of the just brightening sky.

Geraint and I shared a look. This would stop the moment we were out of earshot of Camelot. Else frowned when Arthur patted her backside on the way to his horse but she held her tongue. I felt eyes in the back of my neck and turned in the saddle, Ash moved restlessly under me. I looked up and Guinevere stood at a window. Her beauty struck my heart like a dagger made from ice. As I stared up at her, I felt fear curl in my guts. She meant to hurt me and those I loved.

"God, I bloody hope Kay can control that woman," I muttered.

Geraint followed my gaze, his hand reaching for my arm. "Don't, Lancelot, the woman is poison to you, always has been. Don't let her rattle your cage."

I pulled my eyes down and found Else staring at me. I smiled, a little shaken. She smiled back her eyes alive with the adventure and her regained freedom from Stephen de Clare.

Arthur, always in control, took the lead as we walked out of the stable yard and through another large gate over the moat. My body hurt and my face felt sore but I'd survived and gained his trust. We had met our objective and remained whole. Now all we needed to do was sober him up and find Merlin so we could retake Camelot.

The trouble started even before we were out of earshot from the keep's walls. I watched Arthur pull Willow up next to Mercury and engage Else in a quiet conversation. His hand snaked over to Else's lower back and buried itself under her cloak. Arthur seemed to be rubbing the small of her back. I watched the tension in her shoulders ramp skyward. I pushed Ash forward only to have Geraint hold me back.

"Not here, Lancelot, she can handle him and Arthur isn't going to hurt her," he spoke quietly, while watching our King.

"What the hell is he playing at?" I snarled. Two things made me angry, one, he had his hands on my woman; two, he'd been trying to seduce me. Did he say all that just to confuse me so he could move in on Else? And why would he want her? To hurt me for revenge because he believed we were married.

"Just wait until we are free of this damned city and we'll tackle him together," Geraint said.

So, I sat on Ash and seethed. We walked through the city, watching it rise to face another day of trading. The mighty commercial centre of our world. The noise levels around us increased. The air smelt of bread and autumn frost, the tanners, soap makers, blacksmiths and candle makers were all up and about. Flower sellers roved through the streets looking for their favourite sites and others wove home muttering curses about daylight ending their night's festivities. Arthur wore a hood over his blonde hair, to hide his appearance making certain we were not mobbed leaving the city. When we passed through the last gate, the city dwindled at last.

We pushed the horses to an easy canter and began to ride into the morning while dawn broke the night's hold. The day came to us cold and fresh, as though the weather wanted to begin again just as we did, wiping the slate clean. Else fell back and rode next to me, we were silent but she relaxed when I smiled at her.

Riding south for an hour, we passed through the hills surrounding Camelot and into the woods. Geraint pulled up his big roan, Pepper. "Right, time for breakfast."

"We don't need to stop until lunch," Arthur said, holding Willow on a tight rein to prevent him dancing with excitement. I wondered when the great stallion last left Camelot. Ash looked odd in the dawn light, they tried to wash the colour out of his coat but he'd obviously made it almost impossible for them because he now had faded black patches, pitch black patches and the occasional white splodge.

"Well, I need to stop and Lancelot needs to stop. We can't push him today or he'll become sick. He's been put under too much pressure," Geraint snapped. I'd never seen him angry with Arthur. It was hard to make Geraint angry.

Arthur looked at me. "Do you need to stop?"

"I think we need to talk. I need to know how we are going to find Merlin," I said.

"There's dry wood." Else dismounted and started to gather wood for a small fire. "I'll have something warm brewing in moments."

I dismounted without another word and Arthur harrumphed but followed suit. I watched him. He burrowed into a pack on the horse Geraint led. He came out with a small flask. I glanced at Geraint, he nodded and we both approached Arthur. Else rose and circled around the other way.

Why so sneaky? Arthur is a dangerous man to cross. He's a damned fine warrior and I'd seen no hint of the stable, sensible man I loved inside this shell. I had no idea how bad he'd been or for how long. For Geraint to be this angry it must have been months, therefore we were not taking any chances.

Geraint and I grabbed Arthur in the same moment. Geraint took hold of his left arm and shoulder, I his right. Else appeared and took the flask from Arthur's surprised hands.

"What the hell are you doing?" he cried out.

"Stopping you from killing yourself or us," Geraint said.

Arthur tried to pull himself free. "Let go you damned fools."

"No, Arthur, we are going to dry you out. Else," I said to her as Arthur began to fight and curse, "find all the drink in every pack and start pouring it away."

Arthur realised we were serious when Else emptied the flask in her hand onto the ground in front of him. Our King became inarticulate with anger. He fought so hard I started to lose control. Geraint and I lifted him off his feet and lowered him backwards onto the ground. We rolled him and Geraint tied his hands with a piece of rope he'd been holding in his padded gambeson. Arthur cursed and thrashed. I kept my knee on his back until Geraint finished. Neither of us spoke. As soon as we were done, we neatly stepped back out of reach of

Arthur's legs and left him on the ground. He flipped onto his back, his face puce with rage.

"I'll have your fucking heads for this," he snarled. The first actual sentence for a while.

Geraint and I stared at him. The irony of the situation didn't escape me, a few weeks before it could have been me on the floor ready to kill for a drink. Else lived with me while I found my own way out of my depression. We were going to force Arthur out of his. Geraint just turned and walked away to help Else raid the packs. He seemed unable to deal with Arthur. I wondered what had happened to my friends while I'd been away.

I crouched down and Arthur struggled upright. "You fucking prick. You vowed to follow me anywhere or was that another lie?"

"I will follow you anywhere, Arthur, but only if you are sober," I told him.

Arthur tried to wriggle his hands free. "My circulation is being cut off."

"Tough," I said. "I'm not letting you go until you calm down. We have no intention of fighting you." I considered my options about how to approach Arthur's problems. I decided head on would be a good idea, "Why are you drinking?"

Arthur stilled, his head turned toward me, he looked hunted. "Fine I'll fucking sober up, but you don't have the right to question me."

"I think I do. You've beaten me, threatened me and," I glanced at the others checking they were out of earshot, "and you have told me you love me. What is wrong with you, Arthur?"

He scowled. He looked about five years old, I couldn't help but smile. I wanted to wrap my arms around him and take away the pain this would cause, but I couldn't.

"Fuck off," he snapped and he turned his back on me and the others. I sighed, rose and helped to go through the packs. We didn't speak, none of us were looking forward to the next few days and this was a grim task. We found a great many wineskins, flasks of hard liquor and even some brew in his water flasks. The ground stank by the time we finished.

When we completed our task and reloaded the horses, we looked at Arthur. He'd managed to gain his feet and stood with a mutinous face.

"What do we do with him?" Else asked.

"I think if we release him, he'll just go back to Camelot and send out the army after us," Geraint said.

"Then we tie him to the horse," I said.

The others looked at me.

Arthur, still snarling, said, "You wouldn't dare."

"Arthur, I would dare because it is my duty to care for you and drying you out is not going to be easy." I turned to Geraint, "How long has he been drinking?"

"It's been bad for the last few years, but it's been out of control since you were arrested."

I nodded, "Then we tie him so he is comfortable and we put him on one of the pack horses. If we put him on Willow he'll be able to order the horse to run." I watched Arthur's face fall. He'd had the same idea.

Geraint and I approached him. He moved back and tried to keep us off him with his legs. I received a nice solid kick to the thigh but we wrestled him back to the ground. I sat on his legs, near his hips, while Geraint untied his hands and retied them to the front. Elbows and wrists, then his fingers. Not tight but firm. We lifted him. Else moved the packs on the smallest of our horses and we pushed him onto the beast. Willow looked surprised and affronted as we loaded him up with the bags.

"Well, I've lost my appetite," Geraint said.

"Are you alright?" Else asked me.

I touched her face through my gloves. "I'm fine. You were the one he manhandled."

She smiled and glanced at Arthur. "To be honest I've been handled by worse."

I grunted and we mounted. For the rest of the day we travelled southeast, avoiding towns and villages on the way. Arthur soon gave up fighting but we left him tied. I took control of his horse. Geraint led Willow. At midday we stopped. By this time, Arthur started to suffer. He sank into himself. The shakes began and the sweats soon followed. He stopped talking, well cursing, and I rode beside him to make certain he didn't fall.

After watching him for some time my concern grew to breaking point. I slipped off Ash the wrong way so I didn't have to leave Arthur's side and pulled him from the pack horse. He shivered in my arms, almost gone from our presence in his suffering.

I frowned. "He shouldn't be this bad this soon," I said helping him sit. He leaned into me and I sheltered him, he began to rock back and forth. Geraint knelt beside him.

"Arthur?" he asked. "What have you been taking?"

"Oh, God," said Else. She knelt in front of us all. She pulled Arthur's head from his chest and peeled open his eyes. She forced his mouth open and looked at his tongue, feeling his temperature. "He's been poisoned."

"What?" I exploded. "How?"

Geraint began undoing the ties and dashed off for water.

"It's not what you think," Else said. "This has been going on for months, possibly years. He's addicted to something other than alcohol, although that is probably the delivery method." She raised her voice, "Do you drink from a private cellar, Arthur?"

Geraint appeared with water and I tried to force some of it into my King. Arthur didn't reply to Else's question.

Geraint said, "He drinks at least one bottle of wine from the collection Guinevere gave him. The supplies come from her lands."

"Every day?" Else asked.

"She insists, it's in their marriage contract, a sign of the esteem he has for her father." Geraint frowned. "Guinevere's been poisoning him all these years?"

"It might not be her and it might not have been forever, but someone who knows his routine has infiltrated those bottles," Else said.

"Is there anything we can do?" I asked as Arthur twitched against me, rolled and vomited up the water I'd given him.

Else frowned and looked around her. "I can call on my family for help if we find a grove and a river."

"What family?" Geraint asked.

"Your family has a habit of trapping us," I said, a strong sense of self preservation taking over.

"If we don't find him help, he might die," Else said. "We don't have time to mess about. He needs whatever was in those bottles."

Geraint and I shared a long look, I nodded. "All right, where do we go?"

Else pointed to a wood in the distance, she shut her eyes and screwed her face up tight. When her face relaxed she smiled. "We can go there, they will help."

"I don't want to know," Geraint muttered. We lifted Arthur and put him onto Ash. I sprang up behind him and held Arthur against my chest.

"I'll make it fastest on my own. Geraint can't manage all these horses," I said.

Else nodded. "Alright, I'll tell them to accept you. They are allies to my

~ 113 ~

family, but not my kin, be respectful and ask for help. There is a pool in the centre of the wood, a sacred grove. Don't mess it up and don't expect to see anything. Just strip him and take him into the water."

"It's a bit cold for that," Geraint said, remounting Pepper.

"They will care for him, just don't let him go, we don't want them stealing the King from us," Else said. "I'll join you if I can but they might only allow the two of you there. Your energy intrigues the best of us," she added, frowning.

I wanted to ask more but Arthur moaned and his breathing changed to a pant. I kicked Ash and we sprang into a gallop.

CHAPTER TWENTY

I RODE HARD, ARTHUR a dead weight in my arms. Why hadn't any of us realised he'd been so damaged? His erratic behaviour, his dependency on alcohol, his foul temper. Someone should have noticed his withdrawal from his normal, cheerful, deeply personal leadership. Arthur's finer qualities far outweighed the bad but they died under the onslaught of his drinking, why had no one stopped and asked?

Perhaps because his friends all witnessed how he had treated me and they knew we were closer than brothers. If I couldn't reach him, and I did try, none of us could have done. I betrayed him, made him angry with me and it spiralled from there. My affair with Guinevere lay at the heart of Arthur's sickness.

We slowed as we reached the woods. They were old, unused and clearly didn't welcome casual human interaction. I slid off Ash and carried Arthur in my arms. Leaving my horse behind, I walked a narrow path. Arthur soon became too heavy, so I slung him over my shoulder and continued on into the strange wood.

I realised it held the same qualities as the wood Else and I entered earlier that summer. The trees were bare and the leaves crunched under foot but the sound was swallowed whole by the hush of the place. Old oak, ash, elder and hawthorn filled the wood, but my feet did not trip once, nor were our clothes caught on stray branches. I wandered to the right and I felt a tug on my mind, so corrected my course to the left. The silence wrapped its arms around my body and helped me carry the weight of my King. Things at the edge of my vision fluttered and dived from sight. Images, flashes of colour and even tinkling laughter on a wind, which wove around me, rather than blowing, all increased the sense I had stepped over the threshold into another world. I walked slowly, careful of my intentions, holding any fear or trepidation in my mind at bay. I must do this for Arthur and I would trust Else. Despite the spell I laboured under, I knew how much these places healed a wounded soul. I knew how strong it had made me despite my anger when I realised I'd been tricked.

I found the pool. A fine mist rose from the surface and I knew the water would be warm and kind to my friend. I dropped to my knees and moved Arthur off my shoulder to lay him on the mossy ground. I bowed my head in supplication of whatever guardian this grove contained and breathed evenly, feeling centred enough to ask for help. I didn't move or utter a sound but my intentions were clear in my mind. The wind gusted for a moment and I looked down at Arthur, a white feather settled on his chest. I took this as the sign I needed.

Now, I hurried. Arthur's breathing too shallow and all colour in his cheeks gone. I stripped him and myself in record time, laying our weapons on the bank of the pool. The mist intensified as I worked. The opposite bank vanished in the swirling clouds. I picked Arthur up in my arms, muscles straining to hold him, and walked to the edge. It sloped down into the water and I followed the riverbed. My feet sank into warm mud and the water felt like a bath.

The heat hit my thighs and I lowered Arthur into it even as I walked deeper myself. When it caressed his chest and my own, I stood and released him from my right arm. He lay against my body not across it, his head on my left shoulder, his eyes closed. He felt limp, empty of life in my arms.

I touched his head with my right hand, wrapped my left around his waist and pushed back with my feet so we would float together on the surface of the water. I don't know how long I remained on my back, Arthur inert in my arms, but I realised I felt fingers, not just currents of warm water, on my legs and back. I tried not to flinch and just to accept the magic my friend needed.

Those fingers tickled and prickled over all of me, Arthur groaned and sighed next to me. His hand flexed on my stomach where it lay. If he moved suddenly, we would be forced under the water, so I tried to lower my legs but found I couldn't. We were suspended in the water, held by more than just warmth and steam.

I didn't fight the sensation though it did make me nervous to be this vulnerable. Arthur twisted a little in my arms and his mouth found my neck. All thoughts of possible threats vanished. He kissed my skin, his hands beginning to rove over my naked body. I went hard, my cock reacting our intimacy and my need. I groaned, the first sound I'd made. He stole the sound, his lips covering mine in a kiss of such tenderness and passion I could not deny him. He shifted further over me the firmness of water allowing him to move over me. His lips felt full, his skin rougher than I remembered from when we'd been young, his body firmer, harder, thicker. I felt his cock hard against my thigh, which brought me back to the real world.

"Arthur, wait, please," I whispered, trying to pull out of his grasp.

He looked at me, his eyes the purest, deepest blue I had ever seen them, he smiled. The joy and hope in his face brought tears to my eyes. He kissed them away.

"Wait, please, you are so vulnerable. I can't let this happen, my King." The tears continued to well inside me as he held me. I had loved this man and only this man, for so damned long.

"You have the darkest eyes of anyone I have ever met," he said, running his fingers through my wet hair. "I have seen the death of a hundred men in those eyes and the soul of the man who must bear that burden for me. Lancelot, I love you and I can let this happen, if you will consent. Please consent, my love," Arthur said.

Such small words... I wanted desperately to feel the ground under my feet and my sword in my hand. Right then I would rather have faced a thousand men in battle if it meant I didn't have to allow Arthur access to my heart. While our love remained hidden and unspoken we were safe, he was safe, and I was safe from being drowned by the most powerful man I'd ever known.

If I let this continue he would have all of me. Arthur would own my soul. I wanted to give it to him but should I give it to him? Restraining our physical intimacy was the only protection I had against him.

Dozens of small hands held still. Arthur looked down at me as if I lay on the softest of feather mattresses.

The thought hurt in my head, burned my throat and scalded my tongue as I forced it to move, "I can't."

I watched his eyes dilate in shock. "Please, love, trust me. This is not just about what we want or don't want. *They* need their reward for helping me. If not this, then it will be our blood."

"I don't understand," I managed.

He smiled, all the patience in the world now in his face. "You don't need to. I do, Merlin taught me as a child. Just as Else understands which is why she sent me with you."

I remembered what the fey witch said to me when she healed me and saved Else's life. However, I'd become enchanted by that liaison, I had no wish to add to my troubles.

"I am not fey, Lancelot," Arthur said as though reading my thoughts. "It will not be the same. They just want us, they want our love for themselves. Give them this gift and we will be rewarded."

The hands worked on my skin and began to work between my legs. A hand, which had nothing to do with Arthur, cupped my balls and squeezed. I felt fingers beginning to burrow where fingers didn't need to be, I threw back my head and groaned.

Arthur took that as consent. He lowered his mouth to my neck and moved over my body. I had wanted him for so long, and my sudden surrender felt blissful and easy at last. His mouth captured mine and I felt our tongues explore, a plunging feral kiss, even as our cocks rubbed together, pressed tight to our bodies. My legs spread and wrapped around Arthur's. Our hips moved but we were so engrossed in exploring each other's mouths we felt no need for more in that moment. He felt slick against my hard belly, despite the water. I had one hand on his firm backside, the other tangled in his hair.

The water shifted around us, those small fey hands somehow came between our bodies. They moved up and down our shafts faster and firmer with each passing moment, even as we ground against each other. The wave, the desperate need inside me, built.

Arthur locked rigid in my arms, hard against me, his muscles cording in his chest and back. I pulled him tight against me. "Sorry, I can't hold on," he cried.

He came hard, I forced him to kiss me and my body crashed into its long denied orgasm. I throbbed all over, trying to remember to breathe. Our juices mingled with the water and a hundred voices whispered benedictions over our heads while we held each other. Then they were gone. So was my support.

Water rushed into my mouth and up my nose. I thrashed to find the bottom of the pool. Arthur grabbed my arm and pulled me up his legs more confident as he'd been on top of me.

Spluttering I surfaced. "What the hell?" I exclaimed.

"Their idea of a joke." Arthur grinned, brushing back my hair. I heard the distant laughter.

"Some fucking joke," I muttered.

"Come, let me help you out of this damned pool and we'll dry off." Arthur took my hand and led me from the water. He sat me by my clothes and handed me my cloak. He joined me. "Are you alright?" he asked. I heard a tremor in his voice.

I looked at him. He looked well, really well. Better than I'd seen him in years. I smiled at him and he smiled back. "Thank heaven for that, I was worried you'd be furious with me," he said.

I frowned, "Why?"

"Lancelot, I know how I've felt about you since we were boys, but I couldn't know you would feel the same way. We've never spoken of it" Arthur dried himself not really looking at me.

I reached out and took his hand. Bringing it to my lips, I kissed his knuckles, scarred and calloused like mine. "Arthur, I have craved your touch forever. Cutting me off from your love has to be the hardest burden you ever placed on my shoulders. I knew it had to happen but it's been so brutal. Even if this never happens again, I can live with the knowledge that as men we loved as passionately as we did when we were curious boys."

"More, Lancelot, I love you more now than I did when we were boys. Then it was almost a game, now I know I mean every damned word." Tears stood proud in his eyes. I moved toward him and we kissed again, a soft exploration of the forbidden.

"Hopeless bloody romantics the pair of us," I muttered as I pulled back.

I'd begun to grow hard again and although we shared something unique in that pool, I didn't feel ready for more right now. Not emotionally. I needed to be grounded and certain before we took this any further, if we took this further.

Arthur punched me in the arm. "You are the romantic, I'm a king. I don't have time for sentiment."

I smiled but also shivered, the long day catching up with me. Arthur moved. "Come, you need to dress. You've had a hard few days and I've not made it any easier."

"Any idea who has been poisoning you?" I asked. He helped to dress me as if he was my squire. He knelt before me and laced my boots. Then rose and laid a kiss on my lips before moving to his clothes.

"No, but I have a few ideas. Right now we need to find the others and then really look for Merlin," he said.

I realised night had almost gobbled up the day. We'd been at the pool for hours. "Can you find the others?" I asked, picking up our weapons.

"I know where they will be," he said. "Ash will be with them too."

"How do you know?"

He smiled. "Although I am not fey, like Else, I know them and they know me. Being trapped in Camelot meant I forgot how to feel them, sense them, even use them to help me. Now I am more myself than I have been for years.

Come, it's this way." He took my hand and led me from the steaming pool.

We left the grove and the temperature dropped. Exhaustion stole my thoughts, control over my body and my awareness. Arthur was right; I'd been through too much over the last few days. Just as I saw the fire ahead of us, Arthur stopped me.

"What?" I asked.

"Geraint," he said.

I grunted, "Else."

"She will know," Arthur said.

I thought about that and realised he was right, she would know. How would she react?

"Geraint will be fine," I said. "Just don't make it obvious. He knows what kind of passion we share." Although he'd never said anything.

Arthur stole the opportunity to take my face in his hands, a final moment of intimacy. "I do love you, Lancelot and I am sorry for all the hurt I have caused."

"We have hurt each other, Arthur. Let's call it even between us and be done with the past." I leaned in and kissed his mouth. His lips parted and we embraced once more. He melted into my body and I knew I would ache for him forever if I didn't complete this game and own him. Could my life become any more complicated?

We relinquished the kiss, paused to calm ourselves and walked into the camp. I realised, as I saw Else stand, I hadn't needed her all afternoon. That felt good and bad all at once. Geraint almost tripped over himself to reach Arthur, she walked straight to me.

Else hugged me tight, before rising on her toes and planting a kiss on my mouth. My surprise and the zing between us made my heart stutter. She grinned. "I can taste him on your lips," she said. "I am glad for you both."

I opened my mouth and closed it as she vanished from my side to go and hug Arthur. He returned the hug and the kiss she gave him. Geraint looked surprised, first at them, then at me.

"Don't worry about it," I said, too confused and tired to care. "Just be glad we were all safe and whole, at long last."

That night I slept alone on the cold ground but Arthur and Else shared my camp. We'd eaten well and we felt safe enough this close to home not to have to set watch. At one point, someone curled around my back and held me but my exhaustion kept me docile and my comforter remained anonymous.

CHAPTER TWENTY-ONE

THE SOUND OF SWORDS clashing woke me in an instant. I reached for my weapon but a small hand clamped tight on mine.

"Slow down, soldier, they are sparring," Else said. "You look like a mole emerging from a hill. Good sleep?"

I blinked away the remains of sleep and took a deep breath, trying to orientate myself. "What's happening?" my voice sounded thicker than normal.

"Geraint and Arthur are sparring. It seems he uses the same techniques as you when he needs to regain his self control." Else rose and fetched me water, bread and cheese.

I turned in my sleeping roll and watched them fight. They must have been at it for a while. Both men were naked to the waist and covered in sweat. My body reacted to watching Arthur fight. I coughed and forced my eyes away, toward Else. She grinned at me, making me blush.

"I don't blame you, I'm not certain I'd be able to resist that," she said eyeing Arthur.

"Else..." I still didn't understand what had happened the day before. "I think we need to talk. I've done something and I don't think you are going to be happy about it."

Else turned her head to me as though looking at me not Arthur became almost too much effort. A small smile graced her lips. "If you're talking about you and Arthur making love don't worry."

I frowned. "Don't worry? Is that it? So I can have sex with whom I choose and you don't care?" I remembered she hadn't ever actually agreed to marry me.

Else sighed and turned towards me, her back to the fighting. "Look, our lives are not really our own, not right now. I sent you with Arthur knowing full well what would happen. The two of you ached for each other so much the air was thick around you as soon as we reached Camelot. I am not completely human, Lancelot, things like true love flow differently for me. What you and Arthur have is so special I'm not going to stand in the way."

"But…" I said weakly, even more confused after her explanation.

She smiled and sat beside me, the magic flowed when she grasped my hand. It rippled rather than stung for a change. "You see," she said. "The magic likes your ties to Arthur."

I frowned. "He's going to suffer like I did from the spell?"

"No, but he is being tied to you through bonds as firm as any between two people who are finally allowing themselves to be happy."

"But you are the one I should want," I insisted.

"Not all things are that simple, Lancelot," she said.

"Hey, you woke up," Arthur called. "Come fight, Geraint is blowing like an old horse."

"He's being evil, Lancelot," Geraint yelled. "I think he's cheating but I can't work out how."

I rose on strings, pulled by the opportunity to fight Arthur as his friend and equal. Everything vanished from my mind with the feel of my sword in my hand and the brisk breeze filling my lungs. This was peace for me, this was happiness.

Geraint soon quit the field. Even with my help he'd had enough. Arthur had trained with him since dawn. I'd slept through everything. I faced Arthur and we fought with joy, not desperation. Every muscle in me sang in harmony as we moved back and forth across the glade. His eyes shone in the morning light and he didn't stop laughing.

"Alright, I yield," he said. His arms shook with the exertion he'd put himself through. I'd knocked him over, so I reached down and hauled him to his feet. He sprang up, surprising me and we over balanced, stumbling backward. He ended up nose to nose with me. "Oh, right now I wish we didn't have an audience," he murmured.

I laughed, the heat rising in my cheeks. He released me. I'd become sixteen all over again.

We ate, packed the camp up and moved back to the road. Four happy people, if a little confused. At least I was confused. Else and Arthur seemed perfectly content as they rode together.

"So where are we heading?" Geraint asked.

"Avalon," Arthur said turning in his saddle. "The Sisters of Avalon should be able to tell us more about Merlin's whereabouts. Else and I have no idea where he is, but if the Court is under a spell, or the de Clare's are, then we need him."

"When was the last time you saw him?" I asked.

"He was in the company of a very beautiful young woman he'd been training," Arthur said. "So I assume something happened because that was five years ago."

"He left me in Europe five years ago," Else said.

That's when I'd had the affair with Guinevere, I thought. Is that when the rot set in? When Merlin left us? Did Arthur's enemies finally have the access they needed because the old man wasn't there to hold them back? I hated to think we had all been manipulated that badly.

We travelled with ease through Arthur's lands. We rode with mountains rising in the distance on our left and the sea glittering on our right. The day proved kind, with a sharp breeze but blue skies, kissed by large white clouds. Once more, we avoided towns and villages, we still carried plenty of food and taking Arthur anywhere tended to complicate things. People just seemed to know who he was. We could have been any group of friends travelling together but there is something about Arthur, which makes him a king even to the lowliest of his subjects. Our conversations, when we walked the horses, were light hearted and reconnected us through our shared memories as we regaled Else with stories.

We rode a long way that day and reached the grounds of a mighty Abbey. A brief debate occurred between seeking the beds in monks' cells and beds in the open with no rules. We opted for freedom. We found a large clearing in a wood by a river and set up camp with the night already sweeping the day from the sky. I helped Else with the horses, while Arthur and Geraint collected firewood. Then she and I made dinner. A full, thick potage and hunks of bread kept us content. I wished briefly for a drink but then looked at Arthur and decided I didn't need it after all.

I did however need Else. We'd been separated all day by the others through one thing or another. My hands shook and my belly burned. Arthur and Geraint were talking about some new laws and taxes Arthur had inflicted on his people while he'd been under the influence. Geraint tried to tell him he'd gone too far.

"Else," I called. "I need you."

She looked up from the fire. The glow warmed her skin and made her eyes almost black in the reflection. My breath caught, my chest tightened. She'd never looked more like a being from another world. She smiled, lay down the stick she'd been poking into the flames and rose.

"Are you alright?" Arthur asked me.

"I'm fine," I said, trying to bite back a groan. Geraint fell quiet and my companions watched as Else sat between my knees, her back me. She took my hands, peeled my gloves off and pulled her shirt up, laying my hands on her belly. Her skin felt hot, she squirmed until she leaned into my chest. I kissed her hair.

"That sort of looks like fun and sort of looks like hell," Geraint said frowning.

I chuckled. "It sort of feels like that." My breathing softened. The magic flowed and I sank into Else the only way I could. I closed my eyes and breathed in her scent.

"Is there anything I can do to help?" Arthur's voice sounded strange. I opened my eyes and stared across the fire at him. His gaze shone with hunger. Even with Else in my arms, my body pounded with need for Arthur.

Else stirred against me and said, "Just being here helps, Arthur. He will need you when I move from his arms. The first hour afterward can be hard, we haven't been together for long enough over many days."

Arthur glanced at Geraint. He glanced at me. I didn't know what to say. Nothing had been said which made life difficult. We just needed to know if Geraint could deal with us being more obvious in our affection. He shrugged, "Well, it'd be a nice change if the two of you are able to be honest with each other."

Else rose in one smooth movement and vanished from my hands and body. I felt her imprint on me and her heat. The spell backlashed and I groaned. Arthur moved around the fire. I curled into a ball. He took hold of my shoulders and pulled me close to his chest. His strong arms coaxed my head down onto his lap. He stroked my head and held my hands as I shook.

"You dealt with this alone?" Geraint asked shocked at the effects.

"Sometimes," I said through the shaking. "This is worse than others. I've not been hit this badly in a while."

"They want me to join with you and Arthur," Else said. She stood staring into the fire, the flames coloured her hair red on the tips. Wild and curling around her face. "I am to plant the spell in Arthur, they can use what happened yesterday between you to finalise it."

All eyes focused on Else. I asked, "What will happen if you don't?"

She turned to look at me, where I lay. "You will suffer, you will be used to punish me."

"How do you know?" Arthur said.

She poked the fire with her foot. "I can hear my sisters and cousins through that."

"Then we do it," Arthur said. "You do whatever you need to take the pain from Lancelot."

"No," I said. "Arthur, I cannot allow you to be enslaved by this. You need to think clearly, not be trapped by the damned fey and their desires. Your priority is to your people not them. We don't know their agenda, not completely."

"You are no use to me if you are broken like this," he said, hooking hair out of my face.

"Lancelot is right, Arthur," Geraint said. "I like you, girl," he said to Else, "but I don't trust this magic of yours."

"Neither do I," said Else.

"All we need to do is control the desire the same way you do with Lancelot. It Doesn't have to be a bad thing," Arthur said.

Else turned to him. "It might just be that now, but it could be so much more if they choose it to be. Lancelot can bear the pain and I will do all I can to help. I don't want to do this."

"You mean you don't want me?" Arthur said. I heard a bitterness I didn't understand in his words.

"I don't want to hurt you the way I am hurting him," Else said.

"I'm going on first watch," Geraint said, rising and walking into the woods toward the road. Magic confused and upset him. Although not as practical as Kay, Geraint did not live a life where fey should be so real.

Else moved off toward the horses. "Just hold him, Arthur, you should be able to ease his pain if you remain close."

Arthur moved his bedroll, we didn't talk. I don't think either of us knew what to say. To ease this he'd have to make love to Else and become as entangled with her as I had, not a helpful thought, even if he could manage it. He lay his kit down, took off my thick cloak and placed it over my blankets. Then he forced me down, wriggled his hand under my clothes and placed it on my belly. He stroked me until my breathing started to ease. We were tightly spooned under a thick layer of blankets and I began to calm. He kissed my cheek. I turned my head and kissed his mouth. The kiss grew deep and long.

He pulled back. "Sleep, Lancelot and I'll hold you safe."

Surprisingly, I did.

CHAPTER TWENTY-TWO

I WOKE WITH BONE aching weariness, as though I'd been forced to fight a horde of barbarian's all night without rest. Else tried to take the pain but I found her touch just made matters worse. Arthur rose with me and while Geraint tactfully went to play with the horses, he tried to numb the ache with contact. Nothing worked. I knew we were being manipulated into a situation I didn't want. If Arthur became enslaved to Else, he would do anything for her, or rather those that controlled her. They would have Camelot and Camelot belonged to us, not the fey. The whole situation just made me angry, so what began as a bad day, simply grew worse.

In order to cross the river Severn we travelled north for some distance. Although this land belonged to Arthur, his hold on it remained tenuous. There were bandits in this place by the score and warmongers who did not like paying tithes to Arthur. We rode in silence and on full alert. Geraint took the lead, Arthur rode beside Else and I had our back. We were all fully armoured and carried our shields. Even Else managed the small one we'd packed for her in Camelot. Her bow remained strung and her knives close to hand. One place in particular lent itself to ambush.

We were riding through a gorge without a river. Large cliffs towered either side covered in short scrubby trees, vines and moss. Light found it hard to penetrate the canopy, the trees leaned toward each other on either side like desperate lovers. One particular area widened, and although I'd led a force there myself and cleared the area of undergrowth, it still contained large boulders, small caves and trees for hiding. My tension levels hit critical. I sweated inside the hauberk and the breastplate I wore. My shoulders ached and I felt sick. I had refused to wear a helmet. Breathing came hard enough without smothering me in steel. Geraint held up his armoured hand, we all stopped. Ash snorted and pawed the ground, aware of the tension and hating it. I forced him round so his

Hindquarters faced our companions and we formed a circle. I heard a rustling, from the trees over our heads. Else knocked an arrow and waited for orders. Her eyes focused on a point almost fifty yards from our position. I left her to watch the trees while my eyes sought bodies among the rocks. We knew they were there, we didn't know if they would attack. Would they risk fighting three heavily armed knights and one archer just for the packhorses?

I wanted to issue a challenge, force them into the open and get it over with. This level of concentration made me giddy. Then, a scream tore apart the air from over our heads. Else yelped. A body encased in flame crashed to the floor of the gorge in front of her horse. Yells erupted and men rushed toward us. We prepared to fight, without breaking form, when fire lashed from the ground as though marsh gas escaped from solid rock. We froze. Bodies burned. The screaming and stink of flesh made the horses frantic. The pack animals barged into the warhorses. Mercury's usually passive nature broke. He threw his front legs in the air, almost unseating Else.

"What the hell is going on?" Geraint yelled over the noise. He had his sword in hand and no enemy to face.

"Oh, bloody hell," Else moaned. She tried to calm Mercury. I turned Ash toward her, Arthur on her other side ready to defend her, instead we watched. The first man, who still smoked, rose from the ground a blackened husk.

In his black and shrivelled mouth, a stump for a tongue, thrashed back and forth, miming a scream. The eyes were gone, replaced by pits into hell. Claws reached for Mercury's bridle.

"Run," Arthur yelled. I crashed Ash into the body. He rode it down hard. Mercury leapt forward, with Else close over his neck.

"Arthur, get after her. We'll deal with this," I shouted. Without a word, he turned Willow and charged after Else. The packhorses followed the stallion.

Geraint and I pulled our horses close together and rode for the end of the gorge. Before we reached it, we wheeled the horses and assessed the enemy. All the bodies had risen and were changing before our eyes. The one Ash ran down stayed down, its head a pulp.

"At least we know they can die," Geraint whispered.

The figures stood, and the wind stirred around each burnt corpse, growing stronger with every fast breath I took. Detritus from the floor of the gorge gathered about their bodies. The wind continued to grow, the gorge darkened, each body vanished inside their individual maelstroms, sucking the stink from the air.

"This is not going to end well," Geraint said. "We should leave."

"Wait, we need to see what's going on," I said.

The wind whipped at our cloaks. Ash and Pepper shifted, trying to turn. We held our position. The whirlwinds, eight of them, started to disperse. In their place, stood eight black emaciated horses, with eight black emaciated men. The horses moved, the men all opened their mouths and a silent scream made my skin grow cold.

"Now, we ride," I said. Ash turned so fast I almost slipped off the side. We ran. Arthur had caught up with Else within a quarter of a mile. They were waiting with all three packhorses. One look at our faces and they turned back to the road.

"No, we won't manage it," I yelled while pulling Ash to a skidding halt. "We have to think of something else."

"Is it that serious?" Arthur asked.

"They are no longer human and they have horses," I said. "It is that serious."

"They are golems," Else said. She expanded as she realised we didn't understand, "Basically, they are creations of our enemies and they will be after Arthur, we have to stop them. They will never give up and never leave his scent. They will hunt us, growing stronger the longer they are in this world."

"So, what do we do?" Geraint asked.

"We split up," Arthur said. "If they are after me, I can lead them away from the rest of you."

"Yeah, that's a good idea," I said. "Leaving you on your own against eight monsters." The scorn was not lost on him, "I'll go with Arthur. Geraint, make certain Else is safe. Don't stop until you reach the edge of this damned wood." I realised I would never, ever, be able to go into a wood again without being reduced to a quivering wreck of paranoia.

"I don't think –" Else began looking at me with large frightened eyes.

"No, you don't, you follow orders," I snapped at her. "Arthur, with me."

Arthur glanced at Else and said, "It's what he Does, protect and fight, forgive him."

Then we raced back toward the gorge to force these monsters to focus in on us. We galloped, shoulder to shoulder, Willow and Ash matched to perfection. Finding a fork in the road, we stopped, waiting until our enemy came into sight. When they saw us, we vanished onto the new track.

"How well do you know these woods?" Arthur asked.

"Not well enough," I said.

He nodded and we just worked on staying ahead. The path inclined with a long gradual slope. The light started to fade. I glanced behind us, the black, skeletal horses were relentless and they were gaining.

"We can't maintain this pace," I told Arthur. The adrenaline keeping me upright and thinking would soon run out, replaced by the agony of the spell. With Arthur to protect, I needed to think of something fast. I couldn't afford to be weak.

"We don't have to." Arthur, reins in one hand, pointed. A collapsed bridge covered a huge gulf between us and the rest of the road.

"Are you mad?" I asked.

"Let them get closer." His eyes were fever bright with the fight. "They can't see past us, we slow the horses, allow them to catch their wind and then ride like the clappers for the bridge. Ash and Willow will cover that, no problem. They won't have time to prepare their horses or stop. And if they do they will have to ride around."

"You are insane," I told him as I ducked under a branch.

"I'm alive!" Arthur yelled at the sky, bringing Willow back to a canter. Ash and I followed suit. We were the perfect team, the four of us. I laughed, I couldn't help it. We were about to die, throwing ourselves over a ridge to run from dead men made real. I rode with my King and I was glad to be alive.

The smell of burnt meat from the bodies behind us, laced the air, as if by scent alone they might stop us. Without a word, Arthur and I released the horses and forced them to lengthen their stride. I flattened over Ash's neck and whispered to him to tell him what we were doing. His ears pricked forward and he stretched his neck. He and Willow were in perfect unison. We crested the rise, rode the short flat distance to the old bridge and I felt him gather himself for the leap. He had complete faith in my ability to gauge his capabilities. He hesitated for half a breath when he saw the gap, as did I, but he didn't miss a step. We leapt into thin air. Both horses reached for the other side, Arthur and I leaning back as they approached the ground. I did not look down. The horse's front hooves touched the soft earth and they picked up their stride. Willow stumbled slightly, but Arthur gathered him together and we slowed the beasts down. They quivered and sweated.

Turning in the saddle, Arthur and I watched the pack of riders cresting the rise. They were tight together and the riders at the rear didn't see the gaping hole at the front. They all tried to stop, but the ones in the lead didn't manage.

Two dived over the edge, forced by those at the rear. They fell silently, a long way down.

"That was too bloody close," I said.

"That was fucking great," Arthur whooped. "Come and find me now, you stinky bastards."

"Arthur, don't goad the dead people," I scolded and we both laughed with joy.

Grinning like boys, we turned the horses back to the path and trotted away.

CHAPTER TWENTY-THREE

AS WE RODE, WE talked. This side of the gorge the trees were thinner and dusk seemed to have changed its mind. I held my face up to the sun and smelt the clean air. There are times when life feels too good to be real.

"Do we know anything about who attacked us by using those bodies?" I asked, with my eyes closed.

"I have no idea, but they must have been incredibly powerful. I don't think Merlin could have done that," Arthur said.

"So we are looking at a full fey."

"I don't know," Arthur said. I opened my eyes and looked at him. He frowned and picked at Willow's mane. "I can't imagine a fey being that powerful. They use magic in a sympathetic way and they manipulate minds."

Facts I knew all too well. "They would poison you but they wouldn't send dead monsters after you." I realised the truth of my statement. This had to be an enemy we didn't know or understand.

"It's not a happy thought is it," Arthur said. "And those things will be after us. Once they find a way around that gorge, they will come."

"That's not –" Pain ripped through my guts. It hurt so much I collapsed over Ash's neck and he stopped, surprised, thinking I'd been attacked. I groaned, my hands lost power and my legs turned to jelly.

"Lancelot," Arthur cried out. I felt his hands on my back.

I drew a shuddering breath into my chest as far as I could. "Don't worry. It will be fine," I managed to gasp.

"No," Arthur said. He moved to dismount Willow.

"Don't," I grasped his arm. "We don't have time for this." The pain eased but still left me weak. "I can manage it's just taking revenge for being pushed to one side for too long. We can't stop, those things will be circling back to the place we left Else and Geraint. They won't need to rest as we must."

"You should let me have your woman. Then we can have this under our control," Arthur said.

I struggled to push myself upright. The thought of Arthur inside Else made me feel very odd, it wasn't a good idea if the fey gained control over him.

"You just want her because you'd rather have her than me," I said, trying to make a joke out of it, but even I heard the bitterness.

Arthur gasped, his shock clear. "And I suppose you think all I want is revenge for you fucking Guinevere?"

He had never, ever spoken to me like that. The horses stopped and we sat looking at each other, horrified by our words. The joy of a moment before became a myth I no longer believed.

"Yes," I said, sadness carving a hole in me. "Yes, I rather think I do."

I watched a veil descend over Arthur's heart. His eyes no longer allowed me access to his soul. If my words hurt me, they sliced through him. I realised in one stupid moment I'd carved into our friendship. A thing too fragile for such harsh truths. I could not throw these feelings at him and expect him to love me.

"No," the word burst out of me and I grabbed his hand, which rested on his saddle. "No, I'm wrong. Don't, Arthur, please. Don't cut me out."

Arthur's blue eyes filled with tears. They fell like raindrops from the gods. "I love you, Lancelot, your wife is just an extension of that and if being with her stops this pain, that's all I want. You are the one I would choose to share my bed and life, not her."

"Arthur, I'm sorry, I really am. Please, my King, forgive me." I moved to dismount, enabling me to kneel before him. He stopped me moving and pulled me toward him. Ash stepped into Willow to accommodate my shift of balance. Arthur kissed my mouth. Neither of us had shaved, his skin felt rough, his lips bruised mine. I groaned and held him to my mouth, forcing his lips open with my tongue so I could taste all of him. My desire rippled through me.

When we broke apart, we were both shaking with the intensity. I said, "If you want Else and she wants you, then I will not stand between you. But I won't have you do this just to save me from a little discomfort."

Arthur stroked my hair and nodded. "Alright, Lancelot. But when you can't live with the pain, I will take your wife to my bed and you will be there."

We rode in silence, grim now. Our victory shallow next to the torment we placed on each other. My mind kept up a circle, first thinking about Else and how I felt about her, then about her with Arthur, with or without consequences, then Arthur and my feelings for him. They were galloping out of control for certain. His response to me, his desire for me, just fuelled my own need. I'd always loved him, right from the first moment we met, but now he seemed to accept our desire and it made everything a thousand times more intense.

We cantered down the hill, which led us to Else and Geraint. The trees began to thin and the long flood plain of the Severn opened before us. I saw them waiting a good quarter mile into the open expanse, so we would see them. We rode toward them.

"It went well?" Geraint asked his relief at our appearance clear.

"We managed to kill two of them, but there are still six following us and Lancelot is suffering," Arthur said.

"I'm fine," I muttered through gritted teeth. Else rode to me, pulled off her gloves and held my face in her own. The spell fizzed, but I felt so wretched I hardly moved. It did ease the pain a little.

"He can't keep this up," she told the others.

We heard a noise behind us and six black horses, with riders, burst from the trees. "It looks like I'm going to have to," I said, gathering Ash together for a fight. They were too close for us to run. Willow and Ash would not make it far and the packhorses all needed to rest. We could have left them and tried for the ford in the river but there would have come a time when we had to stop. Far better to fight in the open than be caught in the middle of the night somewhere.

Three of us drew our swords. Else knocked an arrow to her bow and brought her quiver into easy reach. We didn't comment. Arthur rode on my right and Geraint on his left. The horses moved as one and we raced toward our enemies. Else rode behind us, before pulling Mercury up and firing over our heads. She hit one of the foul creatures square in the chest, it fell from its horse but did not die, it rose and ran towards us with an arrow in its chest.

"Aim for their heads," Arthur called out.

Else's next arrow hit the same fiend in the face and it dropped, twitching but not able to stand. Then the fight became real. We crashed into their tight ranks. My sword took one across the throat. His head rolled off and without blood but the stink almost made me vomit.

"Breathe through your mouth," I yelled over the noise.

I realised three of the dead men were trying to take Arthur down. I charged into the medley. The fighting grew desperate, these creatures had him in their sights and it made them single minded. I tried to break their attack, attempting to decapitate them, but they were too close to Arthur. They fought with a wildness and ferocity, which made us vulnerable to mistakes trying to fight them off. Geraint fought another but we couldn't maintain this for long. I caught sight of Else coming on foot. She braced herself and pulled back her bow.

"Duck!" she screamed.

I flattened over Ash's neck. An arrow hissed over my head and my opponent dropped over the back of his horse. Ash lashed out with his rear end and kicked the dead horse. It shattered, once more becoming leaves, twigs and rocks. I forced Ash tight against Arthur's enemy and swung a mighty arc over my head. My sword sliced into the monster's face and carved his head into two pieces. Else shot at Geraint's attacker and we were done. All the bodies collapsed into woodland detritus and scorched corpses of men.

We stopped, surprised by the sudden peace.

"Anyone hurt?" Geraint asked.

"No," Arthur and Else said.

"I don't..." I managed before the pain sweeping through me became unmanageable and I slipped off Ash. My mind went blank and forgot what it was supposed to be doing.

I came to with Arthur holding me to his chest. As my eyes fluttered open, I heard him say, "He's waking, thank God."

Darkness sat over my head, surprising me and a fire danced in my field of vision. A flask smelling of water pressed against my lips. I drank in gratitude.

Else knelt beside me on the other side. "They have realised they've pushed him too far. They were killing him, with any luck his stubborn attitude has made them back off. He might have won this round."

I didn't feel like I'd won anything. I hurt everywhere, my brain considered me a traitor, convinced I'd been drinking heavily for days and this was the world's worst hangover.

"How did I win?" I croaked.

"Just by not giving in, no matter how much pressure they put you under," Else said. She stroked my face. Her touch hurt and made me flinch. She gasped, withdrawing.

I curled into Arthur's body and wrapped my arms around his waist. "Make the pain stop," I begged.

"You are still in pain?" he asked.

"Not from the spell, this is a spiritual hangover," Else said from some distance away.

"What do I do?" Arthur asked.

"We leave the two of you alone for a while," Else said. I heard her speak to Geraint and they left us.

Arthur murmured over me until I felt able to move from his lap. It took a long time. When I sat up I remained inside the circle of his arms.

"I feel fucking terrible," I complained. "If it takes this much effort to fight their damn spells I'm not going to manage it again."

Arthur tightened his arms around me and kissed my neck with soft lips. "I am grateful to you. Bedding Eleanor de Clare would be a complication too far for all of us."

I snorted. "It would make for an interesting conversation when it came to working out who was the father of any offspring."

"I often wondered if that was why Guinevere wouldn't let you go," Arthur said, regret marring his voice.

He must have so many questions about that time in our lives. He had never let me talk to him and I didn't think Guinevere would have told him the truth.

"I made certain she never carried my child, Arthur," I said.

He didn't speak for a long time and I just sat in the circle of his arms, passive, waiting for him to make the next move.

I felt him shift away from me, but only to lie back on the ground. I turned and looked at him. "You can ask me anything."

He sighed. "A part of me wants to know. A part of me thinks it's over so what's the point. The important thing is us."

"Us?" I asked.

Arthur grunted. "So, you don't think this is any more than an aberration in our lives."

I frowned, realising we were having a different conversation to the one I planned. I didn't have the wherewithal for this. "I didn't say that. I don't think our relationship can be easily defined."

Arthur stared at the stars. "No, I suppose it can't."

I had managed to avoid an argument. At least for the moment.

Arthur sat up. "You need sleep, Lancelot." He drew himself out of my space, rose and walked to our kit. He grabbed his bedroll and mine. He laid his down on one side of the fire and mine near it, while I still sat watching.

There seemed to be something going on here I'd missed entirely. Else would have left us alone for a reason. I stood, the world wriggled, I stepped forward, not really seeing clearly.

"Whoa, Lancelot," Arthur cried out and I felt his hands on my chest. "Sit, you almost ended up in the fire."

Not quite my intention but I had him here. "I needed to stop you."

"Stop me?" Arthur asked as my vision cleared and my head ceased pounding.

"I've hurt you." I took a deep breath. I felt him still. I told him I loved him as my king, my warrior brother, but it was time for true honesty between us. "I don't just love you, I am in love with you. I care for Else, I know I do, but what we have." I touched his chest. "Has been a part of me for years. I don't know how to cope with what I feel. When we return to Camelot, I know I am going to lose you again. You can't be with me there and it hurts. Our love is not what should happen between two men, or for a king." My hand found his throat and jaw, feeling the roughness of his stubble.

"I cannot promise you anything," Arthur said, his grief at the thought clear.

"You don't have to. Just tell me how you feel."

"Do I need to? I have loved you since we were boys. I have burned with desire for you. I have craved your body. I don't think you realise how much I have needed you or for how long. Ordering your punishment because of Guinevere broke my heart. Watching it almost broke my mind. I know we are both married but I want you with me, selfish spoiled bastard that I am."

I opened my mouth to tell him Else and I weren't married but decided this wasn't the time. "I will answer any question you have about Guinevere, or Else. And I swear to you, Arthur, unless I have to, I will not leave your side. We will be together the only way we can be, as brothers in arms."

"I want so much more," Arthur said, moving into me. We kissed, he groaned, I pushed him back and lowered him to the ground. I wanted to feel his skin on mine, I wanted to explore, play, tease, I wanted to mark him, brand him as mine. I wanted to spend the rest of the night making him ready to accept my body, so we could join together. We had never managed to be brave enough to try it as squires but I now felt ready. I wanted him, all of him.

His body felt hard and unyielding under me, our hips ground together, we both groaned, then Arthur laughed. "This is insane. I have waited so long for you, Lancelot and now we are going to do this in a cold damp wood."

I grinned, while leaning on my elbows either side of his shoulders. I traced his lips with my finger and he drew it into his mouth. It made me gasp, my bloody imagination on overtime. "Then you want to wait?"

"Not particularly, but I think we should," Arthur said as he rubbed his hips against mine. He felt so hard.

"You can order me to do anything," I said mischievously.

"Don't bloody tempt me, Lancelot. Having you chained up in my dungeon gave me some very bad thoughts." His hands strayed to my backside and held me tight against him.

"If you clean the damned thing out, I'll let you do it again," I told him.

"Just so long as you never ask me to flog you," he said, as his expression darkened.

I frowned and pulled back. "Don't worry, I won't."

The moment died on that one thought. I wondered if what we shared was too ephemeral to survive. I rolled off him and returned to my bedroll. Else appeared as if by magic and said Geraint offered to take first watch. I curled up, feeling bereft and confused, but I found sleep.

CHAPTER TWENTY-FOUR

I STILL DIDN'T FEEL like myself but the journey over the river Severn and down toward Geraint's homelands happened swiftly enough. I found I needed Else less, which put a distance between us. She watched me and I watched her but my affection for Arthur consumed me. I think if we'd had the time and place to deal with our feelings, like a comfortable warm bed for about a week, it wouldn't have controlled so much of me. As it was, Arthur and I couldn't be separated. We rode together, fought together and vanished from sight at every opportunity.

Geraint watched this in a state of mild amusement. He once spoke to me about how it must hurt Else, so I spoke to her. She just said all things would happen in the right way if we let them. I didn't understand but she seemed to be withdrawing from all of us. I would say she'd begun to look different but I couldn't put my finger on it and the fey influence worried me.

When we crested the rise, which looked down onto the wide flat valley of Avalon, the weak sunlight sat high overhead. The cold wind tore into our bodies and the damp leached into everything. We looked over the barren scenery, winter now held the land in its inescapable grasp. To our right, we saw the sloping shape of the odd hump, which drew the eye, rising like an unadorned nipple within the marshes of Wessex. It never failed to make me shiver. I didn't trust Arthur's faith in these people of the older religions, but he needed them, so we would go to them. The Sisters of Avalon.

The range of hills descended into the valley and we needed to stop for the night before reaching the small town nestling under the hill in the distance.

"What if they don't tell us where Merlin is?" Geraint asked for the hundredth time. If I didn't trust these Sisters, his active dislike made him question Arthur's decisions. His lands were shrouded with as much myth as this place but he understood his homeland. This place gave him the creeps.

Arthur straightened in his saddle. "Then, as I have mentioned before, we ask them who can help."

"And what will they want from us in return?" Geraint asked.

"I don't know yet, but we have things in the packs which will smooth the way," Arthur told him.

"You should get the bloody Church down here to tame this land," Geraint said.

"Merlin asked me not to, so I haven't. There are certain places which aren't ready and this is one of them. Their power is old, it is weakening but if I kill it there will be repercussions, far better to let it die a natural death," Arthur said.

We rode close together and I felt the heat of his leg through my own as our horses pressed against each other. Willow and Ash had resigned themselves to having to live in each other's company so a peace developed between them.

Geraint growled but held his tongue. I looked at Else. She stared down into the valley with a hunger in her brown eyes I didn't understand.

I touched her arm. "You alright?"

She jumped, unaware of my presence. "Sorry, yes, fine, let's go shall we." She nudged Mercury forward and began the trek down the long steep road toward the marshes.

Geraint moved off after her. I frowned and said, "There is something wrong with, Else."

"She seems different, I'll grant you that," Arthur said.

"She won't talk to me."

"I'm not surprised, you spend every waking moment with me," he said. "Maybe we both need to talk to her. She is your wife, this can't be easy, despite the fact that you can't be with her."

I felt a pang of guilt over continuing the lie. I should tell Arthur the truth about my relationship with Else. As we walked down after the others, I began to explain.

"So, you aren't married?" Arthur asked to confirm my confession. I'd expected him to be furious with me for lying for so long.

"No," I said. "I still don't know how much of my feelings for her are because of the spell or because I am fond her. Things with you have muddied the waters further. I do know I took her virginity and for that reason alone I should marry her. It is the honourable thing to do. I just didn't want Stephen to take her from me and give her to someone else."

"I wish you'd told me sooner," Arthur said.

"Yes," I said, unable to think of a valid excuse for not telling him.

He watched Mercury carry Else down the steep hill. "You do care for her, Lancelot. I can see that. You need her to. We are different you and I, your interest in women is, I think, stronger than my own. She will provide a family and Doesn't seem to object to our close friendship." His voice sounded strained. This confession hurt my friend. It was a difficult thing to admit considering our stations and responsibilities.

I doubted the validity of his assumption about my desire for women, but I couldn't deal with my complications right now, his were the ones that mattered.

"You need an heir, Arthur," I said, trying to be kind. "You will need to take someone, even if it isn't Guinevere. My marriage or lack thereof is not as important as yours."

"I don't like the thought of sharing you, Lancelot. Even though I know I must at some point. I need an heir and you want a family."

We lapsed into silence. With his marriage a mess, having legitimate heirs would be hard. I felt for him but really didn't know how to help. If he didn't produce an heir he'd need to name one sooner or later on a permanent basis or take a new wife. I had to admit, having him to myself for so many days on the road made it hard to accept he would need to share a bed with someone else at some point. I forced the thoughts away, they wouldn't help us in the long run. We both needed to acknowledge the world we were born into and that meant wives and children, not our heart's desire.

The day drew to a close as we reached the lowlands in the valley. A small town nestled in the shadow of the hills we'd ambled down and we opted for a night under someone's roof for a change. Arthur covered his head with his hood and we found the local inn. The inn offered two rooms, so we took both of them. I had no idea what the sleeping arrangements would be but I knew I couldn't share a room with Else. We sat down to warm food, ale, which Arthur drank rather than wine, and a hearth. I surveyed the room.

A small bar, with large barrels behind the counter sat in the corner. Good quality lamps lit the corners and candles were in a candle stand over our heads. The fire roared without filling the place with smoke and the tables were polished. The bar staff were clearly just that, no doxies in this establishment. There were heavy beams over our heads and the walls were stone. When we'd taken the horses to the stable I'd been impressed with the cleanliness. Ash, clearly tired of being grubby, had allowed himself to taken by a stable lad without argument.

I admitted to being ready for a warm bath and a soft bed myself. I'd been travelling with Else non-stop for weeks, with only a brief respite at Tintagel. Baths were being prepared for us so we settled into a huge meal of roast meats, bread, cheese and winter vegetables. We talked among ourselves as the evening clientele filtered in, consisting of a few merchants, farmers and craftsmen. They were all polite but left us alone. This place was used to travellers but was also used to being civilised. I liked it.

"The two baths we have are prepared," said the soft voice of a girl. The barkeeper's daughter by his hawkeyed stares at us while she served our food.

Else drew her breath in with excitement, I laughed. "Go woman and make yourself comfortable. You should have the other," I said to Arthur.

We had agreed no titles or names should be bandied about. He opened his mouth to argue then changed his mind. "That would be wonderful." He rose and said, "I'm planning on an early night, so won't be back down. I need to avoid drinking too much."

Geraint watched Arthur walk upstairs, as did I, unfortunately we had different perspectives. My mouth watered with the thought of the taste of his skin. Geraint spoke, "It seems you have a decision, my friend."

I tore my eyes from the stairs, which made my heart hurt. "What are you talking about?" I asked.

He smiled and shook his head. "You have no idea do you? Arthur wants you with him tonight. I'm not certain either of you understand what that means but you crave something more. Then," he held his hands up like a set of scales, "there is your beautiful maiden. Else wants you to join her."

I stared at his hands. "Oh, fuck."

Geraint chuckled. "So, who to choose?"

"This isn't funny, Geraint." I took a long draft of ale.

"You want Arthur," he said. I looked at him and realised he did sympathise with me rather than considering me a freak, a man with unnatural lusts.

"Yes." I finally admitted to someone outside my own head. "I do want him, God help me. I don't understand it, Geraint. There has never been another man for me. I ache to hold him, bathe in him, become one with him. I desire him like no other." *And it is making me giddy with joy and sick with fear*, I added silently.

"But…" Geraint prompted.

"But," I said, weighing my words. "There is no future with Arthur and I can see a future with Else. A wife, a mother, a family of my own, Geraint. Something worth fighting for other than Camelot. Other than this foolishness."

"You will have to convince her Arthur isn't as important as he seems to be. Is that fair when it isn't true?"

"I need to convince Arthur he Doesn't really want me. That this is an aberration, just as it was when we were squires."

"Don't do that, don't belittle what I see you sharing with him. It's not an aberration. He won't give you up easily. He burns for you, Lancelot."

My jaw bounced with tension and my knuckles grew white around the tankard. "I will go to Else. I can sleep on the floor in her presence. It will maintain the peace. Arthur and I need more time." Though I was more than ready in some ways to make love to him, in others our emotions were so intense I feared them. I have never felt like this about a woman, not even Else.

"She is easy to love, my friend. Don't blow it. Someone else will take her if you fuck this up."

I grunted and rose. The weight on my shoulders heavy. I walked upstairs, each stair riser feeling higher than the last. I heard Arthur in the bath singing some bawdy ballad. I leaned my head against the door to his room and every instinct in my body made me want to rush in there and take him in my arms. I groaned, hurting deep inside my soul. Yearning for something I didn't understand. I adored Arthur. I placed my palms on the rough wooden door and heaved my body away from the barrier. I walked to the next door in the small inn and knocked. Else called out a welcome. I found her drying herself, her slim muscular legs and arms still dewy with water.

She smiled, with her dark hair slicked back her eyes crystal clear, she looked so beautiful. "I wasn't certain I'd see you tonight."

I didn't say anything. I covered the floor in three long strides and pulled her into my arms. The spell fizzed and spat but didn't make me burn like it had done in the past. Else yelped, her surprise clear. I held her tight. Her small body firm but soft and smooth. I kissed her. I kissed her as though I wanted to devour every part of her being. My raging erection hurt and my hips pushed into her, trying to force my cock through my clothes and her blankets.

Else pushed against my chest, tearing her lips from mine. "What on earth is wrong with you? You've fought so hard to be free of me and now you do this?" she asked her eyes vivid with confusion and anger.

"I would rather be enslaved to you, than to Arthur," I said roughly, unable to articulate my thoughts.

She peeled herself from my arms. "You want me because you fear your desire for Arthur?"

"No, Else," I said meaning *yes*, but I realised she wanted to pull away and I feared the consequences of rejection. "I care for you, I want to marry you."

"You might well want to marry me but that Doesn't mean you love me," she said, using her no nonsense voice. "I don't want this until we know we are free of the spell."

"Else, please. I need release." I found myself sinking to my knees the weight on my shoulders so heavy, driving me to the wooden planks. And I didn't mean just an orgasm.

"Oh, my poor soldier," she said, walking to my side. Her hand on my head. "You really don't understand what you feel for him do you?"

"It's not right, we can't be together," I cried out. "I want a future, I need it, and Arthur will crush me with his love."

"You don't know that. Go to him, Lancelot. Stop being afraid."

My head shot up, I looked into her calm eyes. She smiled. "I am not your wife, Lancelot. I love you but I do not own you and I don't think I want to."

"But I want you." I grasped her fingers in my larger rougher hands.

"And time will allow us to see if that is true."

"I do care for you," I reaffirmed.

She bent and kissed my lips. "Go to Arthur, please."

With her benediction on my lips, I rose and turned in one movement, vanishing out of the door in less than a heartbeat just as Geraint came up the stairs. We shared a long look and he knew he'd be sharing Else's bath water, not Arthur's. I opened Arthur's door without asking permission and walked in with my heart pounding. I trembled and my palms sweated. Arthur stopped singing but remained reclined in the bath water. His blonde head looked almost as dark as Else's and his eyes very blue.

"Can we talk?" I asked. I needed help with Else. Something in her had changed during our journey to Avalon. Her distance toward me over the last few weeks made me realise I was losing her to a life I didn't understand. The nail in the coffin of our relationship was her lack of interest in my desire for Arthur. That couldn't be normal. I walked on stiff legs to the bed and sat on the edge. He watched me without comment, the hunger clear.

"What's wrong, my friend?" He sweated in the steam from the bath. His skin glowed pink. I found myself transfixed by his chest rising and falling. He laughed making the water ripple. "Focus, Lancelot. You have a problem?"

"More than one," I said trying to control myself, leaning forward to hide his effect on my body.

The water heaved and Arthur rose in one smooth movement, disregarding his nudity. "Hand me a towel, Lancelot." His voice tore into me, hooking deep inside my guts and I rose to move toward him, cloth in hand. I focused on his eyes, not the vast expanse of sculpted flesh. A smile played on his lips, knowing and confident of my falling to his private spell. Our fingers touched.

"Tell me what's wrong," he said.

"She Doesn't want to marry me but I've taken her maidenhead. I thought she loved me and yet she has sent me to you." I realised my hands were drying his taut stomach and chest, roaming over his contours.

His eyes were focused on me, concentrating on my words. "Perhaps she knows best, my friend."

"I want a wife and family," I stated, through the chaotic rush of emotion.

"And she might be the one, but not right now," he said. "Besides, right now you need a bath." His hand cupped my jaw. The stubble prickled against his palm.

He stepped from the wooden tub and we were nose to nose. I had never ached so much or been so rock hard for anyone in my debauched life. "Arthur," I managed, my fingers touched his naked chest. He kissed me and I sank. I drowned. His arms came around my back and held me, keeping me safe even as he stole my soul. I pulled back, my heart a mallet pounding against my rib bones. I needed to think, I needed my soul back, but Else would not rescue me, I must rescue myself. I gazed down into his deep, dark blue eyes and knew I did not have the strength left to save myself. I would drown happily inside Arthur's arms.

"Bath," he said, laughter bubbling.

"I love you," the words forced themselves out of my mouth.

He smiled and his fingers laced with mine. "And I love you, but I will love you even more after a bath." He broke the spell his presence created, releasing me. I unlaced my doublet with shaking fingers and stripped my shirt off.

I heard a grunt and looked at Arthur. "Sorry," he said. "I will never be able to forgive myself for allowing this to happen." I didn't comment. He laid his hand on my back and ran his fingers over the scars. I allowed him access. No one had touched them so thoroughly. It left me breathless with the memory of the pain. I found the courage to look at my King. There were tears on his cheeks. I wiped them away and kissed his face. He coughed. "Bath," he ordered.

I stripped the last of my clothing and stepped into the now grubby but still warm water. Bliss after weeks of cold washes and swims in colder rivers. My eyes closed and a long sigh escaped my lips. Something soft brushed my skin and I turned my head, now watching something wonderful. Arthur knelt by the bath, naked, and he started washing my body. He began with my left arm, using the rough soap and a thick strip of old linen. I knew I should stop him. I knew where he wanted this to go, yet I didn't prevent his hands from exploring my chest, neck, belly and finally lower.

The air hissed out of me and I watched his face as he gazed at the work of his hand. His palm, large and rough controlled more of me than any woman and his grip felt firmer, tighter. The slow, measured pace brought me wave after wave of pleasure without tipping me over the edge. I wanted more. I wanted his skin next to mine. His heat burning my flesh. His own desire inside my hands and, I hesitated for a moment, body.

"Arthur, let me finish washing." My words surprised me with their normality.

He pulled his hand back and smiled up at me before moving away. I grabbed the cloth and ruthlessly scrubbed every inch of myself while Arthur banked the fire and lay our clothes out to dry. We didn't speak. I finished washing. Arthur climbed into the bed and reclined, propped upright on the pillows. He made the bed look small. I dried myself and stood staring at him.

The smile on his lips melted my heart. I heard voices from next door and thought about Else in there, alone, with Geraint. I frowned, my life coalescing in this one moment. I felt as though I stood on the edge of a blade over a mighty chasm. One side, Else and a family, a future with children and peace. The other, Arthur. A life of war, of hidden and despised love, of being enslaved to my King by chains so strong around my heart I would be unable to break free. My friend, my companion lay in bed ready for me to make love. Ready for us to voluntarily step over the barrier between what is normal and what is perceived as wrong. Though this did not feel wrong. I wanted to make love to my friend.

"Lancelot?" he asked. Doubt and fear filled his clear blue eyes. My King lay before me. My King, the man to whom I'd sworn my life. The man I fought for and the man who commanded every aspect of my waking life would now control my heart, soul and my passion.

I looked at my hands. They shook. I felt sick. For the first time in my life, I lacked the courage I needed to step into the fray. "I can't, Sire."

What would Guinevere say when she found out we'd stepped over that lace thin line? How would our actions affect Arthur? Would his leadership change, be harmed by sleeping with me? Would he be different? Would the court find out, like they did my affair with Guinevere and how much worse the trauma? It would be more than a lashing and banishment. It would be another reason for Stephen de Clare to fight Arthur for his throne. If they thought their King was aberrant, they would want him gone. I had to protect his throne, over everything. *I had to protect Arthur's leadership.*

I looked up at him and his eyes filled with tears. My own cheeks were wet. "I can't, your Majesty. We would lose everything. Your leadership relies on you being the best of us and I will stop you from being the best." I didn't think that covered the confusion and hurt inside my chest but it was all I could manage. "I love you, Arthur. The throne of Camelot stands between us as it always has and always will. You are King, I am a lowly knight."

"Don't do this." His hands bunched in the rough blankets of what would have been our bed. "I beg you. Please, give me one night. I love you like no other and always have. I know you want a family, a home, but this is just one night. Camelot will never know, I will never let the Court hurt you again."

"It will never just be one night, Arthur. I will always need more, I always have." I bent stiffly to retrieve my clothes, exhausted with anguish and a thousand wounds invisible to the eye but bleeding nonetheless. "I'll be outside, keeping guard. Sleep well, my King."

CHAPTER TWENTY-FIVE

I DRESSED IN THE hallway and descended to the bar. I bought a cheap bottle of grog and vanished outside. A mist lay low to the ground, writhing around my legs, glowing silver in the light of a full moon. The air smelt crisp, hard in my nose and it nipped my fingers like a hungry dog. I walked to the stable and grabbed one of Ash's blankets. He snorted at me over the stable door. I hunkered down in the dry straw and struggled to tear the cork out of the bottle. "Finally," I muttered before choking on the gut rot. The alcohol did its job though and burned my insides warmer than the pain of leaving Arthur alone.

The straw warmed under me and I lay back to stare at the darkness overhead. My mind remained blank. I did not want to think any more about anything.

"Lancelot?"

"Go away, Else," I said. "Go back to Geraint."

"Geraint? Why would I go back to Geraint? What are you talking about, silly man?"

"He's more of a man and will make you a better husband than I ever will," I muttered, slugging another mouthful. The straw shifted and I felt Else lie next to me, removing the bottle from my hands.

"You are a foolish man," she said.

"You just said that." I still did not look at her and we fell silent in the stable.

Else sighed. "You should be with Arthur. He's heartbroken. That's why I came down. He is in my room bemoaning his fate."

"I want you." I reached for her hand, the spell lay dormant. Her fingers laced between mine and the pain in my heart eased.

"But you love Arthur more, desire him more," she said quietly.

"I don't know if it's more, I do know it's wrong."

"Love is never wrong, Lancelot. It's just different. He loves you, wants you –"

"But he is my King." A statement covering all sorts of complications.

"I don't think that matters. I don't think any of it matters."

I became restless once more and sat up. "What about Geraint? I know he cares for you and he'll make you a better husband."

"There is more to life than marriage, Lancelot. I discover things about myself all the time. I am Merlin's daughter after all."

"You feel the power of the fey don't you?"

She sat up and began fiddling with the straw. "I do and I need to understand where that's taking me, but we aren't having a crisis over my love life, it's yours."

"I don't want to talk about it. It's never happening. I'll see Arthur's crown safe and leave England. Leave him."

"Oh, yes because that works so well," Else muttered standing before me. "You need –"

"Wait," I said holding up my hand. "Can you hear that?"

"What?" she asked, her hand going to her knife.

"I smell smoke," I muttered. "And not the good kind." We rushed out of the stable, the mist now a full blown fog. The windows of the inn were hidden but I did see the fitful glow of fire.

Else yelled, "Lancelot, golem." She pointed and chaos erupted around us once more.

I drew my sword, grabbed Else and pulled her behind me. Three men came toward me, their stink arriving first. They moved fast, but not as fast as the monsters from our previous encounter. They were also unarmed. I hacked down one, cleaving him from head to belly. Kicking his body off my sword, I turned and took the next across the throat. His silent scream gave me the creeps. The third slipped past me and headed for the inn.

"They are after Arthur," I yelled.

"So is the fire," Else said, pointing to the window of his room.

"Arthur," I said. Fear burrowed rapidly through my chest. I rushed the nearest golem and I realised these men were different from the last. They were not as visibly dead and they were townsfolk. I took the monster's head from behind and he dropped, his body still trying to walk forward without a head to govern his actions. The inn door stood open, the room filled with them. How had this happened so fast? Else and I could only have been talking for a few minutes and I think she'd have noticed golem appearing when she walked through the bar.

The furniture hampered my fighting style so I drew my long knife. The fire raged from the kitchen. The heat was a wound opening into the bowels of hell. The flames a vision from the deepest pits, making my eyes blur.

"Arthur!" I screamed. Smoke danced down my throat to choke the life out of me.

The golem all turned as one when they heard my bellow and began to target me instead of Arthur. Hands reached for me and fire glinted off a blade to my right. I cut and hacked my way toward the stairs, barely able to see. Pain registered somewhere on the right side of my body. I didn't stop; I simply cut back, picked up a chair and threw it into three of the people attacking. One of those I cut down wore the dress of the innkeeper's daughter. I reached the stairs, gasping for clean air, which rushed in through the vagrancies of the wind's currents. I raced upward and found Geraint fighting two more monsters in the narrow hallway. His great height and width hampered him. I took one from behind by ripping his throat open with my blade and Geraint managed to dispatch the other. A cloth covered his nose and mouth.

"Arthur," I gasped. Geraint just looked toward his door. I smashed into it and saw Arthur, surrounded by fire licking and laughing through the floor. His room sat over the kitchen. He'd collapsed near the tub. I didn't consider anything, I just ran. I don't know if the flames lit my cloak. Don't know if they ate at my boots. I just ran to him, knelt and heaved his body into my arms. His weight was an instant burden but also comforting. I hurried for the door. Fire bellowed its disappointment behind me, the flames reaching for the thatch. Geraint dashed ahead and carved his way through the enemy, an easy task in comparison to fighting the golem in the wood. Whatever controlled these creatures didn't have as strong a hold on the townsfolk.

We exploded through the inn's door, fire racing over the ceiling and floor trying to cut us off from our escape. Our horses were in the street, tack thrown into the yard, Else relying on the warhorses' common sense to keep them close. A wet blanket covered me and Arthur. I stumbled to the ground and dropped him, turned and vomited.

Voices surrounded me in a muddle. I must have passed out for a moment. "Get him moving, Geraint or we will all die!" Else screamed.

I struggled out from under the damp blanket. "Me here," I gasped. My eyes focused and I realised the fire raged out of control and more golem loomed from the red tinged fog. Arthur sat upright, his head in his hands. I stood on wobbly legs and grabbed him under his arms. He wore his shirt, hose, doublet but his gambeson and cloak must be in his room, along with his mail shirt.

I lifted him to his feet. "We need to defend ourselves and we need to leave."

He nodded and reached for his sword, it did not hang from his belt. "Fuck."

"Take mine, Sire," I said pulling my beloved blade and handing it over.

Arthur looked at me. "You saved my life."

I grinned. "My job. Take the blade, Arthur."

He did as instructed and we moved toward Geraint. The big man nodded. "Think we'll be fighting our way out of the town. Else is trying to tack up the horses."

I turned back. She wrestled with the beasts needing to convince them to fight their instincts for running. "Else," I yelled. "Just the bridles, we need to move fast."

"All very well for you to say," she cursed me and Ash.

"Focus, Lancelot," Arthur said, his determination unwavering. The townsfolk descended on us, jaws snapping, hands grabbing and some managing crude weapons. We went to the slaughter and it was a slaughter. Even fire damaged as the three of us were, we outmatched each and every one of our enemies. The horses were soon under control and we mounted one at a time, the other two holding our position at the front of the stable yard. Once all four of us were mounted we began the slow horror of carving our way through the town and out onto the Levels. We were as silent as those we fought, marching the horses forward, a grim progress, protecting Mercury and Else.

When we reached the edge of the town and fought our way through the last of the mobilised dead, we raced the horses into the fog. They ran, relieved to be free of the clawing hands, stink and fire. We covered a league before stopping and turning back. The fog glowed deep red, the town burning to the ground.

"What the hell just happened?" Arthur asked.

Else stroked Mercury's sweaty neck trying to calm his nerves. The whites of his eyes betrayed his thin veneer of control. "Whatever has the power to create those things is not stopping their pursuit. They want you dead, Arthur. To destroy a town, even a small one, is a feat unimaginable. We should press on to Avalon and find Merlin."

"This fog is too thick to move in safety on these Level's," Arthur said. "The road will peter out and the flood plains are dangerous at night. I'll not risk any of you to a boggy grave."

"Just one at the hands of the living dead," Geraint muttered.

We walked on in silence, Else choosing to ride as far from me or Arthur as possible. He eventually spoke, "Interesting night."

I studied Ash's ears for a few moments. "I owe you an apology. I'm a coward, Arthur."

He laughed. "Of all the ways I'd choose to describe you, my friend, I don't think that one comes among them."

I watched my hands, fiddling with my reins. "I am sorry. I lack the courage I need to give you what you want." Those words shot through me as though I pierced myself with arrows.

"Forget it, Lancelot. Forget everything. I was wrong to do this to you. We are different and I need to stop pushing. It won't happen again. You are right, Camelot must come first and she will allow this."

I glanced at him, shocked by his words. His tone had hardened. The decision was clear in the set of his shoulders and back. Arthur Pendragon was cutting me out of his heart. A huge chasm opened before me. A life without Arthur's kisses or his skin rubbing against mine. But it did leave me free to pursue Else, to marry without complications and to work for him as every other one of his knights did. His blue eyes were shadowed, his face stained by smoke and soot.

The fog shrouded me, blinded me and swallowed all of me. I wanted, in that moment to push Ash into the white mists and never return to Arthur's side. A future without him looked so simple and yet so fucking empty and pointless.

The road itself remained quiet. Occasionally we would walk through soft land, almost bog but not quite. Other times we would walk on layers of willow which had been laid down and tied, almost rafts in the mud. Other times we rode on stone, the old Roman road surviving in places. Trees appeared, clawing at the mists with hundreds of naked fingers. Willow was the most common, and looked like manic pixies, with thick trunks and wild hair. I wished I could see the Tor of Avalon, so I knew we were heading in the right direction.

"Arthur." Geraint interrupted my thoughts. "We should stop, the horses are exhausted and we need to sleep tonight."

"We'll stop there then. I dare not take us off the road. We'll set watch and I suggest we sleep armed," he said sliding off Willow.

I dismounted from Ash and took Willow from Arthur's hands. He allowed me possession without comment. I walked the horses a short way from our position, toward a tree, overhanging the road we followed. Else brought Pepper and Mercury, the gelding now calm. Willow and Pepper were the only two with saddles. We loosened their girths and allowed them all long rein, so they'd find their own food. Else touched my arm and before I knew what happened we were hugging each other.

"You should talk to him," she told me. "It's not too late. If you want him, tell him but explain how hard it is."

"Let sleeping dogs lie," I said. "I don't want to cause any more problems. We only just escaped with our lives. I need to stay focused on my job, not my dick."

She sighed and I heard the frustration. "Lancelot, sometimes they are the same thing." Else walked away, kicking clumps of mud into the distance of the fog bound land. I returned to the others just as they tried to make a fire in the middle of the road without moving far to seek wood.

Else chose to settle a long way from the fire. I didn't like her being so far from us. I walked to her and sat. "You need to sleep with us," I stated.

"All of you? My, isn't that asking a little much?" she asked. The sarcasm didn't escape me.

"Else, please, if you are angry I understand but we need to stick together. Don't make yourself vulnerable because I won't play whatever game you require." I realised my mistake as soon as the words dropped to the soil under our feet.

"Game? I have tried to make you understand, Lancelot." Her hand rose toward Arthur in a casual gesture. Her voice resonated and her eyes took on an amber light I'd never seen. We were out of earshot from the others and their fire looked dim in the thick fog.

The tension rose. I reined back my temper, "I don't want to fight, Else. We need to talk." I glanced over at Arthur, so far so good. Nothing had happened to him.

She sighed. "You understand nothing, stupid man. It could have been so much easier for you. I can give you the world."

"Else?" I asked. My scalp prickled and my instincts writhed in fear.

"I can give you everything Arthur has stolen from you, love. I can give you so much power." She smiled and it twisted into something unfamiliar in Else. She walked to me, her hips swaying in a way I'd never seen in my companion.

"And what exactly is that, Else?" I asked backing off.

She studied me as if for the first time. "Albion, Lancelot. Your land and mine. England combined with my own world, united under your leadership."

"Lancelot, I..." I heard Arthur call. I turned my head and began to walk to him. I watched as he fell forward, crumpling like a great golden statue. Geraint groaned and folded over where he sat, bread and cheese still in hand.

"Arthur," I called. My legs turned to ice water under me. I felt my knees sink into the soft wet earth. "Fuck," I cried out. I twisted, fighting the great blackness trying to sweep through my mind. "Else, help us. I beg you don't let this happen." I reached for her, dragging my slow body upright. She just stood, impassive, watching in silence. "Arthur..." I tried to scream but it came out as a whimper. I turned back toward him and pulled myself forward, my arms becoming as frozen as my legs. The mists swirled in eccentric patterns around my head, then burst into colours, reds, greens, purples and dull orange. I hauled myself another foot closer to my King. I reached for his outstretched hand. Our fingers touched as my limbs lost all power and my vision grew so dark not even the mist could penetrate my mind.

CHAPTER TWENTY-SIX

THE WET GROUND OOZED through my bare feet, my toes wriggled into the damp cold soil and spongy moss. For the few feet in front of my nose I could see tufty marsh grass and a wall of white. No breeze blew but the mists shifted. I realised it brushed my naked skin as though begging for the right to caress me.

"Arthur," I called into the fog. "Geraint?"

I waited for a reply. Nothing. Just a sigh from the mist, or had that been my own sigh reflected back? I took a step forward, half expecting the world to shift under me and vanish for good. The marshy ground stayed with me. I started to walk. Nothing changed. I began to run. As I ran, I thought about the White Hart, between one pace and the next I moved from biped to quadruped. The ground now raced under pads and claws, my speed increasing until my black fur became a blur.

I travelled for some miles before I stopped. I lifted my head and howled, knowing Arthur must be out here somewhere. The lonely cry shot through the mists more swiftly than I could run but no answering bark from the Stag returned. I paced a full circle, sniffing the air, praying for a scent to tell me where I needed to go. The air smelt wet, earthy, full of winter death. I walked forward trying to gauge the presence of the sun or moon. The world appeared to be one huge amorphous blob of white.

I howled once more, confused and afraid, still nothing. I drew in my breath for another cry, begging for help and a scent hit my sensitive nose. I froze and sniffed. Summer herbs? Why could I smell lavender? I followed the scent on silent paws. It grew stronger. My body tensed and lowered to the ground, my belly brushed the short spongy grass. The power in my Hindquarters gathered, ready to attack at any moment.

A dark shape loomed before me. I froze, assessing the danger.

"Ah, my Wolf, there you are," said a strong male voice.

I whined and rose, the tension in my body vanishing. I jumped toward the dark figure. The man crouched and laughed. I stuck my face into his and licked him, behaving like a huge black dog.

"Oh, for goodness sake, Lancelot, calm down. I know you are pleased to see me, my old friend, but please stop. Your tail is wagging so hard you are going to fall over." He buried his hands in my ruff and pulled my head back. I stared into the greenest eyes I'd ever known. He still appeared to be twenty years my senior, but who knew for sure. Those intense eyes were crinkling with joy, his smile spreading. A shock of silver hair, long and flowing down his back, with a black streak over his right eye, smelt of herbs. His broad shoulders and strong arms helped make Merlin a great swordsman, not just a wizard.

"I take it you've been looking for me?" he said.

I wanted my mortal form back, then I'd be able to jibber at him about Arthur. Beg his help to save my King. I whined piteously.

"Oh, my Wolf, you can't change with me here. I am in your dream and I shouldn't be. There is only so much we can both do under the circumstances. I'm afraid you will have to listen. I am not strong and we are not as close as I am to Arthur, though your love for him bridges the gap well enough, that and your power of course. You will be able to help him far more than I can help you," he said. Merlin's mercurial nature meant he changed like a coin spinning in the air to land on a gambler's hand. Right now, he appeared happy. I'd seen him angry, I never wanted him to be angry with me, he is the only man who will make me feel fear other than Arthur.

I sat, showing him I was ready for a lesson, panting to enjoy the scent of a friend.

He chuckled. "Right, my Wolf is now paying attention." He paused, gathering his thoughts. "Arthur is in terrible danger and has been for years. Separating him from you was their greatest victory. Capturing me their other great victory. Never chase a bit of skirt which has as many brains as you have yourself." He sounded so mournful. My tongue lolled out of my mouth further and I wished I could laugh. Merlin frowned. "Hmm, well, regardless. This is why I can't reach Arthur, I am held captive. I can only reach you in your dreams because of who you are."

I whined, trying to ask, *'Who am I?'* but he ignored me and carried on. "Therefore, you are the only person I can trust to help both me and Arthur. You must save him, his soul is the sacrifice they need to control Camelot and they will take it while leaving him there as the puppet. If they don't take his soul they will try to take his life. My daughter is being tricked. The family who spawned her are using her, not helping her and she won't welcome your interference. It is the reason I took her away. What I didn't realise is the de Clare's are under the influence of fey as well, which is how I have been trapped."

This all sounded a little bleak to me, so on one side stood a fey family who looked as though they worked with us, on the other stood the de Clare's and their fey friends, and at the end of the line us mere mortals.

Merlin rubbed my ear, I couldn't believe how good it felt, I leaned against his hand. "Now, I know you want to ask how on earth are you going to find Arthur but remember, he is not in physical danger right now, just spiritual. It's his spirit you can save and once that is achieved you can find his body, then come and find me. In the meantime, stay out of trouble and try not to bed anyone else. Have you any idea how complicated you are making my life, never mind your own? I need Arthur to produce an heir and while his heart belongs to you he won't."

I growled in warning and rose, as did Merlin. "Fine, you don't welcome my words but they are true. Listen to me, Lancelot, my Wolf, you will only find your King if you follow your heart. You have to enter his dreams as I have yours. You can because you are tied to him as tightly as two people can be, your shared destiny will ensure you run once more at his side. I must leave now. I have my own battles to face. Just follow your heart and trust no one."

The fog engulfed the man before me, drawing him into its embrace. It grew so thick I lost all sense of direction and found him gone from my side, between the drawing of one breath and the next. I howled.

My body, full of distress and fear, wanted to run. I had to fight my instincts and think, not act. I must reach Arthur and follow my heart. Which meant what exactly? I growled, remembering why Merlin could be such a pain in the arse, he might have given me instructions. Fine, if he wanted me to think about how to enter Arthur's dreams I'd work on that. I realised Merlin had appeared twice in my dreams, I hadn't created him. How would I do that? Concentrate on my friend that's how I would do it. Listen to my heart and its whispers of love. Allow my soul to travel to his mind. And the only way to dream is to sleep. Regardless of what my human body might be doing, this Wolf form needed to sleep if I were to cross into Arthur's mind and save his soul.

I padded forward looking for a den. I had to be comfortable and safe. The fog kept close to me, hugging my fur, making it damp. A great shape loomed out of the darkness, a huge willow tree. I sniffed the air, then the ground, then the tree, looking for possible enemies who may live in the trunk or branches. Nothing, no one lived near this tree. I walked around and found a huge crack in the trunk, large enough for even a Black Wolf to curl up and be safe. I smiled, I suppose it was my dream, so why wouldn't I find something to keep me safe?

I crawled into the hole, walked around in a tight circle and settled down on dry leaves. Tucking my nose into my tail, I shut my eyes and conjured Arthur. Inevitably, my mind tracked back to the previous night. I rewound the events. How it made me feel to have him so close, so intimate. Should two men love each other in such a way? I didn't know. I did know Arthur and I needed to step over that line. There had only ever been him in my heart. With the thought, I felt that familiar and ancient ache, the pain that gives me access to my true feelings for my friend. This pain I carried close for years, as we grew into men. The agony I felt when I finally lay with Guinevere and the horror of seeing his face when he condemned me for the adultery before the court.

Even in my dream, I twitched with distress. I hung onto the feeling, forgetting the mission at hand, my mind roving over old wounds. Those old wounds became so painful I began to run, run hard, racing away from the pain, over polished wooden floors, my claws digging into the surface and making loud clacking noises.

I skidded to a halt. I ran through Camelot. Quiet, lit by daylight, empty of scent. I turned once in a full circle to make certain I hadn't made a mistake. My tongue lolled out, I'd done it. I'd breached Arthur's mind. I knew this couldn't be my world, I didn't dream like this. I trotted forward toward the great hall feeling quite optimistic.

My ears swivelled, catching the first sound. A metallic ring against stone. I paused, I sniffed and fear hit my nose. Long before thinking and planning even entered my head, I raced forward. The great doors to the throne room were shut and I now heard more than just metal clanking. The other noises chilled my bones. I pawed at the door, trying to convince it to open. It swung inward just enough for me to see the hall. I peered in and pushed with my snout to widen the gap. I saw what I feared the most.

Arthur held prisoner. The White Hart captured. He stood with legs splayed, his pristine coat, bloody and torn. His great rack of antlers broken. There were cuffs around each of his legs, forcing him into stillness even as his flanks heaved and sweated. A collar ran around his thick neck, tying him tight to the floor. The chain forced his head down toward a great stone block. Before the mighty Stag stood a woman.

Her long blonde hair brushed the top of her small, round backside. A heavy gold belt slung low over her hips helped to emphasise her small waist. I'd had my hands around that waist, fingers almost meeting as her hips rocked over mine.

Guinevere stood before the White Hart. A blade glinted in her hand. She raised her arms to shoulder height and her head rocked back onto her shoulders. The sunlight, through the great windows danced over her perfect form. Her eyes were closed. From the furthest corners of the room figures walked forward. They all seemed to be members of Arthur's court but horribly changed.

I recognised Kay only because he wore his family colours. He shuffled forward, his legs twisted, his arms pulling him along the polished floor. His face broken and rebuilt as a nightmare. His eyes were glazed and he drooled. There were others. Gawain, another of Arthur's loyal followers, usually young and handsome, now appeared with his flesh torn from his body, his mighty limbs shrunken. Yvain, small, swarthy and the finest horseman I knew, looked diseased, foul fluid leaking from his orifices. Others, who were Arthur's true companions, emerged just as tortured.

Those I thought of as de Clare supporters were all tall, perfect, beautiful versions of what they were in real life. Guinevere stood, shining and glorious among her people. Two men, mighty lords, Lot and Accolon, a man I counted as friend, began to pull the White Hart's head down.

Arthur fought, his legs quivered. He pulled back on the collar around his throat. In painful deliberation they forced his powerful shoulders down. His head twisted to one side exposing his neck. It lay on the stone block. I heard his breathing, smelt his fear and defiance.

Guinevere spoke, "The time has come to reclaim what has been taken from us. Those who follow me, who walk in my path, shall be rewarded." A great cheer erupted from the beautiful people. "Those who have stood against me, who have caused my downfall and stolen my prize." She pointed to Morgan. I knew he had been one of those who had been made to declare me outlaw. "Shall be punished for all time. This will amuse the Court, will it not?" Another cry from the beautiful, those who were ugly moaned and shivered. I watched Kay try to reach the Stag, a man, Guy I think, kicked him hard. Blood crashed to the floor and the Stag twitched.

The Queen continued, "Once we have freed ourselves from the tyranny of Pendragon power we will bring Wessex back to its glory days, under the rule of Albion."

I didn't know what glory days she spoke of, the Romans? Wessex under Arthur's hand had gone from strength to strength and what was Albion? A word I'd heard too often recently.

Guinevere lowered her arms and chanted. She stroked the mighty neck of the Stag. Arthur tried to fight but I watched him beginning to fold under the soft caresses. I stared, transfixed by the sight of his wife, my old lover, raising the knife over her head. Bright light hit the blade and glinted off, blinding me for a moment. The spell, the shock of seeing her, broke within me. I barged into the doors and they swung open. I raced across the polished stone floor, snarling. Guinevere's arms were coming down faster than I moved. I gathered my back legs under me, all that power at my call and thrust up just as she plunged down. I landed on Guinevere's back. She screamed and toppled forward, onto the broken antlers of the Stag, the knife skittered from her hand.

Howls from men's mouths are not the same as a howl from a Wolf. Guinevere died on the antlers and I leapt from her back, tearing through the crowd. All those I knew to be enemies I fought. None were fast enough to lay a blade on my dark form. I became a blur of vengeance. Each body I marked vanished back into the walls of the great hall. Every one of our allies cheered even as they sank into the floor, unharmed and thankfully repaired. When the last of the figures vanished from my sight, I turned back to the Stag. The body of the Queen faded, the beautiful face pierced by a tine from the rack of antlers.

I needed to free Arthur, to bring him back to our world, not his own. I concentrated and felt my limbs grow and straighten, the fur flowing back into my skin, burning hot. I regained my fingers and I moved to the Stag.

"Calm, Arthur," I murmured. I stroked his great cheek. His eye looked at me, wide and wild. I reached for the collar around his neck and snapped the simple fastener open. It slid from his throat and crashed to the floor. He raised his head from the block and stood, legs still splayed, regarding me. I lay a hand on the wide forehead and stroked his face. He pushed his nose into my chest. He had been hurt, cuts bled along his ribs and back. I walked to each of his limbs and undid the clasps. He regained his footing and I wrapped my arms around his neck as he sank to the floor. I held him. The body shifted under my hands. One moment I lay half under the White Hart's neck, the next I sat with Arthur the man cradled in my arms.

"My Wolf," he whispered.

"I will always protect you, my King," I whispered. I kissed his sweat bathed brow.

The air rushed into my lungs, cold and damp. A sharp orange light snarled its way into my eyes and a gruff voice said, "Thank God. I can't find Arthur."

CHAPTER TWENTY-SEVEN

I SAT UP, GERAINT held a candle in his hand. It showed me a world of bleak isolation. Night shrouded the land, the stars a distant meaningless light. The fog had vanished and taken my heart with it. I sat on damp earth, which remained soft under my hands. There were scrubby trees surrounding us, we were not where we had been, on the road.

"What do you know?" I asked, reaching and checking our weapons.

"I can't find Else or Arthur. I've been awake a while. I tried to wake you but you've been out cold." I heard the stress in Geraint's voice.

"Just as well, I've been dreaming again," I said as I stood. "Where are the horses?"

"I don't know," Geraint replied.

"I wish them luck with that then," I said, thinking of Ash and how difficult he'd be making someone's life. "Do we know what happened?"

Geraint shook his head and the candle fluttered. "One minute we were lighting the fire, the next I felt so heavy I couldn't move, then this." He waved his hands around and the candle's flame vanished. "Bollocks."

"Don't worry," I said waiting for my eyes to adjust. I wished briefly the Wolf lived somewhere other than my head.

"How are we going to pick up their tracks without light?" Geraint asked.

"We aren't, we are going to follow my instinct if you will just hold still and let me concentrate," I said. I closed my eyes and thought about the feeling, which led me to Arthur's dreams. The ache sprang back to life. I turned in a circle asking for guidance. The pain flared when I turned in one particular direction.

I opened my eyes. "We go that way." I pointed, uncertain of the direction until we could see the stars.

"What about Else?"

I threw my hands in the air. "What about her? The last I remember, she was the one telling me Arthur needed to be replaced," I said, trying very hard not to think too much about what she had done or why. "Let's not worry about her until we have Arthur back."

"She's a vulnerable woman," Geraint said.

"There is nothing vulnerable about, Eleanor de Clare." I shivered. I realised she might have been tricked and might be working for Arthur's enemies without realising it but equally she might not. And what of Guinevere in Arthur's dream? Was she merely a representation of the evil in the court, or was she queen of our enemies? When would I ever meet a woman I could trust?

"Maybe she's with Arthur," Geraint said. I heard the worry, but didn't care. I had to find Arthur. Merlin had said once I'd saved his soul, I had to save his body.

We had nothing to carry, except the clothes in which we'd fallen asleep. We had lost our swords and our horses. We both had some coin, but no food and the four knives we carried our only weapons. Two of which were eating knives.

We set off along a rough path at a good jogging pace, the mail I wore hardly noticeable. While we ran, I told Geraint about the dream. He cursed. "So you think the Queen is a traitor?"

"I have no idea if she is or if she is just a patsy. Either way she needs stopping," I said. I felt sad for her and for Arthur. How had it all gone so wrong between us?

I felt Geraint's hand on my shoulder. "I am sorry, my friend. You have suffered much for Arthur's sake."

I didn't know what to say, so we fell silent and just ran through the night. I assumed we were still on the Levels because the ground under our feet remained the same. Travelling over such dangerous terrain made me nervous, drowning in the swamp was not something I wanted, but I had no choice. The ache in my chest was the only guide on this journey.

We must have travelled miles at a hard pace, until we noticed the ground rising. I pulled Geraint to a stop and looked around me. "We are not in Wessex," I said.

Geraint peered into the brightening night. A moon appeared over the large oddly shaped hill. "This is Avalon. It's just an Avalon we've never seen. It's like it was before the Sisters came," he said, breathless from more than the run.

I felt the same awe. We were not in the Avalon we knew. The small town built around an Abbey full of women who worshipped things I didn't understand, never existed in this place. "I have a horrible feeling we aren't even in our world," I said.

Geraint stared at me. "We've crossed over into the land of the fey?"

I shrugged. "Can you think of another explanation?"

Geraint paused, clearly wishing he could, he slumped. "No, it is the only explanation. How are we going to find Arthur now?"

"Keep following my instinct, I suppose," I said, moving off once more toward the large naked Tor.

The whole of Wessex grew up on the tales of Avalon. A place of mystery in the centre of Arthur's lands. The Sisters of Avalon were a remnant of the old ways, the old religion, which Arthur protected when necessary and ignored most of the rest of the time. They were said to be prophets, healers, guides for the souls of the lost. I had the feeling Arthur knew a great deal more about them than he told us, but he wouldn't be drawn into revealing all their secrets. Now, however, all Geraint and I faced was the barren hill. Devoid of all except a few bare trees and scrubby grass. We started to walk up the side.

"We could be here forever," Geraint moaned as we slogged in the mud.

"No, I don't think so," I said. "The springs are nearby aren't they?"

"How the hell am I supposed to know? I avoid all this nonsense at every opportunity," Geraint said. "These places are all over my land and they give me the bloody willies. I just let the locals do their thing and avoid upsetting the priestesses."

He talked and whinged, I studied the ground. I had the feeling we needed to be curling around the base of the Tor more to the east and a bit higher. Almost to the base of the main part of the hill. Just as Geraint began another rant about the ills of messing with fey, I found it. A severed artery of water gushed from the side of the hill. My instinct for Arthur pulled me around the water, I walked above the spring and I found a hole.

"Here," I called Geraint to me. "I've found it. There's a stone entrance." I began tugging at clumps of grass and mud, scrambling to pull the earth away from three small lintels of stone, which formed a rough arch.

"Oh, yes, that Doesn't look like a trap," Geraint bitched. "A bit bloody easy."

"If you call this easy," I grunted as I yanked back another sod of earth, "then help."

He cursed once, dropped to his knees beside me and we worked on the hole until we made it large enough for us to crawl through.

Geraint peered into the darkness. "We need a torch if you are certain Arthur's in there."

I rubbed my hands on the grass trying to clean them. "I'm certain. I can feel him." My excitement grew. I ran off to find a branch, needing something to fashion into a torch.

We did the best we could out of what we had, mostly our clothing and managed to light the branch.

"It won't last long," Geraint said. We watched it splutter in the darkness.

I had nothing to say. Crawling into the side of the hill didn't feel like a wise idea but I knew Arthur's heart beat in there and I wanted him back. I crawled through first, the cold wet earth crumbling under my hands. The ground sloped away from the entrance. "Geraint, as you come in –" The ground gave way and I yelped.

Dirt and stones spilled from under my hands and knees. I cursed as I skidded forward into the darkness. It felt like miles but my hands found hard flat stone before my nose did and I stopped, scraping my palms in the process.

"Lancelot?" I heard from above me.

"Fine," I said, cross with myself for being careless. Arthur's survival depended on me. "As I was saying, be careful. The ground slopes away heavily."

Geraint chose to climb in on his backside, wriggling through the gap. The torch high over his head. He slipped the few feet I'd skidded down and landed with a grin beside me. "Glad you're the brave one, going first and all," he said.

"Fuck you," I muttered looking round. We were in a place that should not have existed.

"Oh, God, have mercy on our souls," Geraint prayed as we took in what our feeble light displayed.

CHAPTER TWENTY-EIGHT

WE SAT A MERE hand's width from the edge of a drop into utter blackness. My head spun as we peered down and Geraint pulled me back from the precipice. To our left were steps leading downward and upward. We had entered the hill half way up, or half way down, depending on your perspective. We stood, taking great care, on the only visible platform. The steps curled around the inside of the scooped out hill, matching the shape perfectly. An endless spiral of stone steps. Long and shallow, not man sized and they vanished into the darkness. The utter darkness and silence.

The walls of this great cavern were rough and pitted, whereas the steps were smooth. The only sound came from our breathing and the crackle of our torch.

"This is not good," Geraint whispered. The sound escaped us and shushed around the hollow hill, making the hairs on our arms stand erect and our minds shudder at the possibilities.

I swallowed and looked at him, unable to add to that acoustic terror. He recognised my expression and took a deep breath, nodding agreement. I turned to the steps, placed a hand on the wall for orientation and followed my heart down. To begin with we walked anticipating and attack with each noise we made, waiting with every harsh echo to snap back at us and show us enemies by the hundred. There were no enemies, only the endless journey into nothingness. The torch continued to burn, fitful but surprising us with its longevity, it lit only our small patch of this world. Nothing changed as we circumnavigated the great hill. I did notice a small patch of light when we drew opposite the entrance. It appeared high above us and so far away. Dawn had come. On we walked.

My legs burned with the effort of negotiating steps, which were a pace and a half wide and half a pace deep. Each step became a form of slow torture and a lesson in patience. My legs, already weary from the run, trembled and my knees threatened to give way at any moment, to send me over the edge into the blackness below. Geraint, behind me, pulled me up short. He bent close to my ear, the echoes driving us both a little deranged.

He whispered, "I need to stop, just for a moment."

I looked back at him and he appeared ashen in the light. We had run all night and I knew I must look as bad as he did, we'd be no good in a fight. I nodded and we slumped against the wall, taking a step each, stretching our legs. I had possession of the torch, so I lay it down and watched the flickering light. It hinted at the vastness of the hollow hill. Who or what had done this to the Tor I could not imagine and truth be told, I tried damned hard not to. I wondered if the Tor in our own world resembled this one or if only the fey had a hole in their hill.

I watched Geraint try to ease the burning in his legs by curling them up against his chest. I chose to sit cross legged. We gazed outward, sharing our silence but not our fears. Without comment, we moved together and rose. My back ached, my legs cramped and I felt sick with hunger but we continued our descent. I had no idea how long we walked. I no longer stared around me, just down at the step in front, so I didn't trip in my exhaustion. Down, down, step, step, my left hand sore with the feel of the stone guiding me down, down into the pit. The hill smelt damp, felt cold, remained dark. The ache in my heart for Arthur beat in time to the pain in my legs.

Geraint placed a hand on my shoulder once more. He now held the torch. He raised it high and pointed. I blinked, my eyes unused to focusing on anything other than the steps, steps, steps. I didn't understand, until I saw him grin. "We are near the bottom, look, the wall."

I peered into the dark and realised he'd seen something I hadn't, we were now circling the hill so tightly we saw the other side in the torch's light. I closed my eyes and leaned against the wall. "Thank God." My voice rasped in my throat, I needed water. We took a moment and then started down again, this time faster as the steps began to actively spiral downward. The scent of Arthur drew me onwards, a strong pull on my heart. His name pounded inside my head matching the pace of my feet. I stepped toward a flash of colour at the edge of the torch's capacity. Geraint yanked me back. I lost my balance and crashed to the step.

"What the hell?"

Geraint crouched beside me and ignored my protest. The echoes had become small, almost nonexistent this deep inside the hill. "Look," he said pointing.

I looked, at the floor. We stood on the final step and tiles reached into the distance. The shape copied the strange elongated flat top on the outside of our Tor. "I don't understand," I said. My sense of humour had long since evaporated. I felt Arthur pressing against my heart, pushing me forward.

Geraint rose, walked past me and stood on the last step with the torch high over his head. I saw in the distance a large slab of stone, tall, on a raised dais and a body. Faint light glinted off blonde hair. My legs acted like springs, I rose, exhaustion forgotten. "Arthur." I pushed against Geraint's back.

"No, Lancelot, wait, please." Geraint pushed me back. "Let me think. This isn't as simple as it looks."

"He's there, it's that simple," I yelled, setting off the echo. "He must hear us and he isn't moving, so he's hurt. I have to reach him." I felt frantic with the need to go to my King.

"Just bloody wait," Geraint said. "Let me think. This isn't as safe. See, there, the marks on the floor." He pointed. "It's a maze without walls, a trap. I don't want to lose you because you have no brains and no patience. Arthur isn't going anywhere."

I drew breath to argue when I glanced at the floor. Marks covered the earthen tiles. The tiles were large rectangles and on each was a mark, carved and cast in red. It made them hard to see in the flickering light.

"What is it?" I asked, mollified for the moment.

Geraint knelt down, careful to avoid touching the tiles. "It's an old language, something not used for a long time. I've seen its like at home. My land is littered with these markings."

"How do we get to Arthur?" I asked.

"I don't know yet, Lancelot, this is a dead language and I only speak our mother tongue, Latin and Greek, would you like to take a guess?" His exasperation at my nagging made me back off.

"Sorry," I said. "Just trying to help."

"Well, you aren't helping so sit still and be quiet." He pointed to a step. I sat and watched as he began pacing back and forth across a narrow strip of tiles free from markings. He muttered under his breath and held his head a great deal. Geraint really is the most intelligent of the three of us. Arthur is the natural leader. I am the killer.

I contemplated this as I watched him and realised Geraint should be in a monastery somewhere writing and studying the skies for answers to questions I wouldn't even think to ask. I thought about Arthur's gift of leadership, the inspiration he created in those who followed him and I tried to work out why Stephen de Clare wanted him dead. Jealousy I supposed, a powerful motivator. Me? I sighed. I began to see the faces of some of those I killed, all in the name of my King. I thought about those I had saved because of the death I am capable of creating and I prayed for the strength to save Arthur. "And Else," I muttered to myself.

With my mind focused on Arthur, I'd managed to avoid thoughts of Eleanor. I didn't want to think of her as a traitor. I wanted to believe something, anything else had happened to her. I prayed a reason existed for this madness and I would find her safe but held prisoner somewhere. She no longer occupied my dreams, nor did I see her in Arthur's, what did that mean? Was she dead already? The thought made my mind scream and my stomach knot in genuine pain. I did not want Eleanor de Clare to be dead. I wanted her as my wife. Even if I didn't understand her.

"I have it," Geraint announced. He paused, "At least I think I do."

"About time." I rose on stiff legs. "What do I do?"

"I should go first," Geraint said. "It's my theory that needs testing and it'll be easier for you to follow me than for me to explain."

"Just run it by me, I'm not that thick headed."

Geraint raised an eyebrow but remained silent. I stared him down. "Fine," he consented. "It works like this, these marks are an old language called Ogham, it's a tree alphabet." He pointed to the nearest tile. "This one is oak, here is ash."

I guessed he used these as examples because of our coat of arms. "I understand, but what did you mean about a maze?" I asked.

"Some of these marks are not real, some of them make no sense in this context and some form a pattern."

"What's the pattern?"

"A story, the story of a king, a love and a," here he paused, "a knight who should be king to return the land to the old ways."

"Is it talking about Arthur?"

"Yes, the tiles are using the oak and the ash to represent both of you."

"How is that possible?" I asked as a sense of something horrible swept up my back and sat on my shoulders pulling my hair. I shivered.

"I don't know, Lancelot," Geraint said exasperated, "but we have spent all day walking around the inside of a hollow hill which goes down as far as it goes up, so let's not be caught up in semantics."

"Sorry," I said again. I guessed his temper frayed because of the pressure. I tried to be more sympathetic.

"If we follow the marks that make sense in the story we should reach Arthur safely," he said.

"And if we don't?"

"I don't know, but I really would rather not find out. Fey are known for their tricks so let's not get carried away."

His eyes challenged me to defy him. I stood, both meek and mild, and allowed him his victory. I'd already be dead if I'd been here alone, so he'd won as far as I was concerned. Geraint nodded once and took the first step on the story the fey had written. I followed, attempting to hold my temper and patience. Geraint muttered under his breath and frowned. He translated what he saw as we inched forward. I didn't even try to listen, my attention focused only on Arthur. He lay so still and I found we were going on a circuitous route, making me more impatient.

Geraint stopped and I almost walked into him. "What now?" I asked.

"You need to listen to this," Geraint said pointing. "I know this is hardly definitive but it speaks of the ash taking the oak's place." I was not in the right frame of mind, I stared at Geraint, he sighed, clearly suffering the idiot. "The fey think you are going to replace Arthur."

I snorted. "Don't be ridiculous. I will never and can never replace Arthur. This is madness. Just get me to him."

"Lancelot..." Geraint tried to make me understand.

"No, we don't have time. We need to reach Arthur and wake him up." I refused to believe he might be dead. "Then we find Merlin and Else and leave."

I watched the scholar in my friend do battle with the soldier, who would follow my orders. I have always been Arthur's second and as King's Champion I would always be the one Geraint looked to for instruction. The soldier won.

"Fine, just remember we need to discuss this when we leave this place," Geraint said. He returned to his task.

He walked forward once more remaining cautious. I followed. We grew closer to Arthur. He lay so still, so quiet. We arrived close enough for me to see his eyelashes on his cheek. Geraint studied the ground. I opted for a more direct approach.

My impatience outweighed his common sense. I placed my feet, crouched and launched myself into space. My legs stretched to reach the edge of the dais, Geraint yelled for me to stop. I struck the edge of the low platform and threw my weight forward so I didn't slip backwards. My knees hit the next step, but I'd landed.

"Ha, easy," I said.

"You bloody idiot," Geraint bellowed. "What have you landed on?"

"Nothing, a blank stone."

"And how do you know that's the right place to stand?"

"Oh, for God's sake, Geraint, have pity on me. Not everything is that complicated."

"Are you certain?" Geraint knelt on his tile and banged the torch on the one next door, sparks flew from the torch and the tile smashed into a hundred sharp pieces as a spear shot from the centre. My friend wiped his cheek where a piece of shrapnel bloodied him.

I looked at the spear and I looked at Geraint. I didn't move. "Do you think I'm safe here? Can I reach Arthur?" I still had three steps before I would be at his side.

"Are any of the stone steps marked in any way?"

"No," I said after looking closely at what I could see. "They look the same as the ones we walked down."

"Fine, then you can go, but be careful, Lancelot, please." Geraint began walking again, studying the ground. I sprinted up the stone steps. I finally stood beside Arthur's still form. I touched his jaw with my hand and kissed his brow.

"Wake up, Arthur. I beg you wake up," I whispered. Geraint joined me and took Arthur's hand.

"He will not wake until I allow it," said an imperious female voice.

CHAPTER TWENTY-NINE

LIGHT FLOODED THE INSIDE of the hill. Geraint cried out and I cursed, finding myself blind. Noise filled the cavern and I blinked back tears, trying to focus. Instinct drove me. I grabbed Arthur's still body and pulled it free from the bier, holding him to my chest. I sank to my knees and covered his still form with my back to the room. Sheltering in the shadows, I forced my eyes to adjust. Geraint crouched beside me, his knife hand out, waving it in front of us, acting as a barrier.

A slow hand clap brought my attention toward the woman who'd spoken. On either side of the most regal, the most beautiful creature I'd ever seen, stood an army. Else, gagged and bound, slumped between two of the male fey. The woman's fey heritage glowed from her long red hair, a shade impossible in a mortal, to her eyes, which resembled those of a fox and her slightly pointed teeth. She smiled. Her gaze focused on me. The hunger there I did not recognise or understand. Her tall, elegant form, the narrow waist, firm round breasts and long legs were covered in golden figure hugging armour. It moved like a second skin. She moved like a true predator.

"Welcome, son of Aeddan," she said.

I let my eyes register the soldiers. All were similar. Tall, broad, blonde, perfect and well armed. There were twenty five. Not the best of odds.

"Let her go," I said, waving the knife toward Else.

The woman smiled. "No, I am her mother and I can do as I wish with my flesh and my blood." She wafted a slim pale hand and one of the soldiers holding Else forced her down onto her knees. Tears filled her brown eyes. I heard Geraint curse in sympathy.

"What do you want?" I asked.

"How disappointing, straight to the nub. Don't you want to bargain? Most mortals want to bargain with the fey," she said. Her accent made her voice sing in my ears. She smiled and stepped toward me, her hips almost serpentine in their movement.

"I'm not like most mortals," I stated. "Why have you brought us here?" I reiterated.

Her smile widened. "So, true, you really are like no other. But I am certain you will deal before the end, your nobility will force it upon you."

I did not like the sound of that. What or who would she use to force a deal? I thought about laying Arthur down, leaving me free to rush the fey woman and strike at the heart of our troubles.

The Queen licked her lips and pointed at Arthur. "I won't play games then, Lancelot du Lac. Just for you, I shall keep this plain. I want you to kill him and take his place as king. It is your right. Your father may want you dead, but I need you alive, to be my new consort. Together we will bring Albion back into England. It's quite simple."

Geraint laughed. "You are mad. Lancelot hurt Arthur?" The laugh turned into a giggle. I glanced at my friend, tears coursed down his cheeks and I heard Else make strangled noises. I looked at her, she sobbed.

With my gaze locked on the fey witch, I asked, "What the hell are you doing to them?" With Arthur in one arm and the other hand grasping the knife, I couldn't touch Geraint to bring him back.

"I am showing them, inside their simple minds, with the small gifts I possess, what will happen if you do not kill Arthur. It's sending them quite mad." She stepped closer, immune to the floor's defences. "If you don't kill him England will wither and fade under his reign. Disease will flourish and the land will be barren, as will Guinevere." She stood just beyond my reach. Her skin shone with a strange phosphoresce. Geraint moaned, his knife clattered to the floor and he grasped his head. "I will keep showing them this, and other horrors, until you consent to kill the usurper."

"I don't believe that Arthur living a long happy life will harm England," I said. "Let them go." My rage had begun to turn cold. "Let them go and deal with me, take me, do what you like to me but release them. They have nothing to do with this."

"You see, I knew you'd deal. I had hoped you'd hold out a little longer." Her hand reached for my face and I remained still. I might have cut her with the knife, but with Arthur in my arms, if I'd tried I'd have missed her body. Anything other than a death strike would just make her angry and I didn't think that would be a good idea.

"You are so beautiful," she said. "Your father's perfection made human. I always knew his light would shine bright within your creation." She didn't touch me but the heat from her fingers brushed my skin and I watched the lust in her eyes make her elongated pupils dilate. I swallowed, fear a dark snake sliding around my heart. This woman, this creature leaked power all over me, suffocating me. She smiled, delicate, tentative and brushed the golden curls on Arthur's head. I didn't want her touching him. I drew him closer to my chest.

"Kill him and become king, or I will make your world suffer," she murmured. I so wished she screamed. It would be easier.

"Never," I said, matching her tone. Such a simple word. She blinked and smiled. Else and Geraint screamed. The sound ripped into me, my ears split with the shock and pain it caused. The great wave crashed and broke against my body. I tucked myself into Arthur's shoulder and used him to prevent my mind from smashing apart inside that sound of agony.

The noise died. "Kill him and become king." She hadn't moved.

"No." The word leaked out of my mouth but my body trembled in fear for those I loved. I didn't for one moment consider sacrificing Arthur to save them. I would have taken the pain myself to protect them, but I would not hurt Arthur.

Geraint screamed for so long and so loudly his voice broke and I watched his mouth stretch in soundless agony. Else fainted but her voice reverberated inside my mind.

"Kill Arthur," she said.

"I love him," I said, defiant in my resolution. Geraint lay beside me, his head on Arthur's thigh. Blood trickled from his nose, mouth and ears.

"You will kill him, Lancelot." She smiled. The fey Queen waved her hand and the world turned black.

I woke to agony.

My shoulders and wrists screamed at me and I couldn't breathe. The air stank, fetid and heavy with heat. Sweat dripped into my eyes and I understood my predicament. I dangled from my wrists over a pit full of coals. My shirt gone, my boots gone, my King gone. I tried to call out, the light around me too dim to see, it hid everything but my immediate environment. My weight stretched and crushed my ribs and neck. Just breathing proved a fight, never mind talking. The heat, the pain in my shoulders and the foul air made me sick. I should never have gone blindly into the hill after Arthur. I should have returned to Camelot somehow, raised an army and torn the fucking thing down. My only accomplishment was the near certain destruction of my family.

I strained against the metal cuffs, trying to pull my weight up, my fingers encircled the chain. Every muscle fought for release, but my body weight defeated me, too many large muscles fighting too many small muscles. Next, I tried raising my legs, hoping to use momentum and kinetic energy to alter my odds of escape. The only odds I managed to change were the ones involving the skin on my arms to stay whole. Blood dripped from fresh wounds, tracing elegant lines down the muscles of my arms.

A door opened in the gloom. "Oh, good," the fey bitch's said. "You woke up." She stepped into the circle of light surrounding me. The gold of her armour glowed red in the fitful torch light. She smiled. "You look so perfect."

"Funny, I feel like shit."

Her hand reached out and her fingers, hotter than the coals burning my feet, traced lines over my chest. She caught a little of the blood on the end of one small finger and sucked it clean, watching my face the whole time with those strange intense eyes. Her intimate gestures caused my breath to hitch, sending confusing signals to my brain.

"Tell me you will kill Arthur and I'll let you go," she cooed in my ear.

"He is my King. I am a knight of Camelot. I will never betray him," I said through gritted teeth.

She stood on the edge of the pit, unaffected by the heat, arrogant and beautiful. Her hands turned me around where I swung. I felt her begin to trace the lines of my scars. "Somehow, this tragic imperfection makes you more desirable. The flaw in an otherwise perfect gem."

My skin prickled under her gentle touch. I didn't want her examining me. I didn't want her touching me. Those scars were mine and I horded the memory of the pain they created close to my heart. A deep, personal, and horrific memory. I used it to remember the vagrancies of life. I twitched, then I thrashed, trying to force myself around to face her, so she couldn't trace each line, just as Arthur had done while he wept for our grief.

"You say you won't kill him," she murmured, "but he has hurt you so badly. I don't understand why you won't punish him the way he punished you. He betrayed you. He stole your wife. I created Guinevere for you and he took her. All your grief, your loneliness, your suffering comes from that one selfish, childish act and you won't hate him for it." Her fingers continued to play over the ridges in my skin. I panted for breath unable to stop her fiddling with me. I

~ 175 ~

thought about her words. If they were true, if such a thing were possible, Arthur and I should be mortal enemies. "She is your perfect woman, the only woman in this world you could ever have truly loved."

"Arthur is my life, he can do with me as he wishes," I ground out through clenched teeth.

"I'm sure he can," she said turning me back. I stared down only into her eyes. "After all, you want to fuck him don't you?" she asked her eyes dancing as she planned her verbal baiting.

Feeling like a cat's toy made me grumpy. I hawked and spat at her. I'd never spat at a woman and to be honest it wasn't effective, my mouth being too dry. It made her react though, her hand whipped up so fast I didn't find time to brace. She slapped me hard across the face. The world bloomed with new agony and my stomach lurched with the instant need to vomit. "Fucking animal," she hissed. Stars chased each other around my vision and I tasted blood in my mouth.

"Where is Arthur?" I managed to ask.

"You want your precious King then fine, have him," she snapped. Her hand waved and light washed through an enormous room. My eyes, blurry from the smack, took time to adjust. I saw Geraint first. He hung over a pit like mine, still unconscious. Else hung with him, they were both dressed and dangling face to face. The fey woman waved her hand once more. I considered what it would be like to cut that hand off. Geraint roused, jerked and cried out when he realised his predicament. Else woke and flinched, her small body bucked into his, they saw me and Geraint closed his eyes in understanding and acceptance of his fate. He murmured to Else. I felt love for my friend as he tried to bring her comfort.

Next I found Arthur. Or rather his back. His body lay prone, tied to a post, just like the one used for me all those months ago. His shirt lay torn around his hips, mirroring my own half naked humiliation before the court of Camelot. Sweat gleamed in the ethereal light and his blonde head sagged. He remained unconscious and unhurt. I trembled in the knowledge this status quo wouldn't remain so for long.

"Please," if I had to beg I would. "If you want me, you have me. Let them go, my Lady. Show mercy, I beg you." I couldn't take my eyes off him.

"Nimue, Lancelot, my name is Nimue." She stroked my chest once more. "And I will be your Queen."

"I thought you were already Queen?" I asked, trying to draw her into conversation and away from thoughts of Arthur.

"I am. I am married to your father, but he is an ignorant selfish pig," that came from her perfect lips sounding like a pout, "and I want you not him on the throne of Albion."

Great, I thought, *so we are the pawns in the centre of a game between rival fey who are fighting over our throne and sulking about it.*

"Well, Nimue, if you let them go, I will fight for you and kill this fey king of yours to give you the throne of Albion. We need not involve Arthur at all." It was worth a try.

She giggled. "No," she said and Geraint cried out. My head ripped up to see him and Else lowered several inches toward the coals under their bare feet. I heard Else call out to me.

I watched, impotent, as they hung and twisted now closer to the fire. Else talked to Geraint, his legs moved and he hooked them over her hips, pulling on her small wrists but taking his feet away from the worst of the fire. Blood flowed down her arms.

"I want Arthur dead and I want him dead by your hand," she said, as if speaking to an idiot, poking me in the chest to emphasise each word. "I need Albion and England to become one again. I need the mortals to worship in the old style. I need you to be king. My people will accept you and your people will accept you, with some gentle persuasion."

"Why do I have to kill Arthur?" I asked. "Anyone can do it."

Her fingers played in my blood drawing lines. "True, but I need you to do it, so you understand who and what you are. I need you to kill him and take his place. I'll even throw in Guinevere if you want her that badly. Call it, training," she said, choosing her words. "If you kill him it will stop you from loving him and it will please me. You want to please me don't you?"

Her strange eyes held me captive as she spoke. I wanted to kiss that mouth, those full lips. My brain screamed at me, the warrior in me reacting to something horribly familiar. The spell, the love spell the other fey used to trap me with Else. The lassitude crept over me and my dick stirred. She smiled and I ached for her mouth on my hot wet skin. "Yes, you see, you are weakening for me already," she whispered.

CHAPTER THIRTY

A SMALL WHIMPER ESCAPED me. I hated that spell, more than anything else I did not want to feel it pouring through my body and forcing me hard. Her hand strayed over my growing erection and I closed my eyes in shame.

"Impressive," she said.

I wanted to scream at her that she'd never have me, but I knew that if she continued this game I'd be fucking her on the dungeon floor in front of everyone. Her hand massaged my cock and an image flashed into my head – Arthur pleading with his eyes, wanting to complete our love, to finish what we'd begun. Begging me to help him manifest the unspoken passion we had shared for all these long years. Other than the lovely women I paid, he was the only person to offer me honest physical completion. Unlike my paid companions, he also offered me his heart.

His name did not leave my lips but I did hold him as a talisman against Nimue's considerable charms. If I wanted my lover to be male, so what? So long as we were both happy.

I needed to escape this place and I needed to save Arthur and the others. I relaxed into the spell coursing through me and smiled at Nimue. "Kiss me, my Queen."

Her lips brushed mine and I reacted. The spell tore through me making me gasp. It surged with more perfection and power than anything I'd felt with Else. The fey queen's lips parted and I kissed her, thrusting my tongue deep inside, she tasted of honey and joy. Liquid light spilled into my mouth even as her sharp teeth grazed my lip and more blood flowed. Her hands strayed around my back and great strength pulled me towards her gold encased body. My toes touched the edge of the fire pit. Somewhere far away I heard Else calling to me but I ignored her nagging. All I wanted to feel or see or hear was Nimue. My arms relaxed, the chains to the ceiling lengthened. Their descent enabled me to wrap my arms around my beautiful goddess and hold her close.

She pulled back, arching her neck and I ravaged her pale skin making her cry out. The pain fled from my mind. So far away I barely registered it. Nimue murmured, "Yes, my King, yes. Possess me."

Just one word and the intoxication of her touch vanished. King. I am no king. I loved a king and that love roared forth to devour the witch's spell. My heart would not be tricked again. I gave my body free rein, just as I did when I'd drunk too much to be fully aware. It knew this dance so well it performed its duties without my brain. It raced at full speed, seeking a path through this mess. I needed my hands free and I needed a weapon. I needed a plan. While I worked on her pleasure, I watched the room fill with soldiers and my elation at seeing a way through this mess, vanished.

Her fingers tangled my sweaty hair and she dragged my mouth from her delicate throat. "I have a duty for you, my King," she said.

"Anything," I replied, my hands roving over the golden armour.

"Kill the Merlin first," she said.

I flinched, so he was here, I nodded to cover my movement, pulling against her hand. The pain made me push my hips harder into her body. My nod pleased her and she pulled back from me, the chain giving way under her magic. I found my hands free and aching for her delicate neck. I almost reached for her until she waved her hand and another corner of the room danced with light. Merlin sat in the bottom of a cage on the floor. His long silver hair was filthy and tangled. His strong frame wasted from hunger. A gag sat in his mouth and his green eyes blazed with fury, mostly pointing at me.

"I will need a weapon, my Queen," I said holding her in one arm. My lust, my constant downfall, rode me hard. I wanted to rip her armour off her body and bury myself inside her soft wet cave. I tried to pull her back into my close embrace, the power of the spell fighting my love for Arthur.

"Use your bare hands, Lancelot," she ordered, her fingers stroking my naked chest and teasing my nipples.

I blinked. "You want me to snap his neck?" Shit, and I thought I'd have the weapon I needed to face her guard. If I didn't kill her first, she'd see Geraint and Else burn while I remained occupied by the soldiers.

"I don't care how you do it. Strangle him like an unwanted puppy if you want. Just end his miserable life." She turned away. I dare not do anything other than follow orders. I walked on shaking legs to Merlin, focusing only on his angry green eyes. His lips moved and he made noises but I couldn't understand him.

"I need you to unlock his cage," I said, forcing my mind to concentrate on her desires. The lock snapped open before my eyes. Merlin barged into the door. It swung open but I grabbed him by the neck and hauled him out. He felt terrifyingly light. His legs and arms were shackled, with scars covering his skin. He'd been here a long time. He struggled but I held him, his back to my chest, his ear very close to my mouth.

"Stop struggling you old fool or I'll end up snapping your neck by accident," the words whispered through my lips. I held him tight, one arm around his neck, the other arm pushing against the back of his head. My hand grasped the opposite bicep. If I applied this correctly he'd be out cold in half a dozen heartbeats. He relaxed enough to make it safe, I continued, "Listen to me. We are fucked if you don't do this right. I need you to collapse, fake death if you can, wizard. Then I need you to save Geraint and Else while I pick a fight. Arthur is unconscious at the moment. Geraint needs to save him while I hold them all off. I need Nimue dead."

He made some noises but I'd run out of time, the witch approached. "Kill him, or are you not the great knight they all talk about?" Her mouth twisted in anger and disdain.

"My Queen," I said and tightened my grasp. Merlin fought. I pushed on the sides of his neck and he gurgled before relaxing. I dropped him. "It is done," I said, walking to the vision of female power before me. She stroked my chest, filling my loins with an aching need. The voice in my head, the one which sounded like the Wolf, snarled reminding me of Arthur.

"And now the usurper," she purred.

"Am I to strangle him as well?" I asked.

Nimue smiled. "I don't think so. I think you should have your revenge."

I didn't like the sound of that. I ignored Merlin's body. I ignored Geraint's demands and Else's cries. I followed Nimue, the shepherdess to my lamb. We were in her world, under her power and I wanted us all out alive. She led me to Arthur and I watched her stroke his head. I moved, so did the soldiers nearest us. I forced the bile back down my throat as she brought my King out of his magical sleep. All the time Nimue played games Merlin might find a way to save us.

"Hello, Arthur dear. Remember me?" she asked pulling his head back from the post.

When Arthur Pendragon became aware of his predicament, he fought. I watched and remained mute. He struggled and pulled and cursed and screamed vengeance on Nimue. All his glorious majesty battled with the chains holding him to the post.

When I found myself chained to a post, my back naked, I did not fight. I prayed for Arthur's forgiveness and I closed my eyes against his pain. He had watched every one of the lashes kiss my back. When it ended and I opened my eyes, he stood, unmoved and blank. Our eyes met for a moment before he turned away from me and left. Stephen de Clare laughed. I remembered that, he laughed before they cut down my bleeding body.

Nimue laughed now. "Arthur, I have someone here who wants to help you find your place in our new world." Her hand lashed out so fast it blurred. I jumped. She grabbed me and pulled me into Arthur's field of vision. "Look, the new King of Camelot," she announced, ruffling his hair.

We stared at each other, wordless. Something profound happened, Arthur relaxed. He stopped fighting and smiled. We gazed at each other and just as the Stag and Wolf knew no words with which to communicate, Arthur and I needed no words. His life in my hands and he gave it to me without a fight.

"Ah," Nimue said. "It must be love."

"It is, my Queen," I said to take her mind off Arthur. I stroked her hot skin. She kissed me in front of Arthur. I gave myself over to the passion, forcing my own physical strength into Nimue, dominating her soft feminine body. Delay, distract, confuse, if I couldn't fight, I could fuck. The thought made me want to giggle. I hid my face in her cleavage. Her gasps of delight helped me turn her away from any potential movement belonging to Merlin. I also hoped the fey soldiers were watching me, not him.

"Bad boy," she remonstrated, grabbing my right hand. It strayed down the golden armour seeking a way into her flesh. "Stop trying to distract me from my task." Her hand, so much smaller than mine, flexed. I screamed. "I can taste your love for the usurper," she whispered over the noise of every one of my bones breaking inside my hand. "Thought you'd fool me?" her voice echoed through the chamber, the soldiers cheered in a strangely uniform manner. I crouched at her feet, huddling over my broken right hand. My favoured sword hand.

That devil in female form entwined hanks of my hair around her fingers and pulled me across the floor faster than I could scramble with a broken limb. I reached for the stone ground without thinking and almost blacked out from the flare of white heat crashing into my mind. My broken hand was unable to help me keep up with her movement and stop her pulling hair from my scalp. My mind had learned to cope with so many different forms of pain over the years, even that of my punishment, but this was new and so much worse. I lay, gasping as she cursed my name. The pain washed back. She dragged me upright and I regained my feet. Nimue reached behind her and pulled a single tailed lash toward me.

She smiled. "You are going to have your revenge whether you like it or not."

"No," I almost sobbed.

She forced the handle of the lash into my left hand. "Yes, or they will die." I heard Else scream and worst yet, so did Geraint. The heat must be cooking them.

Where the hell was Merlin? I dare not look but I could delay no longer. If I did not please this fey bitch, saving us all would cease to be an option. Nimue lifted her hand, signalling her intent to lower Geraint further toward the coals.

"Alright," I cried. "Alright, you win. I'll do it." I couldn't say, *'I'll flog Arthur to death'*. I lacked the courage.

"Wolf," he said in tones he used only for ceremonies. "I forgive you. Just do what you must, that is an order."

My hand shook, Arthur bent his head to the post. I raised my hand.

"Now," Nimue barked.

My hand ripped forward. The whip whistled over my head and the point struck home. I tried to pull the sharp end back, but Nimue laughed, the whip controlled by her magic. It found its mark without my help. The whip sliced into Arthur's back on the first pass. His back bowed, his head pushed into the wood of the post, blood flowered, skin split.

I did not have the courage of my King, I sobbed. Tears blinded me. My hand came back with Nimue's order and forward. She laughed and crowed in delight. After five strokes, she danced to Arthur's side and tormented him. I heard nothing but the beating of my heart inside my mind. My right hand grew numb. I felt numb. My left hand came back, no longer under my control and I watched more blood flow down Arthur's back. He grunted under the pain.

"Nimue," a new voice, an old voice, the voice I needed. "I think it's time you let the Wolf stop this silliness." Merlin limped forward, his hand full of something.

Nimue's eyes settled on me. "What is the point of you becoming King if you don't obey me, Lancelot?" she sounded peeved. Her hand twitched, bones cracked and I stopped breathing. Ribs, she'd broken some of my ribs with just a thought. My knees hit the floor. I tasted blood.

"Wolf, on your damned feet," Merlin barked.

"Lancelot, fight," Arthur managed to give an order I understood. I forced myself upright and backed toward Merlin. I fought with the pain and won.

The wizard spoke to Nimue, his right hand stretched out toward her. "You have inconvenienced me for long enough, you damned fey witch. If you don't release us, I will crush this fetch and you will die."

The soldiers took a step forward and I realised they were all one beast. Each man identical, like the golem but they smelt less.

"You sent the monsters after us?" I choked out.

She glared at me. "Traitor."

I needed to understand but Merlin held me back. "Don't, boy. With me you are safe." He waved a small bundle of rags at Nimue. "This fetch is made with my hate and your hair, fey enchantress and seducer. You know I can use this, let them go and send us home or you will die."

"You wouldn't dare you old soak," she snarled. "Your foolish intention to drag the world of men away from the old paths will never work."

"Yes, it will, it has to and Arthur is the answer to that, your time in our world is over. Your power must return to what it was before the worship of man, Nimue. You are drunk on that power and killing your people because of it. This is not the fey path." He waved at the soldiers. "You are selling your souls, you and the rest of the fey nobility."

"You understand nothing, half bred scum." Nimue lunged at Arthur. I yelled and ran toward her, a soldier moved to intercept me, I lashed out with my left hand and punched him in the face with the back of my fist. He toppled, the token resistance not enough to prevent me from taking his sword and plunging onward to Nimue. Her hands were around Arthur's throat, choking the life out of him. I couldn't breathe but I could kill. The sword found the sweetest path through Nimue's guts, straight through the golden armour under my power. Gold, stupid stuff to make armour out of. She screamed and turned, releasing Arthur.

Merlin held the fetch over the fire. Nimue's hair smoked, blood splattering everywhere and I reached for Arthur, pulling the sword from her guts. The hole increased to spill her intestines. I raised the sword, cleaved the stake and chains over Arthur's head. His hands came free and he rose in one movement catching hold of me. I toppled into his arms. My blood mingled with his as he tried to carry me back to Merlin. We shuffled together.

"I will kill you, you fucking meddling wizard," Nimue screeched at the top of her voice, her hands holding her guts.

"How much damage can you heal, lover?" Merlin baited. Her skin started to bubble. Geraint and Else were both unconscious but on the floor, due to Merlin's magic, I hoped. "Home, now," he ordered. His voice swelled into a mighty torrent of sound, far more powerful than the screams Nimue forced from my companions. I found myself cradled within this sound. It protected me and held me like a mother's arms.

The world blurred, the heat grew. Arthur collapsed into me, driving us both to our knees. I groaned in pain but the sound vanished from my lips, I only heard it because I knew my throat vibrated. Merlin spoke words of power I didn't know and soft dawn light with early winter grass under my hand and blue sky over my head turned into blackness.

CHAPTER THIRTY-ONE

ARGUING VOICES, ONE MALE, one female. I heard them from a long distance away. I thought it would be good to visit them. I'd been quiet for a long time. I could always come back to my quiet place if I decided I didn't want to stay with the voices.

I recognised the male voice. It made my heart hurt, it sounded upset. I rushed closer. Oh, now, I remembered. "Arthur..." my lips moved. My hand tried to reach for him but pain coalesced everywhere. My breath hitched.

"He's awake, thank God, he's awake." Fingers encircled my left hand and soft lips brushed the surface.

"I'll find Merlin," said the female voice. I caught sight of a white dress vanishing from a simple stone room. Arthur knelt by my low bedside. He lifted my head from a soft pillow and brought a cup of water to my lips. "Drink slowly. You've been unconscious for days. Merlin said he used you to bring us home. You have real power, Lancelot." His eyes watered and he turned away, lowering my head with tender care.

"Arthur?" I made it a question. My fingers tightened on his and memories flooded me. "Oh, God, what did I do to you?" I whispered in horror.

His head snapped back. "No, don't think about it. Don't ever think about it, I'm healing. I..." His hand touched my face and I winced from bruises, he withdrew his fingers. "I thought I'd lost you. Merlin said you might not come back." He kissed my fingers, then my face, my eyes, my lips.

"Arthur," I murmured between his kisses. "I love you and I am so sorry." Was that enough? Would it ever be enough?

I think I washed away from him because I opened my eyes to look into Merlin's face. He peered at me, startling me to full wakefulness. "There you are, Wolf. Glad to have you home."

"Where's Arthur?"

Merlin smiled. "We finally managed to convince him to sleep in his own room. He'll wake soon enough." His face appeared to have filled out, his skin healthier and his hair shone in the light from a fire and brazier.

"How is he?" I tried to sit up, ribs ground together and I whimpered.

"You should worry about yourself, boy," Merlin said. His confident hands moved around me and helped me to sit upright. I found my ribs bound and my right hand swaddled, with pieces of wood holding my fingers and palm in place.

I lay my head back, exhausted already. Merlin made me drink something bitter. I washed it down with a long draft of water. He also produced some simple food. "Tell me about Arthur," I repeated.

Merlin sighed. "You did well. You need to know that. I know he was hurt but you saved his life, you saved us all."

I placed my left hand on his arm. "What's wrong?" I asked. My heart trembled along with my voice.

Merlin shook his head. "Arthur is hurt, Lancelot. I am trying to understand but it has nothing to do with his back, or maybe it has everything to do with it."

"I flogged him," I said staring at the white stone wall at the end of my bed.

"No, he flogged you but you did all you could not to hurt him."

"He also knows they want me to be king," I said.

"Nimue wants you king, Aeddan wants you dead. There is a difference," Merlin spoke quietly. Lost in his private terrors. "Lancelot," he took my hand, "you need to help him heal. He needs you well and strong at his side. I fear for him and," he paused. "And I understand the love he has for you."

I swallowed, here we go, I thought, the first of Arthur's people to condemn me.

"Lancelot, stop fighting what you are. Who you are. It is making Arthur miserable. He loves you, be that person for him." Merlin's words might sound gentle but I heard the undercurrent of steel. He needed me to let my world become absorbed by Arthur's.

I though, wanted something else. Didn't I? "Where are Geraint and Eleanor?"

Merlin smiled. "They are here. Geraint has sore feet, which is a miracle. Eleanor's magic is not just empathic it seems, she has some juice in there, not that she's going to learn to use it." His great dark eyebrows grew together and a gentle knock distracted me from asking what he meant. Else walked into my room. My heart swelled, she looked battered and bruised but happy. Her soft brown curls danced around her face, she pushed them back. She wore a long simple dress of rusty wool. When she sat beside me, Geraint hobbled in using a stick and wincing. Merlin rose and muttered about Arthur.

Else hugged me but there were no kisses. I found out I'd been unconscious for a week. We'd been spat out of Albion onto the side of the Tor, from there, Merlin and Else limped into Avalon to find help. Arthur and I were worst off, Geraint unable to stand. Of Nimue we had no sign but Else said sightings of a man matching my description made Merlin and the Sister of Avalon set seals of protection around the Abbey. We were not strong enough to confront Aeddan. But we had Merlin back, so facing Stephen de Clare and stopping his fight for the throne of England seemed possible.

While they spoke about events, I watched how they looked to each other for confirmation of ideas. How their hands touched and how my beautiful girl smiled at my best friend. A lump formed in my throat and tears pricked my eyes. "So," I said my voice sounding rough, "when are you two going to tell me about your news?"

Geraint's eyes snapped to mine. An honest man in his heart meant his eyes betrayed him, guilt is not attractive. "Lancelot, you need to concentrate on becoming well."

"No," Else said laying a hand on his. "No, there have been too many lies between us."

"This is one occasion when lying would be a good thing," I muttered wanting to stand and pace the small room. Tension made my ribs hurt and my right hand ached. Whatever Merlin gave me to drink didn't take away enough types of pain.

Else's eyes narrowed. "Don't be foolish. It's the endless lies that have brought us here. Our whole relationship was founded on lies and that's not a place on which to build a marriage."

I didn't want to hear this. "I'm not ready, please go away. Leave me in peace. Come back in ten years or so." I struggled under my blankets and cried out in pain. Geraint rose, equally distressed, Else held her ground.

"It's over, Lancelot. You and Arthur –"

"I gave up Arthur for you," I informed her. "I want marriage, children and home."

"No," she snapped. "You want convention because you are afraid to face the truth of what and who you really are. I will not play this game with you. I watched you in that place, that dungeon, with Arthur." Tears stood proud in her angry eyes. Her sentences broke but they remained lucid and well planned in advance of this moment. "You wanted to save us, but you would have sacrificed me, us, to save him. I deserve to be happy. My bloody step family want me for nefarious reasons, Merlin wants me here learning to be like him and I want love. A love you cannot give me."

"I do care for you." The bleat sounded lost and lonely among her passionate words.

"But you do not love me," she sounded so like her biological mother I flinched. "No," she said more softly as though she'd heard the tone herself. "You love Arthur and that's alright. I have found love, honest love, elsewhere. I will not be a poor second to Arthur, like Guinevere is to you." She rose and took Geraint's hand. "I am sorry and I'm sorry this is going to hurt, but it is the right thing to do."

That was it, except for Geraint's stricken gaze as she led him from my room. Done, over. The squire I met all those months ago, who saved me from despair in France, left me for my friend.

I lay back on my small bed and stared at the ceiling. Tears of loss tracked down my face but I didn't have the energy for rage or heartbreak and Arthur lay next door locked in his own hell. Would I ever know peace? I was certain Arthur Pendragon wouldn't give me peace but he did want to give me something. His heart, his life. I thought about Guinevere and wondered if Camelot would allow us to spend time together. Eventually, I slept once more and woke to darkness in my small room. I swung my legs over the edge of my bed, groaned aloud in pain and saw to my toilet, made more complicated with my sudden left handedness. I hurt everywhere but I could move, so I did, out of my door and into a simple stone corridor, the floor very cold on my bare feet. I considered my nakedness with regard to the Sisters of Avalon, but decided I didn't care when I heard a gentle sobbing from the room to my left. I didn't knock I just walked into a room lit by one small candle.

Arthur lay on his side, with his back to me. Blood stained the cloth bandages wrapped around his body to help the healing of his lashes. His body shook with his anguish. I crossed the small room on silent feet and touched his shoulder, sitting on his bed.

"Peace, Sire," I whispered to him. "I'm here, we will be alright. I promise you, my King."

He rolled over, didn't look at me but curled himself around me and wept for a long time. His head on my lap meant I just sat and stroked his hair until dawn lifted the night sky. When he found his centre of calm Arthur helped me lay down on my back. He stretched out next to me, on his side and rested his head on my chest, a long way from my broken ribs. We both fell into a deep, dreamless sleep, wrapped safely in each other's arms.

The following days kept us both relatively still. The more Arthur moved about, the worst the scars. Merlin hoped with good care, the scarring should be almost imperceptible after a year. That left me relieved in the extreme. Geraint and Else spoke to Arthur about their plans, he tried to talk to me but I ended up shouting at him and then I collapsed. The pain in my ribs every time I drew breath too great. They left Avalon and headed back to Tintagel. They planned on returning to Camelot when they both felt stronger. They would marry formally there in the spring. My anger over their nuptials hurt Arthur but I couldn't help it, I still feared what he and I shared and anger became my only outlet. Losing the use of my sword hand just made things worse. My only consolation was Ash. He and the other horses were soon retrieved from the Levels and happy to come home to somewhere warm and safe. When I managed to leave my room and limp down to visit he appeared to be very sheepish about losing me on the moor.

I slogged through the mud back into the Abbey's living quarters, a wave of exhaustion sweeping over me. I'd been fighting and running from one thing or another my entire life. I craved to be happy but I wouldn't allow it to happen. Arthur watched me constantly, his expression by turns – hungry, fearful and deeply sad. His wounds were healing on the outside but he cried out at night. I found myself waiting for his nightmares. I would slip into his room, curl around his wounded back, and he'd sleep in my arms. I always left before dawn.

"Lancelot," his soft voice called me away from my door. God, I needed him. I turned toward his room. Arthur sat on his bed, his elbows on his knees. He didn't look up at me. "I'm well enough to return to Camelot. I need to return to Camelot, I can't stay here any longer."

"Do you want me to return with you?" I asked. The sudden sharp pain in my chest made my breath hitch. It had nothing to do with my healing ribs.

"You can't ride that far, not yet," he said, still not looking at me.

"My place is by your side," I told him, my throat closing.

"Is it?" he asked, his clear blue eyes rose to mine.

I had pushed him too far, he would rather say goodbye to me than live with the half life he felt I gave him. I walked toward him and knelt. I took his face in both hands. My left touched his blonde stubble, my right protested madly. I winced as I tried to settle. I forced his gaze to meet mine.

"I am sorry," I said.

"Lancelot –"

"No, my turn." I pulled his face toward mine and kissed his soft lips. "Forgive me, love me, help me understand and stop being afraid for you and for me and of Camelot."

"You will never stop being afraid of Camelot, she always fills me with dread." He touched my chest, his lips speaking close to mine, our breath mingling. "As to your other fears, I share them. You can take it all, Wolf. Everything I have, wife, crown, me."

"I only ever wanted to serve you, my King," I whispered and moved into his body. Our kisses grew, no longer tentative or gently loving. Hot, fierce, our tongues fighting for dominance, our hands exploring, what strength we both had pitted against each other. My ribs hurt but my lust hurt more. Arthur pushed me down onto the cold floor. I registered his weight on my bad side.

"Ouch," I groaned.

"Fuck." He rolled off me.

"I hope so," I muttered.

Arthur laughed and I found myself joining him. We laughed long and hard, my ribs moaning the whole time. The pressure left us and Arthur faced me, leaning on one arm, his other hand roving over my chest. "If this is really what you want and what we can accept, then we can wait."

"I don't want to wait, I don't want any more time to think or be afraid. I just want to give everything I have to you," I said.

"And Else?"

"She loves another, it's over. I need to accept it and after all, she isn't a patch on you," I said smiling and meaning it.

I lay on my back, on the cold stone floor and watched Arthur untie every one of the laces holding his clothing in place. I then watched him undress. He placed every item carefully on a chair in the sparse room, no luxuries here for our King. He helped me stand and stripped me naked. He no longer wore the bandages around his ribs and I turned him, looking at his back for the first time. Six deep cuts from right shoulder to left hip carved lines through his perfect skin.

"It's horrible," I whispered. "Why did I do it?"

He turned back and kissed the fingers of my left hand. "You did it to save

Geraint and Eleanor. I would suffer the same fate again if I had to, you did the right thing and I love you for it."

"I hurt you." My hand shook.

"A lot less than I have hurt you," he said. "It is done, in the past. From this moment our futures are together, that's the only thing which matters." My left hand circled the back of his neck and I pulled him toward me.

Our bodies touched, his hands sat on my hips. We were both erect. Our hips met and we shared that intimate touch. My whole existence drew down to this one bright, exquisitely painful moment. His hand slid over my backside, holding us close, our chests rose and fell in the same breath and we shared nothing more than our close physical proximity. I bent my head to his neck and kissed the rough skin, trailing my tongue, tasting the bitter musk so different to a woman's scent. I bit into the huge muscle over his collarbone. He groaned and pushed his hips into mine. I bit harder and his body weakened under the pain. I knew then, he might be my lord and king on the battlefield but Arthur's desires led him to be submissive to me in our private life.

I liked that thought, we had a private life. I moved him, lay him down on the bed and smiled into his trusting blue eyes. "This isn't going to be the athletic ballet I'd like."

He caressed my face. "Just to feel you this close to me is all I have ever wanted. The rest can wait."

"There are some things that can't wait, Arthur," I said feeling nervous about the prospect.

"Have you done this before?" he asked shyly, blushing.

"Not with a man, but I've played this game with some experienced women."

He grinned lopsidedly. "Thank goodness for the dark ladies of Camelot," he said.

"Amen," I muttered my loins throbbing with insistence.

Arthur wriggled under me and reached for a saddlebag, he fished about and pulled out a small glass bottle. I looked at him, my eyebrow raised in question, he smiled. "Oil."

I took the bottle from him and kissed his mouth, grateful for his forethought. I moved, trying to descend his body with some semblance of grace. The ends of my ribs threatened to snap once more. The pain left me gasping and frustrated. I cursed until Arthur rolled me off his chest and rose from the bed. He knelt and pulled me upright, so I sat on the edge of our narrow cot. I'd grown soft because of the pain.

His hand trailed down my chest and stomach. "Patience, Wolf," he said grasping my cock. I growled and began kissing his face, neck and chest with some savagery. Arthur murmured and coaxed encouragement. Within moments I'd grown harder under his hands than I thought possible. He controlled me, never once endangering our completion but keeping me focused on desire.

My hand trailed over his back, I caressed the healing wounds. I blanked my mind and I continued down. His backside so firm and rounded under my exploring touch. A woman never felt like this, Arthur's muscles were perfectly formed, nothing soft and malleable. We were so well matched. For the first time I drew my hand around his hip. Arthur stopped moving and just watched my face. I trailed my hand up and my fingers encircled his engorged phallus. He gasped. I wished I could use both hands, cup all of him. His tip, with skin so soft, made me just want to rub my lips over it, to feel the velvet. I let my fingers explore the foreign world, so similar and yet completely different to my own. Longer, slightly narrower, everything tighter and nestled in fine blonde hair.

"Stand up," I ordered, unable to think beyond my desire. Arthur rose and I sat straight on the bed. Before giving him a chance to speak, I licked up his shaft, every muscle in his strong legs jumped and he cursed. His fingers tangled into my hair. I spent time teasing and playing, just as those wonderful women of mine had tormented me. I knew for a fact the only person Arthur had ever slept with was Guinevere. When I took as much as possible in my mouth, he trembled and I ended up trying to support his weight in one hand. I sucked gently and licked.

"Oh, damn it, Wolf, I'm going to die if you keep doing that," he muttered over my head.

I chuckled, the vibration making him moan again. With just one hand, I couldn't be subtle with the oil. He poured a small amount on my fingertips and I plunged my mouth once more over his straining body. Reaching through his legs, I began to explore, but standing didn't give me enough access considering our inexperience.

I tugged the blankets off his bed and threw them down. He lay back, both shy and confident. I knelt between his knees and guided one of his own hands to play with his erection. He tucked his other arm behind his head so he could watch. The oil made him slick as I explored and my finger gained easy access to his tight body, Arthur melted. His eyes rolled back and he almost panted, fighting for control. I took my time, watching his reactions as I moved into and out of his body. He felt so tight I didn't know how we'd ever manage to complete this, but I worked, first with two then three fingers and he started to relax. Suddenly, I knew we'd found the perfect moment.

I slid my fingers out and lowered myself over his body. He piled up a wad of blanket, tilting his hips up. I kissed his mouth. "You sure?"

"I've always been sure, just never had the courage," he said, stroking my hair and face.

"This will change us forever," I told him.

"Good, I didn't like being a liar and denying you," he said.

I smiled and leaned onto the elbow with the broken hand. My left grasped my own aching erection and I guided myself to his entrance. I kissed him, trying to take away any pain as I pushed, long and slow. He groaned and his fingers dug into my backside.

"I've hurt you," I said frozen over him.

His eyes snapped open. "Yes, no, don't bloody stop, don't you dare stop." His strength matched my own and he pulled me into his body. I stopped him taking it all, not wanting to damage anything. My confidence shaken but my determination strong, I worked it, withdrawing and pushing forward a piece at a time, the oil making it smoother. It felt incredible. All that power, all that strength under me, begging for more. The love I felt for this man overwhelmed me and I bowed my head, tears leaking onto my cheeks. Arthur started to move with me and I knew I never want anything or anyone else. He begged for all of me so I pushed fully into his body, while cradling his head in my left palm. I held still, my face buried against his shoulder. He stroked my back and spoke gently of his love, the tension in my body rose higher and I thrust hard. He gasped and suddenly it was not about tender love but passionate thrusting power. His strength surged against my own.

The chains I'd placed on my orgasm slithered loose and the rush of energy racing through me translated into Arthur's body. He grabbed my face and forced me to look at him. The intense screaming power inside me coalesced into one perfect moment. I fell into the deep blue of his eyes. He locked rigid under me and we both cried out as he tightened around my body and I toppled over the edge, plunging into the sweeping light of my orgasm. It tore through my body, pulsing like I'd never known before. I was lost and alone in a world of passion.

"Lancelot," Arthur's voice came from a great distance. He raised my head off his shoulder where it sagged. "Wolf, are you alright?"

I tried to smile but tears rushed through me. "I love you," I managed, pulling him close to me. Arthur held me, his legs wrapping around my thighs and his arms around my back. He spoke of soft things, of our future and of his love. I returned to myself and managed to separate myself from him both physically and untangling our spirits. My ribs and hand were killing me, the endorphins rushing away too fast. Arthur rose, now silent, washed himself, then knelt on the floor and washed me.

I touched his face with a shaking hand. "Thank you." I didn't know what else to say.

He smiled, bashful once more. "You are welcome." He pulled the mattress off the small wooden bed, went to my room and dragged everything in from there. He arranged both mattresses on the floor.

"You're shaking," he said.

I did, I trembled. All those years, all that time waiting and it was perfect. I was lost and confused and happy and scared and perfect. I wanted to hold him to my heart forever.

For a week, we lived in that happy place somewhere between reality and fantasy. We made love constantly, with long nights spent curled up in our small bare cell. Merlin watched like an indulgent father when we walked around Avalon hands clasped tight, love in our eyes and on our lips. We healed both in body and soul, so much of our pasts vanishing under the onslaught of hope. We both knew it wouldn't last, couldn't last, but damn it felt so good.

I felt complete, happy in Arthur's embrace. It was as though my constant fight against the love I felt for him, took all my energy and now I'd surrendered, life felt so simple. Easy. Painless, for the first time.

Almost a fortnight from when I first woke after our tussle with Nimue, reality once more closed over our heads.

We sat on the top of the Tor. Our daily walks helping us both to regain strength and a way to test my healing ribs. We'd almost run up the steep sides today, slipping in the mud, my hand strapped to my belly so I wouldn't be tempted to use it. Once we reached the top, Arthur won, we lay panting and staring up at the blue sky dotted with huge white clouds. My ribs hurt a great deal and I found it hard to breathe. Arthur sat up, concern for me clear. I watched his face grow pale and his lips thin. His brows drew together and his jaw muscles jumped in anger. His eyes were focused on something a long distance from me.

I levered myself upright and followed his gaze. A horseman raced toward Avalon, even at this distance I could see the clots of mud his horse's hooves thrust into the air and the steam from the beast's nose. I also saw the man's surcoat. Blue and gold, glinting in the pale winter sunlight. Arthur's colours. Camelot's man. Our reprieve was over. England wanted her King back. He rose and I stood at his side. Once more his Champion, ready to defend him and his kingdom to my death if necessary.

Excerpt from

Lancelot and the Sword

Book Two
The Knights of Camelot

CHAPTER ONE

"WELL, THERE SHE IS," Arthur said as he leaned on the pommel of his saddle. "My curse."

We had crested the hills that peered down over Camelot. Rain started to spit from the sky and we were all cold and tired. We'd been riding hard since just before dawn and we'd missed lunch.

"That's a fine way of talking about your home, Arthur," Merlin snapped. They hadn't managed a civilised conversation for some time.

"Do you blame me? I have a wife who hates me and might just be responsible for trying to kill me. I have enemies who I counted as friends. I have the possibility of war hanging over my head. And you want me to give up my one consolation."

"He just asked you to be cautious with what we have between us, Arthur," I said. I'd grown weary of this conversation over the last ten days of travel. I ached all over, my hand hurt in the splints and bandages Merlin fashioned to hold it still and nightmares dogged my sleep.

"So, you too are ashamed of what we have?" he asked. We'd had this exchange at least once a day on the journey to Camelot. I closed my eyes and begged for patience. I think he actually feared his own shame and confusion over our love, rather than mine, but Arthur reflected our anxiety into the light.

"You know the answer to that. I am not ashamed, Arthur, but I am aware of other people's opinions. You have a wife and crown to save," I said.

His eyes swivelled to take in the city swarming down toward the river and the sea. "I know, Wolf, but I don't want it."

There we had the final confession. Arthur Pendragon, King of Camelot and England, wanted to throw his crown into the sea. When the messenger arrived in Avalon to say we had trouble brewing at home and Kay needed help, I watched Arthur close down before my eyes. When it had just been the two of us in the Abbey, we'd grown so close and we were so happy, we'd both forgotten the real world waited to close its jaws on us once more.

"They need you, Arthur," I said gesturing to the city and meaning the people.

"I know but I need you," he whispered.

"I will always be at your side, my King," I said, laying a hand on his bowed head.

He nodded and pushed Willow forward. Merlin clucked his shaggy mountain horse, Daisy, into a walk, and I gave Ash his head. If I were honest, I didn't want to return to Camelot any more than Arthur did but that was not my decision. Where my King went I followed, always would.

As we rode into the city, during the busy afternoon rush in the markets and around the inns, Arthur kept his ears open. We walked a circuitous route and he maintained his anonymity. Merlin watched and listened just as hard. He'd not been in the city for more than five years. I rode behind them; hand on my sword, ready. I knew how restless and unhappy Camelot had grown over the months. Even having been in prison for almost a year, then banished, it didn't make me ignorant of the problems we faced. The evidence of Arthur's neglect lay everywhere.

The city guard were not guarding, they were chattering with whores. The women in question offered themselves on the streets, rather than quietly in the houses, which made ignoring them impossible. Litter, mud and shit covered the paved roads and we heard endless arguments about prices and guilds taking advantage of the power vacuum. There were more beggars, more obvious hunger, more poor. We found an area of the city which didn't even have houses, just shacks thrown up against each other, streets too narrow to ride through. We witnessed crime, cutpurses, the illegal sale of narcotics, unlicensed alcohol, and theft. Merlin bought some of the drugs we found and almost choked on the foul smell.

"It's fly agaric and poppy. It'll kill in these doses if someone Doesn't know what they're doing," he said.

"I had no idea it had become this bad," Arthur said.

"I told you, if the king is sick the land is sick and Camelot is the first place to turn bad when the king is bad," Merlin lectured for the hundredth time.

"It wasn't exactly my fault," Arthur snapped.

"You didn't have to drink the poison, Arthur," the old wizard snapped back.

"It seemed like a fine idea after I almost killed my –" he paused and bit back the word he wanted to use to describe me. "What do I do to fix it?" he asked instead.

"Rule, bring leadership back to Camelot. Stop the fey from poisoning our people, in mind and body. These people would welcome Stephen taking the throne from you if he promised them health, wealth and happiness. So, you need to give it to them but make them proud of it, make them work for it. Don't just hand over money to the churches to care for them in their sickness. Make them proud to belong to Camelot by forcing them to invest in their city, in you. They are your greatest defence against Stephen and the fey. Use them, Arthur. Woo them. You know how to do it, you've just lost the common touch because you've been in pain for too long. Now, you are free of that pain, so help them help themselves." Merlin's grey eyes shone as he guided Arthur. I remembered watching almost exactly the same scene when Arthur had just gained the throne all those years before. Merlin had told him the same thing to help him become the great king I loved.

"We need to start with the guard. We give them back their pride, give them something worthy of the uniform," I said. "Give them a reason to police their city."

Arthur nodded and I knew as we walked through the city to the great keep, he already had a list of orders a mile long to give us all. He'd always held to the law and maintained a tight rein on the detail of his government. I had the feeling any slack which may have occurred would be banished.

The walls to the entrance of the keep could be seen at the end of the road we rode up. Arthur stopped. We stopped. Merlin looked at him.

"What is it?" the wizard asked in that voice I'd grown wary of over the years. It meant Arthur tapped into a part of himself connected to another world.

I watched as Camelot's King drew in a deep breath and closed his eyes. "There's something wrong in there," he said. He turned to me. "We go in there armed and we stake our claim to my city." His blue eyes shone with an inner power.

I grinned. "Yes, Sire." My right hand groused that fighting didn't seem a sensible idea, I ignored it.

The three of us turned the horses and rode back to a nearby inn we'd all been drunk in at one time or another. I slipped off Ash and entered through a discreet door at the back. I spoke with the innkeeper. He came out, bowed briefly before Willow and Arthur and took us to a small set of private rooms he kept for his more illustrious patrons, when they were doing something they shouldn't.

We piled into the rooms and I found myself alone with Arthur for a moment. I looked around. "I should keep these rooms on retainer for our private enjoyment," I said.

Arthur tried to scowl but gave up and laughed. "Think I'm becoming your whore?" he asked.

I frowned, considered and said, "More like mistress." Then Merlin walked in.

"You are quite correct, Arthur." His presence dominated the room. No mean feat with two huge warriors in there as well, "Camelot is sick and the sickness is at her core. We are going to have problems, my friend."

Arthur, his moment of jovial silliness fleeing before the wizards unhappiness, said, "Tell me."

"There have been countless arrests throughout the city. Men are being held without charge and decent women are avoiding the keep. Those that work in the keep but live in the city are scared. There is foulness in the stones."

"I haven't been gone that long," Arthur complained. "How can things be as bad as that?"

"Your spirit has been gone from Camelot for a very long time," Merlin stated.

Arthur glanced at me. "My spirit almost died in Camelot," he spoke with such emotion, my own heart ached in sympathy for the golden young man who had to become king.

"Well," I said, trying to control Arthur's anguish, "it Doesn't make much of a difference what kind of malaise is in Camelot's walls, we have to stop it." I grabbed my breastplate and began buckling it on. "If we are facing an enemy in Camelot, whether it can be defeated with a sword or with our spirits we need to put on a display of victory and that means looking shiny and fierce."

To be honest I had no idea if I was right but I'd far rather face anything with a sword in my hand than complicated politics. Displays of strength I understood. In the end, Arthur helped me into the armour, the fingers of my right hand too damaged. I worried I'd never be able to function as a warrior again, but Merlin seemed convinced I'd heal given time. Something of a luxury.

When Arthur finished dressing he turned to me. "What do I do about Guinevere?"

The question came from nowhere and I had nowhere to hide. My heart rate shot up. We'd not spoken of Guinevere for weeks. I'd shied away from thinking about her and the consequences of caving into Arthur's desire. Correction, our desire, I couldn't blame Arthur for this mess.

"I'm not certain I'm the person to ask," I said, hedging around the subject.

Arthur's eyes narrowed. "I want your opinion not a tactful withdraw from the field," his tone hardened.

"Arthur..." I tried to escape but the look in his eyes gave me no retreat. I puffed air out and stared at the beams in the ceiling looking for inspiration. "Alright, if you want my honest opinion here it is, don't fight her. Find out what she wants. Find out why she is so angry. Talking, not screaming or fighting. One day at a time and give her space to be angry with you." I grabbed Arthur's steel shoulders. "You need to try to save your marriage, Arthur. You loved her once."

His gaze dropped. "Now I love you," he said.

"We share something different," I spoke to the top of his head, "but you still need a Queen, a wife and an heir."

He nodded and turned away, burying whatever conflict he suffered under the armour of a king. Wearing my own armour made me feel invincible. When Merlin returned, in his formal black cloak rather than riding leathers, the three of us walked from the inn and I revelled in the feeling of being at home with my King at my side.

I'd buckled my sword onto my right hip, ensuring I'd have a clean draw with my left, but it made an untidy remount of Ash. He danced and pranced around the inn's yard, the armour and Willow's company making him think we were in for a fight.

Arthur grinned at me. "I have the best at my side once more, Wolf."

"I will always be at your side, Sire." I smiled in return.

We clomped from the yard and into the streets of Camelot. All three of us had our heads bare, no great helm or coif. Each of us recognisable in our own way. As one unit, we returned to the curtain wall of the castle and followed it around toward the main gate.

The sun sat low and squat in the western sky on the short winter day but people began to realise their sun rode the streets. Arthur sat, straight, strong, proud and the epitome of knighthood. Damn it felt good to be home.

News of Arthur's appearance in the city spread more swiftly than fire, water, or air. People filled the streets in moments and the cheering started. With bare heads, we watched the people and they watched us. My name rushed from lip to lip as Arthur walked ahead, my coat of arms as familiar to the people as the king's because we were so close and I won the tourneys. Arthur smiled and waved to those he recognised of the traders and craftsmen. People adored him and he adored them back. A king is his people and the people are their king.

By the time we reached the keep's outer walls, a surging living tide of humanity cried out our names. Except for Merlin. Mother's invoked his name to scare their children but I felt their relief in his presence as much as my own. The old team were together, now all ills would be cured.

I only had to hope they were right. The welcoming committee at the gates made me think they might be proved wrong.

**Find Sarah Luddington on <u>Facebook</u> and
<u>http://romanticadventures.net</u>**

AND

***Welcome to the Newsletter
of Sarah Luddington's Romantic Adventure Books***

Sign up for the newsletter and you will receive every month, author news, competitions and free downloads!
I promise on Lancelot's honour I will NOT spam you, sell your email address, become a monster troll and I will make sure you don't regret committing to my strange new worlds.

<u>www.romanticadventures.net/newsletter/</u>

**And if you enjoyed this story, or even if you didn't, could I trouble you for a review? I know it can be annoying but they are the life blood of authors and they matter, they really matter.
Many thanks.**

Made in the USA
Coppell, TX
31 October 2019

10805996R00125